BURY THE TRUTH

DI RYAN HALE CRIME THRILLERS
BOOK 1

R. K. LYNOTT

For my Family

*Thanks for sticking around through the "purely hypothetical"
and increasingly frequent body disposal chats.*

CHAPTER ONE

Emily Astley woke to a persistent drip.

Her head throbbed, each pulse sending needles of pain through her skull. She struggled to swallow. Her tongue felt swollen, and her throat sandpaper dry.

She tried to open her eyes.

Nothing.

She strained again, but the lids remained shut. Her heart hammered against her ribs. She fought to lift an arm to touch her face. Her body refused to obey.

An icy dread hit her. Had she been in an accident? Was she in the hospital? In a coma? Or worse, had she slipped? The old fear tasted sour at the back of her throat.

Slowly, she noticed the chill seeping through her clothes. Again she tried to force her eyes open and felt a pull at her eyelashes.

Was there tape over them? Why did they throb so much?

She jerked upright, or tried to. Her body barely responded, limbs heavy. Something metal rattled.

Emily went rigid. The scent of damp earth and mildew filled her nostrils, mingling with the faint smell of bleach.

Wherever she was, it felt underground.

Memories flickered at the edge of her consciousness, just beyond reach. The knock at her cottage door. The face was blurry, but she could still remember the familiar voice had made her stomach tighten even as she'd plastered on a smile. Polite as always, she'd invited them in for tea.

She remembered the way the room had spun as she'd lifted the half-full mug to her lips.

Had she been drugged? A fresh wave of panic coursed through her. How could she escape if her body wouldn't obey her?

"Hello?" Her voice emerged as a dry whisper, swallowed by the thick walls.

She tried again to move her arms. The rattle was louder this time, followed by a sharp tug at her wrist.

Handcuffs.

Her breath hitched as her fingers searched until they found a solid rail where the other end of the handcuffs was attached. Her fingers brushed against fabric. Was she on a hospital bed?

The fog in her mind cleared, making way for growing terror. This wasn't right. This wasn't supposed to happen to people like her. People who helped others. People who'd turned their lives around.

Emily tugged at the handcuffs, and the metal bit into her skin. The rail didn't budge. She pulled harder, ignoring the pain as the cuff dug deeper.

"Let me out!" Her voice bounced back at her from unseen walls. "I know you're there! Let me go!"

Silence answered her.

For once in your life, Emily, get it together. Think.

Her free hand weighed a tonne as she raised it to her face

and picked weakly at the edge of the tape across her eyes. Her fingers felt thick and uncooperative, sluggish to obey even the simplest task. She focused on that corner of tape, using her fear as fuel to keep going. Millimetre by millimetre, she peeled and dragged the tape loose with clumsy, fumbling movements until a shred of weak light appeared at the corner of her left eye. Her fingertips felt numb, but eventually the tape came away. She blinked.

Not much of a victory, but a tiny little fuck you to whoever had taken her.

She sat back and looked around.

She lay on an old hospital-style bed covered in a lumpy quilt. The handcuffs attached her right hand to the bed's metal rail. Bare stone walls surrounded her, stained with mould in places. High above, a single lightbulb cast a weak glow.

She scanned the rest of the room. In one corner squatted a chest freezer, the kind that held sides of butchered animals. Emily decided not to think too hard about what it might contain. Along the opposite wall, a workbench held neat rows of jars filled with screws and nails, with cardboard boxes stacked underneath.

She twisted to look behind her. An old porcelain sink stood against the wall, its rusted tap the source of the dripping sound. Beyond it, a set of wooden stairs led upward into the shadows. At the top, she could just make out a heavy timber door.

She shifted position. Her flowing skirt had twisted around her legs, constraining her movements. She kicked them free and winced as her bare foot struck something hard.

Water sloshed as a plastic bottle rolled off the bed and out of reach.

A sob ripped from her lips.

I'm going to die.

The realisation made her limbs go limp, and she flopped

back onto the mattress. Her mum's last memory of her daughter would be her screaming down the phone at her to get her over-sized nose out of Emily's business.

A heavy scrape sounded from above as the door opened. Emily froze. Should she pretend to still be unconscious or plead for her release?

Heavy footsteps descended the stairs. The boards groaned under the weight. The air shifted as the footsteps reached the bottom of the stairs and stopped.

She stayed still for now, keeping her face towards the wall to hide the missing tape, but lying there blind to her captor's movements was agony. She tried to control her breathing, using the drip behind her head as a counter. In through her nose. Four counts in, six out. The steady pace was at odds with the frantic beat of her heart.

Footsteps crossed the room, and she could sense someone standing over her. The low hum of the freezer motor kicked in across the room.

Hot breath tickled her neck as they knelt beside the mattress.

"Been a naughty girl, have we?"

Before she could stop it, a whimper escaped her lips. The person yanked her head around and pressed the piece of tape firmly back across her eyes.

The voice was bitter, mocking. And familiar.

Not him. Please God, not him.

The fight drained out of her, replaced by a cold, absolute certainty. This was her fault. She should never have let him into her life. She'd known it was a mistake from the start, a reck-less decision born from her pathetic need to see the good in everyone.

When she had finally found the courage to tell him not to come round anymore, the mask had dropped for a second, and the pure hatred in his eyes had chilled her to the bone. He'd called her stupid and naïve. She had known then there'd be consequences. But in typical Emily fashion, as the days had turned into weeks and then into months, she'd buried her worries under layers of forced positivity and affirmations of self-love.

The mattress dipped beside her.

"I visited some friends of yours." His voice slithered into her ear. "They see the truth now, Emily. And soon, so will you."

CHAPTER TWO

Hannah's voice cut through the morning quiet. "What do you think they sacrificed here? Back in the old days, I mean."

She spoke German. Her pink hair bounced as she dodged puddles on the muddy track. The cold bit at her cheeks, painting them a healthy red she knew would look fantastic in a selfie.

When she turned, Lukas was too far behind to have heard her.

The light was almost perfect. Liquid gold bled beneath the cloud edge and spilled across the dark contours of the moor. It set ablaze the dormant heather and thick mist that blanketed the landscape. Hannah snapped a few quick photos on her phone. Her followers would love it.

"Hurry up, Lukas! We'll miss it," Hannah shouted down the path, her breath fogging in the cold air.

Lukas grumbled back. "Miss what? Hypothermia? I can't feel my fingers. This entire country is just... damp."

Hannah stopped at the tree line and turned, phone held

aloft. She framed him on the screen. A lanky figure bundled in a dark coat, his face pinched against the moody backdrop of the Derbyshire dawn.

"It's for the 'gram', you moaner," she said, her accent thickening with playful exasperation. "Imagine the caption: 'Chasing ancient gods at golden hour.' It'll be fire."

"I think the ancient gods had the sense to stay in bed." He drew level with her, his breath pluming in the crisp air. He picked at a loose thread on his sleeve. "Can we just take a few pictures and go back to the van for coffee?"

"Patience, mein Liebling." She gave him a quick, cold kiss and spun back towards the path. "The stones are just through these awesomely skeletal trees. The sign said so."

She darted behind a tree, then leaned out and raised her arms. "Wooooo! I am the ghost of the moor, come to steal your soul!" She wiggled her fingers at him.

Lukas didn't crack a smile. "Halloween was last night. And it's a capitalistic money grab imported from America, anyway." He hunched deeper into his coat. "If you want to see a real ghost, just wait until I die of pneumonia out here."

Hannah stuck out her tongue and forged ahead, dodging gorse bushes and ferns that encroached on the path. Lukas followed, dragging his feet. The trees opened out, and she saw them. Nine squat, weathered stones, arranged in a lopsided circle in a clearing of flattened grass. They were smaller than she'd imagined. Less dramatic. More forgotten teeth than towering monoliths. The tenth rock beyond the circle, called the king stone, wasn't any more impressive.

Disappointment flickered through her.

"Is that it?" Lukas's voice was flat. "We froze our arses off for a pile of tiny rocks."

Hannah ignored him as she searched for an angle that

would transform the stone circle from the mundane into the magical.

Then she saw it.

In the centre of the circle.

"Oh, wow." Her breath fogged. "Lukas, look."

It wasn't part of the ancient monument. It was something new. Purposefully arranged. A star, its five points etched deep into the dark earth. At each point, a thin wooden stake stood sentinel. In the middle, two small statues sat back-to-back, facing away from each other.

"What is this?" Lukas moved to her side, his earlier crankiness replaced by caution. "Some kind of prank?"

"It's art," Hannah breathed, her photographer's eye alight. The disappointment vanished as she felt a surge of adrenaline. This was better than a few old stones. Edgy. Weird. Unforgettable. "Like a land-art installation for Halloween. It's brilliant. So pagan."

She unlocked her phone and switched to the camera, then stepped inside the circle. The composition was perfect. The ancient stones created a natural frame for the rising sun. It cast long, dramatic shadows from the stakes, the installation an interesting focal point.

Bizarre. Super creepy. Her followers would go wild.

She moved around the edge of the star and snapped a few pictures. A wide shot to capture the whole scene. Then closer, focused on the detail of the statues. One a horned man, the other three women intertwined. She crouched to angle her next shot up the length of one stake towards the sky.

Two circles were impaled just down from the tip.

The objects were smooth, roundish. Maybe glass or resin? She took a close-up as the sunlight glinted off their moist surfaces.

"This is amazing," she murmured, more to herself than to Lukas, who hovered at the circle's edge.

She stepped back and reviewed the images on her screen, swiping through them with a frozen thumb. The wide shot looked incredible. The one of the statues was moody and evocative. She stopped at the close-up of the stake. Her thumb and forefinger pinched the screen, zoomed in to check the focus.

It was sharp.

Too sharp.

The objects weren't polished resin... or glass. She could see... threads. Tiny fine red lines on each circle, spreading out from their dark centres.

Her mind refused to accept it. It searched for alternatives. A masterful sculpture. Hyperrealistic special effects for a student film. Animal parts from a butcher, arranged for shock value.

It had to be.

She zoomed in further, her fingers shaking, until the pixels broke apart. But before they did, she saw it. The unmistakable, intricate lattice of an iris.

A human iris.

A strangled gasp escaped her throat. The world tilted, the golden light now sick and yellow. Her phone slipped from her numb fingers and thudded onto the damp ground.

"Hannah? What is it?" Lukas rushed over, his hand on her arm.

She couldn't speak. Could only point; her shaky finger aimed at the stake. At its grotesque decoration.

He followed her gaze, his brow furrowed. He squinted. His eyes widened. His face, already pale from the cold, bleached to bloodless white. He stumbled back, one hand flying to his mouth. A violent, retching sound tore through the morning's silence as he doubled over and vomited into the ferns.

Hannah stared at the scene, her brain a frozen knot of denial.

It wasn't real. Couldn't be.

"It's a joke," she croaked, her voice thin and reedy. The words sounded hollow even to her own ears. "A Halloween thing. For a TV show."

She forced her limbs to move and picked up her phone. Her eyes swept the bare trees and fern bushes that surrounded the clearing. "There will be cameras. Hidden somewhere. We have to look for the cameras."

Lukas straightened and wiped his mouth with the back of his sleeve. He shook his head, his eyes wide with horror that brooked no argument. He took another shuddering breath, and the smell... a faint, foul-sweet scent they had barely registered before, seemed to fill the air, thick and cloying.

The smell of meat left out too long.

"Hannah," he whispered, his voice trembling. "But... what if it isn't?"

He ignored her frantic scan of the bushes, his own phone already in his shaking hand. His thumb smeared a drop of vomit across the screen as he swiped to the emergency call function. He held it to his ear.

"Emergency. Which service?" The tinny voice from the speaker was calm, official. Worlds away from the nightmare in the circle.

Lukas swallowed hard, his gaze fixed on the stakes. On the grim trophies they displayed.

"Polizei," he whispered before he caught himself. "I mean the police."

While he gave the details, Hannah stood frozen, staring at the installation. The careful geometry. The deliberate arrangement.

Someone had built this. Recently.

Someone who might still be watching from the trees.

CHAPTER THREE

"You!"

Detective Inspector Ryan Hale sighed. Of all the petrol stations at seven in the morning.

He regretted not having settled for the expired tin of baked beans. Ryan tugged his corgi, Winston, away from the uncooked pork sausages protruding from the paper bag he'd placed on the concrete, and untied the dog's lead from the post.

He hadn't left Chesterfield with many admirers, but the vitriol in that single word, coupled with the nasal tone, narrowed down the speaker to one likely suspect.

"Nice to see you too, Lampton." Ryan turned to face Stuart Lampton, the man who'd played a large part in his departure for London over a decade ago.

Lampton gave one of his trademark wet sniffs. "That's Chief Inspector Lampton to you now, Hale."

Ryan shrugged and glanced at his wristwatch. "Not for another hour at least."

Lampton's eyes fixed on the light scarring on Ryan's face.

Ryan knew the damage would be stark under the fluorescent lights of the petrol station.

Time hadn't improved Lampton's appearance, and he'd been no oil painting to begin with. His bulging forehead paired with his pinched facial features made him look like a sentient lollipop from a toddler's nightmare.

Ryan nodded towards the packet of Liquorice Allsorts in Lampton's hand. "Still fond of the sweets."

Lampton ignored the comment. "You've got some nerve coming back here after what you did to that girl."

Ryan resisted the urge to throw a right jab straight into the man's dripping nose. A close-run thing given Lampton's head created a perfect round target. Only Lampton could reduce an extraordinary woman to 'that girl.' He wondered if it was possible to be fired for gross misconduct before he'd even started.

Instead, he kept his expression neutral and remained silent. He loosened Winston's lead.

As expected, the corgi lunged forward, drawn to an old puddle of sticky ice cream on the ground at Lampton's feet. The sharp tug on the lead sent a stab of pain through his injured fingers. Ryan swapped hands and tightened his grip on the worn leather strap.

Lampton leaped back with a shriek, clutching the bag of sweets to his chest as if Winston might somehow overcome gravity and his stubby legs to rip it out of his hands.

The corgi ignored the man and pounced on the dried creamy mess, tail wagging furiously.

Lampton's eyes narrowed. "Don't think I'm going to make this easy for you," he said over the sound of Winston's frantic licks.

"I wouldn't expect anything less." Ryan pulled a reluctant Winston back from the ice cream and reached for the paper bag containing his breakfast. Forcing the stiff fingers of his left hand to grip the handles, he said, "Well, good chat."

He turned and walked towards the road, his attempt at a nonchalant stroll undermined by Winston's determination to get back to the sticky puddle.

As Ryan hauled the corgi away by the collar, he questioned his decision to return to Chesterfield. Twelve years had passed since they'd chased him out of town. Or at least shown him the exit.

Back then, he'd been naïve. A mug who'd believed in the system. He'd thought that if his colleagues from the CID team couldn't find the answers, there was nothing to be found.

He knew better now. They'd overlooked something, and he was going to find it.

CHAPTER FOUR

Ryan took a deep breath and steeled himself. Of all the shit ideas he'd had over the years, and there were many, this one might be the turd that topped them all.

He gazed up at Chesterfield Police Station. The uninspired red-brick building loomed on the corner, its shadow stretched across the pavement in the early morning sun. A frigid breeze ruffled his dark hair, and he pulled his woollen overcoat tighter.

Too late to back out now.

He plodded up the steps, with all the enthusiasm of a man fitted with concrete boots, and headed for the end of the pier, pushing open the door.

Back when Ryan had been a sergeant, the station had always carried a particular scent. Stale coffee, printer toner, and floor polish. So familiar, it felt like coming home. Now it was gone, replaced by an unsettling blend of plastic, fresh paint, and an indefinable odour.

Corporate renovators had gutted the place recently, dispensing taxpayer money and buzzwords like "synergies" and "open-plan" until any sense of personality had been obliterated.

A row of bright blue ergonomic chairs lined the walls, each designed with profound ignorance of the human backside. Instead of the mishmash of posters and notices pinned to a sagging corkboard, a pair of video screens flashed community updates no one would read.

Behind the sleek laminate counter, a florid-faced man in a sergeant's uniform sat hunched over a computer screen. Sergeant Barney Goody.

Ryan's leather shoes squeaked on the linoleum as he approached.

Goody looked up, eyes travelling over the scars on Ryan's face. He gave a derisive snort. "Well, look what the cat dragged in. Heard you were crawling back from London with your tail between your legs."

A waft of pungent breath reached Ryan. He took a step back. The source of the unpleasant odour permeating the reception area became immediately apparent.

Some things never changed. Barney had treated him with unbridled contempt even before everything fell apart all those years ago. In a way, Ryan appreciated the consistency.

"Thanks for the warm welcome, Barney. Buzz me through and point me towards DCI Lee's office."

Ryan moved towards the door and waited. He looked back at Barney. The custody sergeant's finger hovered over the button, as if weighing whether to invite a vampire across the threshold. With a resigned slouch, Barney pressed it. The door buzzed.

Ryan pulled it open and stepped through.

"Escort this plonker to the DCI's office, would you?" Barney called out to a young, uniformed officer unfortunate enough to be within his line of sight.

As Ryan followed the constable down the corridor, he overheard Barney as he spoke to someone in the back office. "Did you see the state of that bloke's face? Couldn't have happened to a nicer arsehole."

———

THE CONSTABLE GESTURED towards the lift. "Third floor, Sir. DCI Lee's office."

"Ryan?"

He turned. Fiona stood in the stairwell doorway, folder in hand. The years had been kind, though he noticed she still wore the same unflattering pantsuits.

She nodded to the constable. "I'll take it from here."

"Yes, DS Bennett." The young officer retreated the way he'd come.

"Change of plans," Fiona said, her tone all business. "Something urgent's come in. Lee wants you in the incident room." She jerked her head towards the stairs. "She'll brief the team as soon as she's got the details." Fiona paused for breath and smiled. "I'm glad you decided to come back."

"Thanks." Ryan gestured to the stairs. "Lead on."

Of all the familiar faces at Chesterfield Station, Fiona was the only one he'd looked forward to seeing. A few more laughter lines creased the corners of her hazel eyes, and silver threaded through the pale curls she'd wrestled into a tight bun with little success, but the mischievous spark in her eyes remained.

"So it's Bennett now? I take it Nathan stuck around for the long haul?"

She'd been dating the mild-mannered software engineer for only a few months before Ryan left for the Met. He'd encountered him once at the pub during one of those gatherings where colleagues sized up a teammate's new partner. Nathan had passed in Ryan's books.

She grinned and twisted her hand, catching the fluorescent light on the delicate white gold bands. "Six years ago, in the Cotswolds. Sent you an invitation."

Ryan felt heat creep up his neck. "Must've got lost in the post."

"It was an email," she said without accusation. "To your work address."

"How did it go?"

"Terribly." Fiona hauled open the heavy fire door to the second floor. "Pissed rain the entire weekend, and one of the serving staff gave half our guests norovirus." She glanced back at him. "So you dodged a bullet, really."

Her warm smile stripped the sting from the words. "But despite turning into a Carnival Cruise nightmare, it was lovely."

She stopped and faced him. "I'm sorry for what you went through. The whole torture and maiming business. Thought I'd get that out of the way." She studied the thin scars on his cheek. "Can't properly see them with the stubble. Shame."

Ryan raised an eyebrow. "Why's that?"

She tilted her head. "After what I read in the papers, I expected you to look like a Bond villain. The bad guys would've been quaking. Instead, you've got more of an old Heathcliff vibe."

"Old? I'm only two years older than you." He held up his hands, showing her the ropey red scars crisscrossing his knuckles and how the pinky and ring fingers of his left hand bent at unnatural angles. "I won't be learning piano anytime soon."

From the moment he'd woken in hospital, he'd been determined to wear his scars as a badge of honour. Marks earned in the line of duty. He refused to hide or feel ashamed.

Fiona regarded his injuries without pity, and he found himself respecting her more.

"Ouch," she said.

"Ouch is right." He nodded at her outfit. "Same pantsuit you were wearing when I left?"

She looked down at her pinstripes. "Hey, at least it still fits. This look's coming back into fashion. Hanging on to it for a decade will pay dividends any day now." She eyed his long brown woollen coat. "Not sure you can talk. Doctor Who called. Wants his coat back."

Ryan laughed. "Fair point."

Fiona's friendly manner and short stature masked an unflappable nature and terrier-like tenacity. Back when they'd worked together, she'd smoothed his rough edges and reined in his more impulsive ideas while giving him the support to push cases through despite Lampton's interference. He could only hope they'd work the same way now.

"So what happened to Dobby?"

"Dog bite."

Ryan blinked. Given the man's waistline, he'd expected a heart attack.

"According to his wife, he got bitten on the arse by a greyhound when he was snooping around the kennels at a dog meet. Didn't tell anyone. The bite got infected, and he ended up in hospital with sepsis." She chuckled. "I shouldn't laugh. He almost died, but it's so..."

"Dobby?"

"Yeah." She pointed to a door marked 'Major Crimes.' "Come on, I'll introduce you to the rest of the team." She flashed him a grin. "Let's see who irritates you most in the first hour. My money's on Cal."

CHAPTER FIVE

The incident room had been updated since Ryan's last stint. Soft cream walls and charcoal carpet replaced the previous flaking paint and worn paisley in a shade that Ryan had optimistically called mustard. Only the meagre outside view through the narrow windows remained unchanged. At the back, one of the four whiteboards displayed details of an open case.

"I thought Dobby didn't believe in case boards?" Ryan remarked. He'd heard enough of Dobby's complaints about boards to know the man's views.

"He didn't. I do. He's been gone for over a month now."

"Good." Ryan liked to let his eyes roam over the details of a case laid out in one place. It helped him connect seemingly unconnected pieces of evidence. Like a crossword. Across first, then down. Test the surface meaning, then hunt for something deeper.

He walked over to the board detailing a series of robberies and studied the photos and scribbled notes. "Two vets, a dentist, and a doctor's surgery?"

Fiona joined him. "Hit once a week for a month straight. Cleaned out all the painkillers they had." She pointed to a fuzzy CCTV photo of a blurry black shape.

"Any leads?"

Fiona grimaced. "They left no evidence. We analysed the most likely places they'd hit next, staked them out for two weeks. No one showed."

Ryan surveyed the rest of the space, wondering if Fiona felt any animosity towards him about stepping down as acting DI.

The desks were arranged in two facing rows in the middle of the room. Only one was occupied. A young black man sat before a computer, his fingers flying over the keyboard as his eyes flitted between three monitors decorated with fake cobwebs and a huge black plastic spider. The pair of massive headphones over his short, tight dreads left him oblivious to their arrival.

"When Dobby left, I shifted everything into this open layout." Fiona bit her lip. "I thought it might help with collaborating. We can move the desks back if you'd prefer?"

Ryan shook his head. "No, the current setup is perfect."

At the Met, he'd used something similar with his homicide team. It made it easier to throw ideas around and keep the team unified, as well as spot anyone not pulling their weight in an investigation or struggling with personal issues.

Fiona frowned at the empty desks.

"Digit," she called across the room.

The man glanced up and swung around in his swivel chair. His eyes widened in surprise, as if they'd teleported in front of the whiteboards. He pushed his gold-wire glasses up his nose and took his headphones off.

"Where's Cal?" Fiona asked.

"I believe he is presently escorting the new Detective Constable upstairs," Digit replied, his posh accent a stark contrast to his inner-city styling. Ryan placed the polish in his vowels somewhere in the Midlands private-school belt. He wondered how the lad had fitted in there. Was the streetwear armour chosen on purpose?

Fiona turned to Ryan. "Oh crap, I forgot she was starting today. Lee's assigned us an extra set of hands. DC Dewan. Just wrapped up her probie phase stationed out of St. Mary's Wharf CID." She paused. "Now Dobby's gone, we should get something meatier than smash and grabs. I haven't met her in person."

Both of them knew without saying that Lee was banking on his relationship with DCC Cliffe to deliver more high-profile cases to the team. Ryan already knew about the addition of DC Dewan. Lee had sent him all the team's personnel files.

She moved to introduce the man behind the monitors, who had already risen politely to his feet. "Ryan, this is DC Mathias Asare, though as you might've guessed, we just call him Digit around here. Digit, our new DI, Ryan Hale."

Ryan held out his hand, and Digit shook it as briefly as possible.

"Sir, I've been anticipating your arrival since 08:02. Very pleased to make your acquaintance." He bobbed his head and sat back down.

"Is there a story behind the nickname?" Ryan asked.

Digit's forehead wrinkled as he mulled over the question. "Yes, well, I suppose you could say there is a twofold rationale behind the name."

He launched into a long, jargon-laced explanation involving coding, binary representation, and a grisly encounter six hundred and thirteen days ago with a closed door that had resulted in 'the avulsion of his distal phalange'.

Ryan had no idea what it all meant and wished he hadn't asked.

"Long story short," Fiona cut in. "On DC Asare's second day, DS Moore accidentally slammed Mathias's finger in the door. He ran around for ages yelling, 'My digit, my digit!' and the nickname stuck."

"Do you prefer Digit or Mathias?" Ryan asked.

"Initially, I preferred Mathias, as it is my given name and the one I've responded to for twenty-six years, seven months, and eleven days. However, after a month of consistent usage by the team, I found the neural pathways associated with name recognition had successfully adapted to 'Digit'. I now respond to it with equal efficiency, but I appreciate your enquiry into my preference, Sir."

Before Ryan could think of a response, a man with artfully tousled hair strutted into the room like a peacock into a flock of pigeons. He wore a three-piece suit with trousers so tight Ryan figured he would have had to lie down on his floor this morning to wriggle into them.

He stopped just inside the door, paused like a model on a catwalk, and smoothed down his suit jacket. A lanky Indian woman in a loose grey suit with a thick black puffer jacket over it peered around him and gave the occupants in the room a tentative smile. A small notebook already clutched in her left hand.

"DC Pine," Fiona said. "Thank you for collecting our new recruit. Ryan, meet DC Cal Pine and the other addition to the team, DC Shriya Dewan."

Ryan looked DC Pine up and down. He knew the type. The detective who spent more time polishing his shoes than polishing his investigative techniques.

"Alright, Guv?" Pine replied in a Mancunian accent so thick it could knit itself a woolly jumper for the chilly northern nights. The DC might be dressed like a London footballer on a night out, but his accent was pure northern housing estate.

"Sir is fine, Cal," he responded.

Meanwhile, Dewan hurried forward with her hand outstretched, brown eyes shining with unbridled enthusiasm. Her other hand touched the small ruby pendant at her throat before dropping to her side. *Still keen, this one,* Ryan thought as he accepted her firm handshake.

"Please call me Sheri. The only person who calls me Shriya is my mum when she's mad. I'm so excited to be here, Sir." The DC's words tumbled out. "I read up on some of the big cases your team solved in London. Your investigation into the Red Hand murders was a masterclass. The way you established the victimology patterns...I mean, based on what was in the reports." She cleared her throat, seeming to catch herself.

"Ah?" Ryan said. He wasn't the kind of boss who needed smoke blown up his backside, but Sheri's nervous patter seemed earnest.

"Suck-up," Cal fake-coughed while he walked towards the filing cabinet with some paperwork.

Sheri's cheeks flushed. "I just meant—"

"All right, DC Pine, let's hear it then," Ryan said, turning to Cal.

The DC spun around. "What?"

"The best-man speech."

Beside him, Sheri let out an involuntary snort, then gasped. Her hand shot up to cover her mouth.

Cal's eyebrows knitted together. "What?"

"I assume with that get-up you're off to a wedding later?"

Cal looked down at his waistcoat as if surprised to see it. Fiona came to the confused DC's rescue. "Cal has...what do you call it, Cal? An eye for fashion?" Her smile widened.

Cal lifted his chin. "The ladies appreciate some effort."

"And how many women have you picked up at crime scenes or canvassing for witnesses?" Ryan asked.

"What? None!" Cal protested, shooting Fiona a look as if pleading with her to back him up.

"Good. Keep it that way," Ryan replied. He turned to Fiona and raised his eyebrows. "A Manc with a Vogue subscription. I guess someone needs to balance out your fashion sense."

This time it was Cal's turn to laugh, while Sheri looked between Fiona and Ryan with wide eyes. She'd taken a half-step back during the exchange, her fingers rubbing the edge of her notebook.

Fiona wagged a finger in Ryan's direction. "Play nice, guv. The kiddies aren't used to your dry wit yet. Sheri, choose an empty desk and get settled in while I show the boss here his new office."

Ryan had forgotten that the incident rooms at Chesterfield had separate offices for the detective inspectors who led each team. When he'd last worked here, it had been Lampton's domain and a place he'd avoided stepping into at all costs.

"Yes, Ma'am. Sir." Sheri gave them a quick nod and moved towards the centre desks, scanning the case board as she walked past. She paused mid-step, her gaze lingering on a CCTV photo. "The pattern suggests..." She glanced back at them and stopped herself. "Sorry."

"Something catch your eye, DC Dewan?" Ryan asked.

Sheri hesitated, her hand moving to her necklace again. "It might not be important, but the timing of the hits. Weekly, always a Thursday evening between eleven and midnight. That's quite specific for an addict looking for their next fix." She glanced down at her notebook as if second-guessing herself. "But you've probably already noted that pattern."

"We had," Fiona said. "But it's good to see you're paying attention."

"Go on and settle in," Ryan added, making a mental note. Observant. That would be useful.

Before they could enter Ryan's corner office, the incident room door opened.

CHAPTER SIX

DCI Olivia Lee strode in, with a faint hint of expensive perfume trailing after her. She was average height, immaculate in her navy suit and white blouse, with sleek dark hair brushing her shoulders. She shouldn't have commanded attention, but she took it anyway.

Most of Ryan's intel on his new boss had come from a fellow detective at the Met who had worked under her in the Northamptonshire Major Crimes Team, where she'd been the Detective Inspector.

The detective had described Lee as having a big personality and an almost Machiavellian ability to manipulate the press and the upper brass to get what she wanted.

The light atmosphere from moments before evaporated. Sheri straightened as if she'd been prodded. Cal leaned against the filing cabinet, and Digit swivelled in his chair, his attention absolute.

Lee held up a tablet. "Call came in twenty minutes ago. Two German backpackers on Stanton Moor stumbled across this."

She angled the screen so everyone could see.

Ryan stared at the close-up photo, an icy knot tightening in his gut. The raw horror of it bypassed rational thought, hitting something primal. Beside him, Fiona drew a sharp breath. Sheri's hand flew to her mouth, the colour draining from her face. Cal let out a low whistle. Only Digit studied the screen with analytical curiosity, his head tilted as if examining a complex equation.

"This is from the Nine Ladies Stone Circle," Lee said. "Pathology's seen the image. They think we're looking at human remains, but can't confirm until examination. Forensics is on the way from Derby, but we're closer. I want you over there now to secure the scene."

She lowered the tablet. "A constable is with the backpackers at the Birchover Road entrance to Stanton Moor. Get their preliminary statements, get them out of there, then head up to the circle."

Her eyes landed on Ryan, then flicked to Sheri. "DI Hale, DC Dewan, welcome to the team. Sorry we couldn't do a softer launch."

She turned and strode out, leaving silence in her wake.

The team sat frozen. Ryan scanned the faces of his new colleagues. Fiona, already composed, met his gaze. Sheri looked shaken but resolute. Cal's bravado had returned, a mask sliding back into place. Digit was already tapping at his keyboard, pulling up maps and aerial views of Stanton Moor.

"Right." Ryan's voice cut through the quiet. "Who knows where the Nine Ladies Stone Circle is?"

Sheri's hand shot up. She flushed, then lowered her arm, clasping her wrist as if trying to restrain it from independent action. "I've been there a few times. Not recently, though."

"They're hundreds of years old. Doubt they've moved." Ryan's lips quirked. "How long to get there?"

"Maybe twenty-five minutes?"

"Do you know the Birchover Road entrance?"

She nodded. "I think it's the one closest to the Cork Stone."

"Good enough." A thought occurred to him. His eyes narrowed in Fiona's direction. "Do you still drive like a getaway driver with their eyes closed?"

Back when they'd worked together, Fiona had driven with the aggression of an F1 racer and a complete disregard for road markings, lane etiquette, and pedestrians she considered were 'dragging their butts'.

Cal piped up before she could respond. "I used to play rock-paper-scissors with DS Moore. Loser had to ride with DS Bennett."

Judging by the look Fiona levelled at the younger man, he was one unsolicited comment away from becoming the victim in a fresh murder.

"Speaking of," Ryan said before Cal could cram his foot even deeper into his mouth. "Where is Graham?"

There were only three occupied workstations. Digit's was covered in screens and tech gadgets that had crept onto the empty desks either side of him. Fiona's desk was neat, organised to an almost obsessive level, and the spot that looked like a bomb constructed from sketch pads and charcoal pencils had gone off had to be Cal's. The other five workspaces sat empty.

Fiona's cheeks coloured. "He asked Lee to be transferred back to Serious Fraud."

Ryan nodded, ignoring the sharp pang in his chest. DS Moore had been one of the few detectives he'd thought was on his side. He knew Graham wouldn't have made the decision lightly. Most would consider going from Major Crimes to investigating dodgy tax returns a big step down. He pushed the feeling away. They had work to do.

Fiona's phone buzzed on her desk. With an apologetic

glance at Ryan, she picked it up. Her expression tightened as she listened. "Is he okay? Right. No, I'll figure it out. Keep me updated."

She ended the call, pinching the bridge of her nose. "Sorry, Sir. That was daycare. Liam cut his forehead open, and Nathan's stuck in a meeting in Sheffield. I have to go pick him up and get it stitched."

Ryan's mouth dropped open. "You have a kid?" When he'd known her, Fiona had been allergic to anything under three feet and snotty.

"Twins. Max and Liam." She sighed. "Long story."

"It's okay, we'll manage," Ryan said, feeling an unwelcome stab of envy at Fiona having a life outside the job. "Go. Keep us in the loop."

It'd give him a chance to assess the junior members of the team on his own terms. He turned to the others. "Digit, you're here starting the research." He knew from the files that research and analysis were Digit's strengths. "Sheri, Cal, you're both with me. We'll take a pool car. Sheri, you're navigating."

Sheri pulled her puffer jacket back on. Ryan looked out the small window at the rolling black clouds forming on the horizon, then back at Cal's best man get-up. "You might want to grab a coat?"

He shrugged. "From the North, aren't I? Don't feel the cold, boss."

Ryan decided not to point out that Manchester wasn't geographically much further north than Chesterfield.

"Suit yourself."

An anticipatory fizz thrummed beneath his skin. The familiar cocktail of excitement and dread that accompanied a new case. A feeling he'd sorely missed these last five months, buried beneath the wreckage of his disastrous last case and the long, brutal recovery that followed.

After all, if experience had taught him anything, the best way to drown out his demons was to bury them under a pile of suspects and paperwork.

CHAPTER SEVEN

The Nine Ladies. Why there? A connection to the place or just convenience? Either answer might help them down the line. Ryan had a vague memory of being dragged through the bracken by his parents to see some decidedly unremarkable lumps of stone, but they hadn't left much of an impression on him.

The familiar Derbyshire landscape rolled past the window as he followed Sheri's directions, a patchwork of green fields and weathered stone walls. Cal was blissfully silent in the back, tapping away on his phone.

"You did psychology at Derby, didn't you?" Ryan asked, glancing at Sheri.

"Yes, Sir." She looked up from her notebook. "Switched from a business degree. My parents still think I should've stuck with it and got a finance job in the city." She frowned, suggesting she didn't agree. "My mum sends me job listings for HR and office positions at least once a month."

Ryan could tell from her tone that she struggled with her parents' disapproval. "They'll come around," he said.

"That's what I keep telling myself," Sheri said quietly.

They turned off the A6 onto a narrow road lined with woods on one side and fields on the other. A few minutes later, Ryan pulled onto the verge opposite a marked police car. A battered light blue Ford van with German plates sat on the gravel shoulder in front of the car. Garish pink and yellow flowers were spray-painted across its sides.

Through the windscreen, Ryan saw a uniformed officer standing behind the van, gesturing as she spoke to a young couple. The PC had a solid build, dark hair and the no-nonsense expression often worn by rural police officers.

The girl slouched against the van's rear doors, arms folded. Her shoulder-length bright pink hair was at odds with her compressed lips. The boy had short hair dyed platinum blond at the tips and a more anxious air. He picked at a loose thread on his sleeve, eyes fixed on the ground. As Ryan and the others approached, the constable glanced up, relief on her face. She stepped forward to meet them, leaving the couple by the van.

Ryan introduced himself and his colleagues and showed her his Met warrant card.

"PC Tobin, Sir, from Matlock Station. The pair are from Germany. Travelling around the UK on a backpacking holiday."

"Have you been up to the stones?"

"No, Sir," she replied. "I got the impression Pinky over there would convince her boyfriend to do a runner if I didn't stay here and monitor them."

"So it was the girl who took the photos?"

PC Tobin nodded. "The Katy Perry wannabe with the pink hair is Hannah. She's still under the impression the whole thing's a practical joke. Kept going on about pigs' eyes resembling humans or something daft along those lines." She ran her fingers through her short hair. "Lukas was less convinced. He's

the one who called the station and reported it. After I got here
and realised it wasn't a hoax, I contacted my superiors."

"And the photos?"

"I emailed the photos on Hannah's phone to myself,
forwarded them to my boss, and deleted the originals from her
phone and cloud storage. They both swear they didn't post it to
social media before I arrived, and I believe them." She paused.
"Well, I believe Lukas would have looked more guilty if
Hannah had been lying."

Ryan made a mental note to get Digit to double-check. The
gruesome images weren't something they wanted out in the
public domain. Especially if the remains were human.

"How do we get to the site?"

She pointed up the road to a path leading into the moor.
"The stones are that way. About fifteen to twenty minutes at a
trot."

"How many entrance points does Stanton Moor have?"

The PC thought for a moment. "Maybe six or so from
memory?"

Ryan frowned. They'd need more manpower to keep the
scene secure and canvas any witnesses living close to the
various entry points.

Sheri poked her head around the side of the PC. "I spent a
year in Germany on a foreign exchange programme in high
school. I could see if I can get anything more out of the couple
and eavesdrop while they're speaking German?"

Ryan nodded. "Cal, you come with me to secure the crime
scene. Lee said the forensics team is on the way, but they're
coming from Derby. I don't want the rain to wash away our
evidence."

He turned to Sheri and PC Tobin. "Sheri, see what you can
get out of them. Find out if they passed anyone walking in or
out and make sure you have their contact details recorded in

case we need to speak to them again. I'll call Lee for some extra manpower. When they arrive, I want you to coordinate with PC Tobin. Send them to check as many of the entrances and exits to the moor as possible and knock on the doors of anyone living in the vicinity. It's a long shot, but someone might have seen something."

CHAPTER EIGHT

ONE TRICK RYAN HAD LEARNT FROM DCC CLIFFE WHEN he'd first started at the Met was to bring a duffle bag of crime scene essentials with him.

He pulled on the waterproof jacket and hiking boots he kept in the bag for remote crime scenes and loaded up a small rucksack with plastic booties and crime scene tape.

Cal was reading an information placard on the side of the path when Ryan joined him.

"Hey boss, have you ever been to the Cork Stone? According to this map, we should walk right past it. Someone added rings in the nineteenth century so people can climb it."

"Anything about eyeballs on that?" Ryan pointed to the sign.

"No."

"Then I don't need to know about it. Come on."

The wind picked up, and the black clouds rolled closer as they followed the muddy track into a wooded area of spindly trees. A tangle of overgrown briars and soggy weeds crept onto the trail, snagging on their trousers.

Ryan settled into the steady pace he used when he walked Winston, his long legs eating up the distance. The familiar rhythm helped to clear his mind, focusing his thoughts on the case ahead.

"There's no signal out here," Cal said, tapping furiously at his phone.

"The countryside. Shocking, I know."

Cal frowned. "I've got sixty-five thousand followers who expect daily content. Missed a day last week and lost three hundred."

"Sixty-five thousand people follow you? Why?"

"Started back when I was at the academy. Football fans followed me then, but now it's mostly true crime enthusiasts and aspiring coppers. I do educational posts too. They even let me do them during work hours to build awareness of careers in the police. DCI Lee thinks it's impressive how I'm inspiring the next generation of law enforcement."

Ryan rubbed his face. *Christ, now we're treating criminal investigations as content opportunities.*

Soon the trees thinned, and the Cork Stone appeared in the distance, thrusting out of the ground to tower over the surrounding landscape. Crisp moorland air filled Ryan's nose with the scent of damp earth and dormant heather. The moor probably looked nice in the summer when the heather bloomed in a riot of purple, but right now it clung to the boggy ground in miserable dull brown clumps.

Cal's eyes lit up as they drew level with the historic gritstone. Without warning, he thrust his phone into Ryan's hands.

"Oi, Guv!" Cal called out, already clambering up the metal rungs embedded in the rock face. "Take a pic of me, will ya? It'll be mint for the 'gram'!"

Ryan made a show of lifting the phone. "Oh, absolutely.

Then shall I get your good side while you pose next to the evidence from our murder scene?"

Cal shook his head. "Wouldn't fit my vibe. I keep my feed PG-rated so I can reach the next generation of police." He drew out the last word to poe-leece like some wannabe gangster.

Ryan studied the DC's face, hoping against hope he was taking the piss. It didn't look like it.

"Get your arse down here, you muppet. We're not bloody sightseeing."

Cal rolled his eyes. Ryan heard him mutter 'Okay boomer' under his breath as he reluctantly climbed down and took the phone Ryan held out.

As Cal stomped off ahead, Ryan opened his mouth to point out he'd been born in the eighties, not straight after the Second World War. He shut it again. What was the point?

Had he ever been that young and stupid? Probably, but at least he'd had the decency not to constantly share his idiocy with the world at large.

Ryan caught up with Cal. They continued up the track in silence, occasionally walking on the edge of the heather to avoid the thicker patches of mud.

Ryan trudged along, lost in thought. His new team was like a box of mismatched socks. All technically functional, but a bloody nightmare to sort out. He'd known coming back to Chesterfield would be a challenge, but this lot... Christ.

Still, buried beneath the layers of inexperience, attitude, and possibly, in Cal's case, a social media addiction, there had to be some promise. He just hoped he was up to the task.

He hopped over a deep puddle and looked about. The DC had fallen behind.

"Preserving the crime scene is more important than your Italian brogues," Ryan called back. White steam from his huff of impatience blocked his view of Cal picking his way through a muddy section.

When Cal reached Ryan, he was gulping like a landed fish.

Ryan sighed. He eyed the DC's biceps bulging through his tailored jacket. "Don't you go to the gym?"

"It's a different type of fitness," Cal wheezed, his hands pressed hard on his thighs as he leaned over.

"Just for show then?"

Cal scowled but said nothing, still trying to catch his breath.

The air felt heavier. The dark clouds were almost on top of them. Ryan shifted his focus to beating the rain to the stone circle. "Right, follow along when you're ready."

"For what it's worth, boss," Cal panted, hurrying along beside him, "I reckon you're in the clear." The words came out rushed, but his usual swagger was back.

"For what?" Ryan asked with fake innocence. There was only one thing Cal could be talking about.

"Ah, the disappearance. I don't think you killed her, I mean."

A slight hitch in Cal's step.

Ryan stopped. "Are you limping?"

Cal waved him off. "Nah, it's nothing. Old football injury. Flares up sometimes."

Ryan swallowed a snort. More likely, a blister. "Do you want to head back and send Sheri instead?"

"I'm fine," Cal said, gritting his teeth. He picked up the pace as if to prove his point.

"I'm not trying to suck up to the new boss," he said a moment later. "By saying you didn't do it. DS Moore let me read the case file after we found out you got the job. He's still technically on the case."

"And what did you deduce, Detective?" Ryan asked,

fighting to keep his words casual when all he wanted to do was reach across and start shaking the kid till he spewed out every little detail he'd gleaned from the file.

"That you didn't have time to do it based on your neighbour's testimony about when you left home and the CCTV footage."

Fuck, nothing new then. "The neighbour could have got the time wrong," Ryan said, playing devil's advocate.

"Maybe," Cal conceded. "Yeah, but she'd have to be out by a good twenty minutes for that to work, wouldn't she? Old folk don't mess about with their routines, do they? Me nan gets up, has her brekkie, walks her Cockapoo round the block. Same time every single day, like clockwork. That neighbour was seventy. If she's saying she clocked you at twenty past seven when she were making her porridge, then she probably did, didn't she?"

What I'd argued with Lampton, Ryan thought. *There might be a brain cell or two rubbing together under that floppy fringe.*

"They said I had an accomplice."

"It still doesn't add up."

Cal's limp was getting worse. Ryan took in the lines of pain around his eyes, at odds with the determination on his face, like he was fighting an invisible battle. Not a blister then. He got the feeling there was a history behind the injury, and he made a mental note to ask Fiona if she knew anything about it when things calmed down.

"Go on." At least talking seemed to distract the lad from the pain.

"According to Graham, you were already a detective with a reputation for clever solves. He made you out to be some genius with puzzles. If you'd wanted to kill someone, you could have done it without involving someone else. Too risky. The problem was Lampton didn't have any other suspects, and his smartest detective was benched."

Ryan laughed. "That sounded a lot like sucking up to me."

Cal grinned. "That last bit, sure."

"Well, thanks for the vote of confidence. Be sure to spread the word with all my old colleagues who still think I did it, will you?"

A large raindrop hit his nose. Then another. Shit.

Ryan looked at his watch. If PC Tobin's time estimation was correct, they should be there.

They jogged down the path through the middle of a stand of ferns and into a grassy clearing. Nine stubby stones lay in a rough circle.

"That's it?" Cal gasped, breathing hard again from the short run.

"It's no Stonehenge." The circle was even more unimpressive than Ryan remembered, but as they got closer, the sight that greeted them in the middle of the circle captured his full attention.

Ryan gestured to Cal to stop walking and handed him a pair of plastic booties before pulling a pair over his own hiking boots. At least the DC had the sense to fall in behind him as Ryan approached. He monitored the ground to avoid stepping on any fresh prints or evidence.

He reached the centre of the circle. Somehow, the stark reality was worse in person.

Happy that their approach had done minimal damage, he studied the display, trying to lock the details in his memory before the rain compromised the scene.

In the heart of the stone circle, a meticulously carved five-pointed star scarred the soil. Five thin wooden stakes, each driven into the ground at the precise points of the pentagram, stood like silent sentinels. At the centre, a pair of small bronze statues sat back-to-back, separated by a bundle of partially burnt herbs and leaves and an empty metal chalice. The statue facing him depicted a horned, faun-like man sitting cross-legged, surrounded by animals.

Carefully placing each foot, he circled to the far side of the pentagram while Cal hovered in the background. The second statue came into view. Three women standing beneath a tree. If this had been all, Ryan could have passed the ritual trappings off as harmless Halloween shenanigans.

But now he could see what Hannah's photos had hinted at.

Not one pair of human eyeballs, but four.

Ryan's stomach churned as he took in the grisly sight. Four of the five stakes were adorned with a pair of eyeballs, two impaled on each tip and pushed a hand span down the shaft. As he continued his slow, methodical circuit of the display, Ryan fought to maintain his professional detachment. The irises, clouded and lifeless, seemed to stare outward accusingly. One green pair, and three blue.

The implications made his blood run cold. Were they looking for four victims who'd been maimed, or four bodies? And why was the fifth stake ominously empty? A message or someone the killer had missed?

CHAPTER NINE

RYAN CONTEMPLATED STRINGING CRIME SCENE TAPE between the trees around the clearing, but a series of fat raindrops hitting his head changed his mind.

Aware the rain could wash away evidence, he pulled out his phone and shot a dozen close-ups of the ritual. The camera flash illuminated the scene in stark bursts, searing the images into his memory. He retrieved a plastic sheet from his rucksack and handed it to Cal.

"Thanks, boss." Cal went to pull it over himself.

"It's not for you." Ryan pointed to the grisly display. "It's to protect that."

As the scattering of raindrops turned into a downpour, they stood across from each other, holding the clear blue sheet between them above the stakes. The rain drummed against the plastic and pooled in the middle, mocking their efforts.

Cal looked miserable as icy rain soaked through his blazer and thin cotton shirt. He flipped his head futilely, attempting to shift his floppy fringe from where it sagged across his eyes. His arms seemed to hold up better than Ryan's, though. Ryan prayed the crime techs arrived soon as he fought to hide the burn growing in his muscles. His shoulders screamed in protest, but he gritted his teeth, determined not to let the evidence wash away.

Cal glanced down at the nearest stake and swallowed. He looked away.

Ryan knew the feeling. The pair of blue eyes closest to him, so similar to his own, seemed to follow him wherever he looked, pleading with him to find their missing owner and make the perpetrator pay.

Something white streaked through the trees behind Cal. A moment later, a small dog bounded out of the bushes, its ears flapping up and down.

"Head's up, there's a dog incoming," Ryan said.

Cal looked over his shoulder, his eyes widening with alarm disproportionate to the creature barrelling towards them. Some sort of miniature poodle cross from the look of it, that could easily be mistaken for a wet lamb. And annoyingly friendly.

"Argh." Cal yelped. "Get off." He cowered away, desperately fighting to keep his side of the sheet in place. The dog jumped up on him, leaving muddy paw prints on his trousers as he tried to shake it off. The dog ignored him and carried on snuffling upwards, its nose heading towards his crotch.

"Think you could stop it destroying our crime scene?" Ryan asked, trying to hide a smile.

"I'm trying. I'm not a fan of dogs," Cal replied through gritted teeth as he batted ineffectually at the dog with one hand.

"It shows."

The dog started humping Cal's leg.

Male, Ryan noticed.

Cal let out a shriek that should've been too high-pitched to have come from a grown man and dropped the sheet. He threw the dog off and jumped away. Luckily, there was just enough plastic on his side for the edge to catch on the top of the closest stake. The pooled water gushed down the sides and filled in the shallow lines of the star carved in the dirt.

Ryan sighed. Not ideal, but better than the entire scene getting rained on. The dog shied away from Cal and went over to a stake. He cocked his leg.

"Sit," Ryan said in the voice he reserved for when he wanted Winston to know he meant business.

The dog's backside hit the ground before his brain registered the command. He turned his head in Ryan's direction. His tail swished along the ground, but he stayed seated.

"Grab him," Ryan said to Cal.

"Um..." Cal looked from Ryan to the muddy dog and back again. Probably worried about his bloody suit.

"For Christ's sake, grab this side, then." Ryan nodded at the plastic sheet.

Cal gave him a grateful look and hurried over.

Ryan leaned over and scooped the dog up. Mud-caked paws scraped along his jacket as the dog tried to lick his face with a tongue long enough to make a frog proud. Ryan wasn't enjoying the dog's attempts at French kissing or the overwhelming aroma of wet dog fur, but at least it wasn't pissing all over their crime scene.

"Fiddles, come," a woman's voice rang out from the trees. "Fiddles? Where are you, you little rascal?"

A spry-looking elderly woman with a pair of hiking sticks and a bright purple dog lead hanging around her neck marched out of the trees. Her weathered face was pink from exertion, in stark contrast to Cal's blue-tinged lips.

Spying the dog in Ryan's arms, she gave a yelp and rushed in their direction. "Yoo-hoo! Young man, that's my dog."

Fiddles spotted the woman and wiggled. Feeling his grip slipping, Ryan gave up and let the dog race over to its owner.

"There you are," the woman said. She knelt down and gave the little dog a body rub as it licked her face.

She obviously didn't share Ryan's aversion to canine tongue kisses.

"Was the strange man bothering you?" She glared at Ryan with a look that suggested she'd foiled a dog-napping attempt.

Ryan bristled but said nothing, hoping the woman would go on her way without noticing the scene behind him. Instead, she straightened and marched over, no doubt ready to give the strange man a piece of her mind.

Ryan held his hand out as she approached. "Madam, please stay there." His tone was firm but polite, a trick learned over years of dealing with the public.

The woman puffed up, her lips pressing together. "I'll have you know, young man, that Stanton Moor is part of the National Trust and accessible to everyone all year round."

"It also said on the sign at the entrance that dogs should be on a leash," Cal called out.

"Pish posh," the lady replied. "He's hardly going to bother the sheep."

More likely they'd mistake him for one of their own, Ryan thought as the woman realised there was something odd in the centre of the circle. She tried to lean past him. He moved to obscure her view, grateful the edge of the clear blue plastic mostly hid the eyeballs from sight.

She must have seen something, though, as her eyes narrowed. "You two aren't those people, are you?"

Ryan was quite interested to hear who those people might be as soon as he'd got her away from their crime scene. "Madam, I'm Detective Inspector Hale, and this is an active crime scene. I have to ask you to leave."

"You don't look like police officers," the woman replied, her gaze now fixed on Cal's muscular torso prominently on display under his soaked shirt. The hint of a large tattoo showed on the left side of his chest under the wet cotton. If Cal's pecs distracted her from the gruesome scene in front of her, she could stare away as far as Ryan was concerned. He took out his warrant card and gave it to her.

The woman studied his ID as if she suspected it was a forgery. "This says Metropolitan Police on it."

"I transferred to Chesterfield Station recently. DC Pine and I are both with the Derbyshire Force. You're welcome to call the station and check." Hopefully, Barney would admit he worked there.

"That won't be necessary. I'm sure you're both Derbyshire's finest." She drew out the last word and gave Cal a long up and down.

The young detective looked scandalised.

Ryan felt his lips curling up and fought them back under control. "Mrs?"

"Ms Lavender. I'm still on the market. Call me Maggie." She looked over at Cal again. "Both of you."

"Maggie. I'll need you to put... Fiddles, is it?...back on his lead, please." Ryan led her in a half-circle until the ritual site and Cal's distracting bulges were at her back.

"It's short for Mr Fiddlesticks, actually," Maggie said. She clipped the lead onto the dog's collar. "He got his name because when he was a puppy he kept fiddling with himself."

Cal's mouth dropped open behind her.

"He wouldn't stop chewing on his paws," she continued. "The vet thought it was anxiety."

"As I said, we're trying to secure this area until the forensics team arrive, so maybe you could help me with our enquiries over there?"

"Forensics. Like CSI?" Maggie asked as he led her to the edge of the clearing. Her head turned from side to side as if technicians in white suits might spring from the bushes shouting 'Surprise!'

"Something like that," Ryan replied. He didn't know many techs who appreciated the comparison, but he wasn't going to get into that now.

"Do you walk Mr Fiddlesticks on the moor regularly?"

"Every day, rain or shine," Maggie replied proudly. "I live in a little cottage in Birchover." She waved a hand vaguely over her shoulder.

"Are there many entrances to the moor?"

She thought for a moment. "Five main entrances and at least a dozen more unofficial entry points."

Ryan groaned. More than PC Tobin had thought. Maybe he could use Maggie's nosiness to their advantage and get rid of her in the process.

"Maggie, you know the Birchover Road entrance near the Cork Stone?"

"Of course. I'm heading that way now."

"One of our colleagues, DC Dewan, is there coordinating uniformed officers to stand at all the entry and exit points to the moor while we conduct our investigation. With your in-depth local knowledge of the area, any advice you could give her would be invaluable."

He wondered if he'd laid it on a bit thick, but the slight woman preened under his praise.

"Of course. Mr Fiddlesticks and I will head right there." She stole a long glance at Cal, as if committing the sight to memory.

"Before you go," Ryan said. "You mentioned those people. What did you mean by that?"

"The weird ones who come and chant in the circle at all

hours. I should have realised you two weren't with them. No velvet cloaks," she finished with a knowing nod.

"Are they up here often?"

."Mostly in the evening, when it's a full moon." She leaned forward and lowered her voice to a whisper as if they might hear her. "Devil worshippers. They like to prance around the stones naked. All sorts too. Old, young, male, female. Not a stitch between them." Her lips pressed together in disapproval.

"And you've seen them doing this, have you?" Ryan could easily picture Ms Lavender crouched in the bushes, tutting away to herself, as she spied on the wicked goings-on.

"Well, no. What if they went after Mr Fiddlesticks? They perform animal sacrifices, you know. Probably summon demons as well. But everybody talks about the dancing." She showed much less concern about demons and animal sacrifices than about the naked prancing. She gestured to the dog. "They can smell things we can't. Mr Fiddlesticks went mental last month. Hackles up, growling at nothing. Well, I say nothing, but my mother would've said he saw something wearing a face that wasn't its own."

A chill crawled up Ryan's spine. He brushed it off. "Do you know the names of these devil worshippers?"

She looked scandalised at the thought. "They aren't locals, but Terry might know their names."

"And where can I find Terry?"

"He runs The Forest Sage Inn over in Stanton-in-Peak. I think they go in there for a pint afterwards. I imagine it's thirsty work calling up Satan."

CHAPTER TEN

"You were right. You do have a way with the ladies," Ryan said as he relieved Cal from his post. "Even if she was old enough to be your nan."

Cal shuddered. "I was worried she was going to come over and take a bite out of me at one point."

Ryan directed Cal to use the surrounding trees to string up crime scene tape around the perimeter of the clearing. A few minutes later, his arms ached. He was about to call the detective over to switch places when a pair of crime scene technicians in white paper overalls appeared at the edge of the clearing, on the opposite side from where he and Cal had entered.

The taller of the two, a beautiful black woman with a scowl that would send Winston scurrying for cover, caught Cal's eye. He fumbled with the tape, nearly dropping the roll as she approached. From her curt gestures, it was obvious she was asking him about their approach into the circle. She turned and spoke to one of the other techs, who started laying down stepping plates along the route, checking for existing footprints or other evidence as he laid each one.

From now on, this would form the common approach path inside the inner cordon.

The short male tech gave Ryan a nod but said nothing as he placed plastic plates in a circle around the ritual site.

Once the plates were laid, the scowling tech came over, carrying a crime scene kit. She strode along the steps, her slim hips swinging like a runway model, as if she'd put on the white suit as some kind of avant-garde statement. She stopped in front of him and somehow the scowl deepened.

"And who are you?" she asked in a thick French accent.

"DI Hale. I'm the new DI for Major Crimes."

She looked down at his drooping arms. "Can you continue this?"

"Not for much longer," Ryan admitted. The burn in his muscles had receded to a dull ache, but he could feel his damaged left hand shaking.

"Jeff," the woman called out to the tech who'd just finished laying the plates, the name coming out closer to 'Zheff'. The man jumped and then hurried over. "Exchange your place with the detective while I get the tent."

The woman looked young to be the senior crime scene officer, Ryan thought, or maybe it was sunscreen use or Botox? He didn't know and didn't care. All he hoped was that she'd got the position because she was very good at her job. After years in public service, Ryan was a firm believer that merit should override seniority, even if it rarely happened.

She disappeared into the bushes. There was an awkward shuffle as they switched positions, but eventually Jeff was holding the plastic edges and Ryan let his arms drop to his sides with a sigh of relief.

A minute later, another pair of techs arrived with a large white tent. They worked together with practised ease and soon had it erected over the stakes and the stepping plates.

Cal returned to Ryan's side with an armful of unravelled crime scene tape and a dejected expression. "I got demoted."

Ryan glanced over at the trees. Jeff was now stringing the tape around the glade.

Cal held out the wad of tape to Ryan.

Ryan looked at him.

The DC huffed, then smoothed the tape and started winding it back onto the roll.

The scowling French tech reappeared beside them.

"I should introduce myself." Her face implied she'd prefer to slit her own throat, but she pressed on despite her obvious distaste for the whole affair. "Eloise Durrant. I'm the SOCO here." She waved a delicate hand around the clearing like a queen from the royal balcony before her gaze slipped down to Cal's wet shirt as he wrestled the tape.

Ryan fought the urge to roll his eyes. Despite her beauty and aloof demeanour, the young SOCO appeared no less immune to Cal's chest on display under his wet shirt than Maggie.

"I'll be the SIO on this case." He pulled off his plastic gloves and flexed his fingers. "I'd shake your hand, but my fingers have lost all feeling."

Cal noticed Eloise. He gave up on the tape and instead tried to hide it behind his back. "DC Cal Pine," he stammered out. He reached out his hand, then remembered the tape and changed his mind. Redness rose up his neck.

"Celtic, oui?" she asked Cal.

"Huh?"

"Ze tattoo?" She gestured at his chest.

Cal looked down at the design showing through the soaked fabric. "Ah... I dunno. I just liked the pattern, so I worked it into the design." The flush reached his cheeks.

Keen to move away from whatever this was, Ryan glanced at his watch. "You made good time. Lee said you were coming from Trent-upon-Burton, and it took us fifteen minutes to hike in."

"As you had the attention to put on overshoes, gloves and attempt to protect the scene from the rain, I will share with you my petite secret. There is a hidden entry to the moor on Lee's Road three hundred metres in that direction." She pointed in the opposite direction to the one they'd come from. "Paul, my boss, likes to... how did he say... ramble on the weekends, and apparently he has rambled here in the past. He gave instructions to my team where to go."

Ryan took a deep breath, cursing PC Tobin for not being more familiar with the area and cursing Paul for not thinking to inform the detective team. But at least he wouldn't need to hike the longer distance if he needed to visit the site again or put up with Cal and his social media escapades on the way back.

Ryan followed Eloise into the tent, leaving Cal outside. The SOCO walked around the stakes, studying the scene.

"Pretty weird," Ryan said. "A dog walker mentioned satanic rituals."

"It is not satanic," Eloise replied, crouching down for a closer look at the statue of the faun man. "This is Wiccan."

Ryan blinked. "Wicca? As in witches?"

Eloise frowned. "Sometimes witchcraft. In the majority, it's simply persons who desire to honour nature and explore their connection to the ancient past, before Christianity. An alternative to the patriarchal monotheism of more recent traditional religion."

She pointed to the star shape in the circle. "Look at the pentagram. The five points of the star represent the four classical elements. Air, water, fire, earth, and the fifth element, aether." She tapped her chin thoughtfully. "This fifth element, it can also mean spirit or the self. Maybe this is why they left one stake empty? To represent their own place in the ritual?"

"Is Wicca your belief system?" Ryan asked.

Eloise lifted her chin, her eyes narrowing. "Pourquoi? You have a problem with that?"

"No," Ryan replied. "Your insight into this case could be valuable."

Eloise's lips shifted into something that was nearly a smile. "I am not a follower of Wicca, but my grandmère was a Nganga in Cameroon, a Westerner might say a witch, before she moved to France with my grandpère in the sixties. Spirituality fascinated me from an early age. My dissertation compared spiritual practices between Western and African traditions." She frowned again. "But no, no human eyeballs involved."

"Wow, you really know your stuff," Cal said, crowding into the tent behind Ryan.

Eloise tucked a stray strand of hair back under her hood and looked down her nose at him. "It is all in the petits détails, you see."

Ryan agreed. "Does your grandmère still practise?" Ryan asked. If she did, she might be a useful source of information.

"Non, she is dead."

"Oh, I'm sorry," Ryan said, as the photographer arrived with her camera.

The SOCO gave a Gallic shrug, then directed the photographer where she wanted the woman to start.

"Can you tell us anything about the statues?"

"Wicca usually follows a duotheistic structure, though there are branches with different beliefs. The Triple Goddess and the Horned God are central to British Traditional Wicca. These statues, they represent these deities."

"Hmm, yes," Cal said in Ryan's ear, nodding along with her words. Ryan cleared his throat, and Cal shuffled further around the plates. The tent was cramped with the two detectives, Eloise and the photographer.

"Don't you have a job to do, DC Pine?" he asked the constable.

"No."

Ryan gave him a look that suggested he should find one.

"Right, I'll just... go check the perimeter again," he said, reluctantly leaving the dry tent.

"What about the dried leaves?"

"It looks like a sage and lavender smudge. The burning herbs are used in rituals to cleanse negative energy and to increase spiritual awareness."

Ryan imagined the killer had racked up plenty of negative energy that needed cleansing after gouging the eyeballs out of their victims.

When Eloise was sure her tech had captured the scene to her satisfaction, she opened her kit and prepared evidence bags for the statues.

"Is the pathologist coming?" Ryan asked.

"Non, he is occupied with a drowning victim in Derby. He has authorised me to collect everything and bring it to him at the morgue."

"Will you call me if you find anything unusual?"

"More unusual than eyeballs on stakes?"

He reached into his pocket for a card, the stiff fingers of his left hand struggling to grip the thin cardboard. He managed to grab one and held it out. "I haven't got my new cards yet, but my mobile number's the same."

"I will call if we find anything of interest," Eloise replied. She paused as if she wanted to say more.

Ryan waited.

"My grandmère always said the stones demand a price. She'd say, 'Feed the stones or they'll feed on you.'" She looked into Ryan's eyes. "Be careful, Detective."

CHAPTER ELEVEN

RYAN THANKED THE TECH THROUGH THE OPEN PASSENGER window. The driver nodded and drove past the line of cars, executed a three-point turn, and headed back the way he'd come.

The German backpackers and their flower power van had disappeared, but Sheri remained beside the police van, talking to Ms Lavender while Mr Fiddlesticks cavorted in circles around them. Further down the road, PC Tobin coordinated with a small group of uniformed officers standing in front of a pair of patrol cars.

Ryan glanced at Cal, who stood shivering and looking more miserable than Winston at the vets. He took pity on him. "Grab one of those patrol cars and swing by your place for a quick change, then head back to the station. See if you can find any recent Misper reports that could match our victims. Sheri and I will head to the pub and track down this Terry bloke."

Cal nodded gratefully and hurried off.

"You'll want to hear this, Sir," Sheri said as Ryan approached.

She gestured to Maggie. "Could you please tell DI Hale what you saw this morning?"

The woman preened. "I was out with Mr Fiddlesticks at five. He's got a weak bladder, bless him. I saw a little car creeping along without its lights on, which I thought was odd. Whoever was driving it was so hunched over the steering wheel, I'm surprised they could see where they were going."

"Did you notice the make or model?" Ryan asked.

"Sorry, it was still dark, and cars aren't my thing, dear."

———

The Forest Sage Inn stood half a mile down the road at the edge of Stanton in Peak. An English pub with hanging baskets of herbs framing the entrance and ivy trailing down brown brick past white lattice windows. In the side courtyard, benches sat stacked on empty picnic tables. Two high-end SUVs occupied one corner of the car park.

A life-size wooden statue stood by the door. An old man with a flowing beard and cloak, polished smooth where countless hands had touched it in passing. The pub's namesake, Ryan figured.

The window sign read 'Closed,' but the door stood propped open.

Inside, the pub suffered from an identity crisis. Like Ye Olde England and Paganism had clashed in battle, then both limped off the field with no clear victor. Dried herbs hung from exposed beams. Ancient farming tools lined the dark panelling above benches carved with Celtic knots. A gnarled staff was mounted over the open hearth. Behind the bar, taps offered English lagers, ales, stouts, and ciders, including, Ryan noticed, a local brew called Druid's Head.

At the end of the counter, a folded paper lay open to the

quick crossword. Someone had bungled 6 Down. For 'moorland bird (5)' they'd pencilled GROUSE when the crossings wanted SNIPE. Ryan's fingers itched for a pen, but he forced himself to focus on the task at hand.

He was about to call out when a large man with a jovial face stepped out from the back room. If he'd been an actor, he'd have been a shoo-in for 'innkeeper of a medieval pub'.

"Canna help yer?" the man asked in a broad Irish accent. "The bar doesn't open for another hour."

"Are you Terry?"

"Aw, that's me all right." He looked Ryan up and down. "Not the tax man, are yer?" He laughed nervously.

"DI Hale." Ryan gestured to Sheri. "And this is DC Dewan. We'd like to ask you a few questions about some of your patrons."

Terry nodded and pointed to the nearest table.

They sat, and Sheri pulled out her notebook and pen.

"Is this about Willy?" Terry asked. "I told that gobshite riding a horse while drunk counts as drunk driving. That's true, isn't it?"

"Technically, he could be charged under the Licensing Act 1872," Sheri replied before Ryan could admit he had no idea. There weren't many people riding horses through London outside of ceremonial parades.

Sheri continued. "The act states a person is guilty of an offence if he or she is drunk on any highway or other public place while in charge of any carriage, horse, or cattle."

"Ha, see!" Terry slapped his leg. "I told him, so I did."

Sheri shrugged. "More likely, he'd be charged with being drunk and disorderly."

"That's not why we're here," Ryan interrupted. "Tell me about the group that carries out rituals up at the stone circle. I was told they come here every full moon after their ritual at the Nine Ladies."

"Aw, Old Potty and his mad witches? Sure, they're a harmless bunch of eejits if ye ask me. Sometimes they pop in for a bit of food or a pint before or after, but it's not every full moon, like. I reckon they head off to Bamford Moor or the Grey Ladies now and again."

"Were they in here last night for Halloween?"

He shook his head. "Ah, not a sausage. Dead quiet, it was. I don't go in for theme nights."

"When was the last time you saw them?"

Terry thought for a moment. "They were in here about a month ago. I think it was the full moon."

Ryan felt a stab of disappointment but pushed it aside. The group hadn't been in, but that didn't mean one of them hadn't visited the circle.

"Does Old Potty have a real name?"

"Lawrence, I think? Lawrence Potts. Lives in Matlock or thereabouts. Calls himself the high elder priest, if ye can believe it. His missus used to be the high priestess, but she didn't seem all that arsed about it, like. Haven't seen her in a while, though. Word has it she caught him playin' away. Dirty oul' dog. Probably with one of the initiates. That's what the rest of 'em call themselves."

"Are all the initiates female?" Ryan asked.

"There's been the odd fella come and go. There was a new one here the last couple of times, actually. I remember him 'cos he comes with this stunner of a blonde and he didn't look like he should be her cup of tea at all. Goth-lookin' fella with long greasy black hair and more slap on than me sister. There's an older pair that comes too, regular as clockwork. Husband and wife. Odd thing to do as a married couple if ye ask me, but sure, live and let live. But they do tend to be women. Nice little number if ye can get it, eh?"

He gave Ryan a knowing nod, then turned to Sheri.

"Sorry, love. No offence meant."

Sheri ignored him.

"What age are the initiates?" Ryan asked.

"All sorts. Young, old, middle-aged. Some of them ye'd never guess they were into all that new-age craic if ye passed them on the street. Look as normal as you and me."

Ryan handed Terry his card. "Thanks for your time."

Outside, he called Digit before they reached the car. "I need you to find me some information and an address for a Lawrence Potts. Possibly living out Matlock way."

"Consider it done, Sir," Digit replied.

CHAPTER TWELVE

"Come in."

Ryan entered DCI Lee's office. She sat behind her glass desk, laptop open, surrounded by neatly stacked paperwork. Behind her, an artful arrangement of houseplants in bright pots gave the room a splash of personality. A departure from the usual bland offices of the upper brass.

Lee gestured to a chair. "Thanks for coming up, Ryan. I know we barely had time for introductions this morning before I threw you straight into the deep end." She grimaced. "Not quite the welcome I'd planned, but murder has a way of ignoring our schedules. There are a few things we need to cover now that you've caught your breath."

"Appreciated, Ma'am. Though I can't say I'm complaining about hitting the ground running."

"Keen. I like that."

Ryan noticed her expensive navy suit was offset by a chunky jade necklace that hinted at a rebellious streak. His gaze drifted to the only personal item on her desk. A photo of

Lee grinning beside a short black woman, both clutching an amusingly shaped marrow.

"My wife, Sandra," Lee said, catching his look. "Two-time champions of the spring fair's largest marrow competition. In this job, it's important to have hobbies. Work-life balance and all." She studied him with knowing eyes. "Do you have any hobbies, DI Hale?"

Ryan scrambled for an answer. Walking Winston sounded pathetic. Did browsing the craft beer aisle at Tesco count? "I enjoy trying new craft beers."

The words came out more like a question. Christ, now she thought he was the stereotypical alcoholic detective.

If Lee suspected he was all work and no play, she kept it to herself. "Let me be upfront, Detective. You prefer straight talk, yes?"

"Yes, Ma'am."

"Chief Inspector Lampton was vehemently against your appointment. He spoke at length about your perceived failings."

"I'm surprised he's not still in here listing them off."

Lee smiled. "He advocated strongly for another candidate. Superintendent Dockery disagreed. According to the superintendent you once saved his mother from being buried alive. I look forward to hearing that story one day. His willingness to take you back on, along with DCC Cliffe's support, tipped it in your favour."

Ryan exhaled slowly. DCC Cliffe, the head of EMSOU, had been the one to piece Ryan back together twelve years ago when he'd started at the Met, smoothing his rough edges with patience and the occasional boot up the rear. It had been Cliffe who'd visited him in hospital and planted the seed about returning to Chesterfield.

"I trust my superiors' judgement, but I'm still on the fence about you," Lee continued. "I asked DCI Hardlow about your time at the Met. He said while your team were devoted to you, half of Scotland Yard wouldn't piss on you if you were on fire."

Ryan laughed. That sounded like Hardlow. "Fair assessment, Ma'am."

"However, he admitted you have an uncanny ability to see connections others miss, and that made you worth the hassle." She fixed him with a pointed look. "But I will not tolerate any shit. Clear?"

"Permission to be frank?"

She nodded.

"I'm not here for games or red tape. That's your job, dealing with bureaucrats. I'm here to close cases and help victims. Nothing else matters." He leaned forward. "I expect a lot from my team, but I'll be in the trenches with them. If you're good with that, we'll get along fine."

"I can work with that." Lee pressed her lips together. "Now, there's something I should address. I've reviewed your wife's case. There's no evidence pointing to your involvement, but you're still listed as a suspect."

His fingers curled into fists in his lap.

Don't say it. Don't say it.

Her voice was steel. "To be clear, DI Hale, you are not to investigate your wife's disappearance."

Fuck. She said it.

For a moment, Ryan's heart seemed to stop.

Jaime.

His eyes fell to the pale band of skin on his ring finger. A sight he still hadn't grown accustomed to, even five months after the surgeon had cut through his wedding band to save his mangled hand.

He'd known the warning would come, but he'd expected

more preamble. Not a straightforward order delivered before his feet were under the desk.

"Yes, Ma'am." The words tasted like sawdust.

Lee leaned back. "Good. I'm glad we understand each other." She paused. "So why Chesterfield?"

The unspoken question hung heavy. Why return to a place where half the force thought he'd murdered his wife and hidden the body?

Ryan's jaw tightened.

Justice. Closure. Redemption.

Possibly vengeance, if it came to that.

All answers the shrewd DCI wouldn't appreciate.

"I wanted to come home," he said.

Even as the lie slipped out, he realised it held a sliver of truth, so small it was almost imperceptible, but there.

Lee's dark eyes held his for a long moment. "It was no secret that DI Dobson had one foot out the door towards retirement and little interest in his job between dog meets."

She frowned. "I didn't enjoy seeing our Major Crimes Unit sidelined from the more complex operations. Now that Dobson has thankfully taken early retirement for medical reasons, our unit needs a kick up the arse. And from what I hear, you're the detective to deliver it."

Ryan allowed himself a faint smile. "My boots have been mistaken for steel-caps in the past, Ma'am."

"Good." Lee straightened in her seat. "There's one more thing."

Something in her tone made the hair on the back of his neck rise.

"You've been through a traumatic experience."

Her gaze flicked to the faint scars cutting across his cheek, then dropped to his hands.

Without a word, Ryan turned his palms down on the glossy

surface of the desk. A silent dare for her to take in the ropey red scars crisscrossing his knuckles, to notice how the pinky and ring fingers of his left hand bent at unnatural angles the surgeon couldn't fully correct.

Lee regarded his injuries without reaction.

"Everything has healed as much as it's going to, Ma'am. I've been officially cleared for active duty."

He didn't mention how he still jolted awake most nights, heart pounding, as fragments of his captivity replayed in a loop in his head.

"Your physical wounds may have healed, but you don't go through what happened to you without lasting psychological effects." Her tone was blunt but not unkind. "When I agreed to this appointment, the only condition I required from DCC Cliffe was that you attend counselling sessions with one of our force-appointed psychologists."

Ryan stiffened. He folded his arms across his chest. "No."

Her eyes met his, unwavering. "Twice weekly appointments for a minimum of six months. Non-negotiable. Your first appointment is tomorrow."

He pushed back from the desk, rising halfway out of his seat. "You expect me to march off to see a psychologist one day into a possible multiple homicide? How will that look to my new team?"

Lee's expression hardened. "Like a detective following his commanding officer's orders."

Briefly, he considered throwing down his warrant card and walking out. But acting like a petulant child wouldn't get him any closer to the answers he sought.

He settled back into his chair. "Once a week for three months."

A ghost of a smile touched her lips. "Agreed."

He suppressed the feeling he'd played right into her hands.

"I'd like to think that will be the last time I need to pull rank on you, but I doubt it." Her expression sharpened. "Keep me informed about the case. And do your best to stay off Chief Inspector Lampton's radar, if possible."

CHAPTER THIRTEEN

RYAN TOSSED EMPTY TAKEAWAY COFFEE CUPS ONTO THE backseat of his old Range Rover as Fiona pulled open the passenger door. He brushed in vain at the ginger and white corgi fur coating the seat cover.

"Sorry about the hair. Winston knows the rules. Stay in the back when I'm driving. But the minute I leave him alone, the little chancer jumps up front." Ryan eyed Fiona's dark suit. "I could put down a towel?"

Fiona waved away the offer and climbed in. "Wait. Winston's still alive? How old is he now?"

"Two. He's actually Winston the Second."

It had been Jaime's idea to get a dog. Ryan hadn't been keen, given their long work hours, but as soon as Jaime brought the corgi pup home he'd been smitten. Not that he'd let on, of course. There'd been no question about him taking Winston to London when he'd left. After the original Winston had died, it had taken him six months to realise there was a corgi-sized hole in his life that needed filling.

She raised an eyebrow. "You named your dog the same name as your previous dog?"

He shrugged. "Seemed easier."

"And they say men aren't sentimental." She buckled her seatbelt.

Ryan cleared his throat. "How's Liam?"

"Six stitches, but he's fine. Currently in his happy place watching Paw Patrol on the neighbour's couch with a bowl of popcorn." She gave him a tired smile. "Nathan's on his way home now."

"Kids. Never a dull moment."

"You got that right." She paused. "Sorry I had to bail on you like that."

Ryan waved it away. "Life's messy. We managed." He turned to face her properly. "Before we head off, I wanted to clear the air. Why didn't you go for the DI job?"

Her eyebrows rose. "What makes you think I didn't apply?"

"Because I know they would've given it to you in a heartbeat." When Lampton had first paired him with Fiona, she'd been a newly minted detective constable, but anyone, barring a blind numpty like Lampton, could already see she had the makings of a brilliant lead detective.

"Are you asking me if I didn't go for the job because of what you did for me before you left?" She sighed. "Despite what you might think, DI Hale, the world doesn't always revolve around you."

"So why didn't you apply?"

"Two reasons."

Ryan waited.

"The twins." She smiled and then sighed. "We accidentally got pregnant, and then I let Nathan talk me into it. I thought I was only agreeing to one, though." She stabbed a finger into the dashboard. "A week after my thirty-sixth birthday, I gave birth to two of the little buggers."

"Congratulations?"

She gave him a wry grin. "Thanks. They can be so sweet. A real pair of tiny comedians, but the rough days... God. On those days, I could happily murder Nathan for convincing me to go ahead with it."

"At least you know how to hide a body."

"There's that," she agreed. "But to answer your original question, it sounds so cliché, but after having Max and Liam, my priorities just shifted, you know? I reassessed what I really wanted out of this job. Out of life, I suppose."

She shrugged. "Turned out I was pretty content being the best sergeant I could be. Doing my bit to protect and serve without having to make the 24/7 sacrifice of being a DI or higher. Things can be stressful enough juggling family commitments."

"Sure. I get it." For a moment Ryan wondered if he and Jaime would have had children by now if their life together had continued as planned. Before they married, they'd talked hypothetically about maybe having a kid or two, but they hadn't been in any rush. Would he have been content to stay a sergeant to spend more time with his family?

"Well, thanks for leaving the door open so I could come back."

She patted his arm. "You're welcome."

"Do you know where I'm going?"

She pulled out her phone. "Digit sent me a pin. Head towards Matlock."

"What the fuck is a pin?"

"I've warned them to keep in mind that you're technically challenged. Luckily, Digit's savvy enough in that department to make up for your deficiencies."

"Right." Ryan threw the Range Rover into gear and navigated out of the Chesterfield Station car park. Easing out onto the main road, muscle memory kicked in, guiding him towards the A619.

Ryan's brain did what it always did on a drive. Making anagrams from words, testing letter patterns and turning problems over in his head until a new connection appeared.

Keeping his eyes on the road, Ryan asked, "Was there ever any blowback after I left?"

"You mean after what I did?"

Ryan nodded then stole a glance in her direction.

She rested her head against the headrest and squeezed her eyes shut. "No, and I feel guilty about it every damn day."

CHAPTER FOURTEEN

Ryan read the small hand-painted sign nailed to the wooden gate.

Mystic Wellness Lodge.

No building or driveway in sight. Just an uneven path of rough paving stones weaving through dead brambles and skeletal trees.

"This is the place according to the map pin Digit sent me," Fiona said. "Maybe we should have called ahead to check Potts is in?"

"Better to catch him off guard." Ryan flexed his left hand once, tendons tugging like wire, then lifted the latch. A bare branch scraped his shoulder as he stepped onto the path, which didn't look like it got much use. "Even if he's not involved, he might know who is. Small community and all that."

Ryan pulled out a printout of an 'About Us' webpage that Digit had helpfully supplied him with. In the photo, Lawrence Potts sat in a Buddha pose in long grass, meditating. Scraggly blond hair hung past his shoulders, his beard plaited down to his chest. He wore a loose-fitting top made from undyed cotton, the neck ties loosened to reveal a series of rune tattoos circling his collarbone.

"Right, let's go chat to Dumbledore."

After a minute of walking, the trees thinned. Ryan startled a chicken from the overgrown weeds as a large, whitewashed stone building came into view. More chickens scratched around the courtyard between piled bags of potting mix and a wooden wagon with broken spokes, filled with half-dead plants. The building had seen better days. Cracks marred the stonework, and lichen grew in patches on the paintwork. Down the side, the nose of an older model white transit van poked out.

Ryan nodded in that direction. "There must be a driveway off one of the back roads." Made sense. Carrying supplies up and down the path they'd just climbed would eventually end in a broken ankle.

He made his way over to the van and glanced through the windows. On the passenger seat lay a crumpled velvet cloak that might have started life midnight blue. A scattering of junk food wrappers suggested the van needed a good clean. Ryan straightened. The van had a smashed left headlight, but nothing inside screamed I recently murdered someone.

Parked behind the van was a shiny new BMW SUV with a Nottingham registration.

"No convenient biohazard cool box in the back," Ryan said.

Fiona pursed her lips. "I have a feeling this won't be that easy."

Ryan felt the same. Despite what Hollywood would have people believe, in most homicide cases there was often a clear-cut suspect from the outset and his team's responsibility was simply to prove their guilt beyond reasonable doubt.

This case felt different. The Wicca aspect unsettled him,

though he couldn't pinpoint why. Until the bodies were found, Lawrence and his coven were their only lead.

A blood-curdling scream echoed from inside the wellness lodge.

Ryan and Fiona shared a look, then both ran for the front door. Ryan reached it first and shoved it open to reveal a short, empty hallway.

"Should we call for backup?" Fiona asked.

Another scream split the air.

"No time." Ryan headed down the hall towards the open door at the far end.

He burst into a spacious studio. A couple in their thirties sat cross-legged on a mat in the centre of the room. The man was sucking his thumb. Lawrence hovered above them, with a hand resting on each of their shoulders. All three looked up, startled. The man's thumb slipped from his mouth.

Lawrence looked the same as in his photo, with the addition of a pair of baggy hemp trousers with a low-hanging crotch and a noticeable pot belly poking out of the bottom of his shirt. Somehow, the overall look ended up more comical than spiritual.

Lawrence removed his hands from the couple and straightened. His wide eyes narrowed as Ryan skidded to a stop.

"Can I help you?" he asked in a refined London accent at odds with his appearance. "We are at a delicate stage of our session."

Ryan held up his warrant card. "Mr Potts, I'm Detective Inspector Hale. This is my colleague, DS Bennett." He gestured to Fiona, who had arrived on his heels and was now taking in the scene with interest. "We heard screams."

"Of course you heard screams." Lawrence rolled his eyes as if people shrieking at the top of their lungs was normal. "This is a scream therapy session. I am guiding my clients back to infancy to help them access the traumatic experience of their primal pain at birth. Only there can we release our repressed anger and frustration through the healing power of scream."

Beside him, Fiona tried and failed to suppress a snort.

Ryan felt his own lips twitch. "I apologise for the misunderstanding."

He'd rather pay Lampton to be his therapist than shell out hard-earned cash to this wannabe extra from Vikings. The idea of pretending to be a baby and wailing like a banshee held no appeal. But people were free to pursue whatever floated their boat so long as no one was getting hurt or breaking the law.

Lawrence's lips pressed together. "Did Mrs Tubbs next door make a complaint again?"

"We're here on a separate matter. If we could have a few minutes of your time?"

"We are at a fragile stage of the session. To leave my clients in this regressed infant state would be unconscionable."

Ryan sighed. "And how long will it take to reach adulthood again?"

"How long is a blade of grass? Can a sunset be rushed—"

Ryan cut him off with a raised palm. "You have five minutes or we're doing this down at the station."

"We'll wait in your office over there," Fiona added, pointing to an open door across the room.

Lawrence looked like he wanted to protest, but nodded.

Ryan glanced over and saw what had attracted Fiona's attention.

———

Fiona waited for Lawrence's focus to return to his clients, then closed the office door, muffling the moans and wails coming from the couple, who appeared unfazed by the police interruption. She crossed to the woven rattan cabinet and gestured to the three statues on the middle shelf.

"Look familiar?"

The centre statue depicted a woman with full breasts, cradling the world. To the left stood a young woman with flowing hair, perched on a crescent moon with a crow on her outstretched hand. The right statue showed three satyrs kneeling at a tree's base, with a snake coiled in the roots.

"Eloise said the Triple Goddess and the Horned God on his forest throne were the most important figures in British Traditional Wicca," Fiona said. "Lawrence is supposed to be his coven's high priest..."

"So where are they?" Ryan finished.

Fiona indicated two spots between the statues on the glass shelf with less dust. "Two are missing."

Ryan pulled out his phone and brought up the crime scene photos. The bronze statues on the shelf matched the size and craftsmanship of those at the scene. They could be from the same set.

Fiona photographed the statues while Ryan examined the office. Faded canvases with insipid inspirational quotes hung haphazardly on the walls. An old wooden desk, more charity shop than antique, sat in one corner cluttered with New Age books. He scanned the titles. Nothing about Wiccan practices.

He considered checking the desk drawers when Lawrence swept into the office. Through the doorway, Ryan saw the couple had already left.

"How can I assist the police?" Lawrence gestured towards the three chairs arranged around a rickety coffee table.

Ryan eyed the flimsy woven rattan chairs matching the display case, unconvinced they'd hold his weight. Fiona, weighing barely eight stone, sat without hesitation. Lawrence followed suit. Ryan lowered himself into the last chair, grimacing as it creaked.

"Mr Potts, you're the high priest of the local Wiccan coven?" Fiona asked.

"Please call me Vidir." Lawrence made an elaborate hand gesture.

"It says Lawrence on your most recent driver's licence." Fiona opened her notebook.

"Vidir is my craft name. I use it in all my occult dealings."

"Mr Potts," Ryan interrupted, "answer the question."

Lawrence sniffed. "Yes, I am the elder high priest of the Coven of the Crescent Moon."

"Spells and dancing naked under a full moon, that sort of thing?" Fiona's face remained earnest.

"Devotees of Hecate pursue a significant spiritual journey, coexisting peacefully with nature." He leaned forward and patted Fiona's hand as if she were a child. "Our practices are grounded in the traditions of our forebears. We venerate pagan deities through ceremonies, incantations, and spiritual rites. And yes, for those who choose it, attire is optional."

He sat back.

"Now, you're probably thinking we're an odd bunch who play with dolls and burn incense, but trust me, detectives, we're quite normal." He chuckled. "Kidding. We are weirdos, but the good kind."

Great, Ryan thought. *The Wiccan Bill Bailey.*

"Were you and your coven at the Nine Ladies Stone Circle last night?" Fiona asked.

Lawrence frowned. "No. We were last there for Cinco de Mayo." He gave an exaggerated wink. "That's the Day of the Dead to the layman."

He pulled up an off-centre image of a blurry stone circle with a tiny ball of light Ryan assumed was the moon.

"Took this myself last night. Quite artistic. A special trip to the Twelve Apostles Stone Circle. The experience was transcendent, the ley lines—"

"The Twelve Apostles. Where is that?" Fiona cut in.

Lawrence huffed at the interruption. "In the north of West Yorkshire."

"What time did you finish in there?" Ryan asked.

"Sometime before the witching hour."

Ryan resisted the urge to strangle a straight answer out of him.

"When, exactly?"

"About ten thirty."

"Long drive home," Fiona observed.

"We stayed the night at a hotel outside of Leeds and drove back this morning."

"Name of the hotel?"

"The Greymoor, I believe. What's this about?"

"We'll come to that. Did anyone drive back home to Derbyshire straight after the ritual?" If the circle was in West Yorkshire, above Leeds, it had to be at least ninety minutes away.

"No. We all travelled up together in my van."

"Did any regulars miss the ritual last night?" Fiona asked.

Lawrence shifted, and his rattan chair groaned. "Emily didn't show at the meeting point. I was surprised. She was set to play the maiden. She's still a novice, but she did a cracking job penetrating the chalice with the athame at Mabon."

Ryan closed his eyes briefly and decided not to ask.

Oblivious, Lawrence rattled on. "Ashling stepped in, Goddess bless her, but she doesn't have the same energy flow. It's the teeth. I know she can't help it, but they're distracting..."

"Back to Emily. Does she have a surname?"

"I'm sure she does."

Ryan gave him a pointed look. "If you'd rather do this at the station?"

Lawrence sighed dramatically. "We call her Sunshine. That's her craft name though, not her surname."

"So you don't know her surname?"

"Many have stepped out of the broom closet in recent years, but some members prefer to keep their Wiccan personas and everyday identities separate. Emily wouldn't be involved in whatever you're investigating. She has the purest spirit." He beamed at them as if that settled it.

"Do you have pictures of Emily? Any contact details?" Ryan asked.

Lawrence shrugged. "I post upcoming events on the centre's website and our social media groups. I think she posts some things about wellness and spirituality on Instagram, but that's all I know."

"Can you give us her description?" Fiona held her pen ready.

Lawrence glanced up at the ceiling. "Young, long blonde hair, beautiful."

Ryan sighed.

"I have an idea," Lawrence said, leaning closer. "Why don't you join us for our next ritual, detectives? We promise not to hex you... or at least, not too much." The high-pitched chuckle resurfaced.

They were getting nowhere. Given Lawrence's appearance, the hotel staff would remember if he'd stayed last night. If confirmed, he'd have a solid alibi. Ryan went for it. "Recognise these statues?" He thrust his phone under Lawrence's nose.

Lawrence's eyes widened. "I... ah..."

"We couldn't help noticing the resemblance to your collection." Ryan pointed to the shelf with the statues. "Two of your statues are missing. These two statues." He waved the phone.

"How could you know that?" Lawrence's face drained of colour.

"So the statues in these photos belong to you?"

"Yes. They did until a couple of months ago." Lawrence stared at his hands. "Someone broke into my van and stole them at the Grey Ladies Festival. They also took my grimoire."

Hiding something, Ryan wondered, or embarrassed about being robbed?

"Did you report it?" Fiona asked.

"No..." Lawrence stuttered, eyes pleading. "They took only the statues and the book. Would you have taken me seriously, Detective? If I'd turned up at your place of employment? I figured there wouldn't be anything the police would do."

Unfortunately, he wasn't wrong.

"Your statues were used in a ritual left at the Nine Ladies last night. The crime scene officer believes the ritual includes Wiccan aspects. Do you have any knowledge of this?"

"No," Lawrence replied vehemently.

"Can I ask you to look at some pictures from the scene and give us your opinion on whether the ritual looks Wiccan? I need to warn you, the pictures are disturbing."

Lawrence nodded.

Ryan showed him a series of shots from different angles.

Lawrence swallowed. "Are those... human eyeballs? Why would you show me that?" His voice rose to a squeak.

"Yes, those are eyeballs, and the pathologist suspects they're human." The pathologist hadn't made such a claim since they hadn't examined them yet, but Ryan deemed it a safe inference.

"I...ah..." Lawrence seemed lost for words.

"Is it common to use eyeballs, human or otherwise, in Wiccan rituals?"

"What? No. Never. I've never performed or heard of such a ritual. The only thing I can think of is a local legend."

"What legend?" Ryan asked.

"If you visit the Mermaid's Pool on Kinder Scout, she'll grant you immortality, but she requires a sacrifice. In most stories, she demands the visitor's eyes so she can see the world above. But the legend speaks of sunrise at Easter, not Halloween."

Ryan made a mental note to get one of the team to look into it. "What about the rest of the elements? Do they look right to you?"

"Ur..." Lawrence glanced at the photo and looked away. "We use pentagrams, and the statues are correct, but a few things look off."

"What things?"

"That crystal." Lawrence pointed to a yellow stone tucked beside the Horned God statue. "That's citrine. All wrong for a full moon ceremony. Lavender and sage are a strange choice for this type of ritual, and the chalice is in the wrong location. It would sit in front of the goddess, not in the centre."

He ran both hands down his face and exhaled.

"None of my regulars would make these mistakes. This was set up by someone trying to mimic one of our rituals, or a newbie."

"Anyone recently join the group?"

He fiddled with the carved stone hanging around his neck. "No one comes to mind."

Ryan glanced at his notebook. "What about the man with long black hair and eyeliner who came to the Forest Sage?"

Lawrence screwed up his face. "Robbie? He's not part of the group. He came along with Emily to a couple of rituals to see what they're about. Bit of an odd fellow."

Bit rich from a man with plaited facial hair and oversized harem trousers, Ryan thought. "Did Robbie come to the Twelve Apostles last night?"

"No. Like I said, he's not an initiate."

"Know anything about him? Like a surname?"

"No, but I think I overheard him saying he worked in transport. Derby Railway Station, maybe?"

"Alexandrian covens have a high priest and a high priestess, right?" Fiona asked, showing off the knowledge she'd gained during her ten minutes of googling on the drive over. "Who's the current high priestess of your group?"

Lawrence shifted uncomfortably. "We're looking to fill the position."

"What happened to the previous high priestess?"

He sighed. "My wife left the coven when we separated in June."

"Getting a little too cosy with your initiates, were you?" Ryan said.

Lawrence's cheeks flushed. "I don't like what you're insinuating, Detective. Now, I have to ask you to leave. My next session starts in fifteen minutes."

"If we have more questions, we'll be in touch." Fiona placed her card on the desk.

Like any detective would, they took a lingering look around as they left the property.

"What do you think?" Ryan asked once they were back in the car.

"He got worked up about the last question, but he didn't deny it."

"Exactly. Get Sheri to check his alibi and Digit to look on social media for a pretty, blonde Emily or this Robbie. Without surnames, it's a long shot, but with his talents you never know."

As they reached the outskirts of Chesterfield, Ryan's phone rang. Fiona glanced at the screen. "It's DCI Lee."

"Can you answer it for me?"

Fiona listened as the DCI spoke.

"Yes, Ma'am. We'll head straight there." She hung up.

"We have a body."

CHAPTER FIFTEEN

RYAN DROVE THROUGH THE OUTSKIRTS OF BAKEWELL. Above the tree line, the steeple of All Saints' Church came into view as the road followed the meandering River Wye. Beside them, the river's glassy surface reflected the dull pewter of the overcast sky. He turned onto Plumstead Lane. The road narrowed, hemmed in by stone walls that leaned inward, as if trying to squeeze out unwelcome intruders. Marked police cars and white forensic vans gave away the address.

The synthetic voice on Ryan's phone announced, "Your destination is on your right."

A dark blue late-model BMW sat in the only parking space allocated to the property. Ryan eased the Range Rover in behind a vintage Jaguar tucked up against the wall, praying he wouldn't lose a wing mirror to a passing car. He sucked in his gut and squeezed out of the driver's side.

Bloody hell.

His coat caught on the rough wet stone wall. He wrestled it free and shuffled down the length of the SUV.

Fiona stared at him from the passenger side. "Christ, that

was undignified. I feel like I made pushing out two children look easier."

She smiled, no doubt trying to soften the blow, then cocked her head towards the Jaguar. "Odd Bod's here already."

"Dr Gates is still the pathologist?" Ryan replied.

She nodded. "And as enthusiastic as ever."

Despite the grim circumstances, Ryan perked up at the news. Odd Bod might be as odd as his nickname implied, but he owned his eccentricities with pride. He was a brilliant pathologist with an uncanny talent for coaxing secrets from the dead. Unlike some of the clock-watchers Ryan had dealt with back in London, Odd Bod treated each case like a personal crusade.

If Ryan were ever murdered, he could only hope Odd Bod was the pathologist on call.

A uniformed constable in a yellow hi-vis stood huddled in on himself by the front gate, manning the outer cordon. The young man's face was ashen, his eyes fixed on some distant point, working to erase whatever he'd witnessed.

Poor bugger.

Ryan knew the look well. No amount of training could prepare you for your first gruesome crime scene.

"Hey Bobby. How's Matilda?" Fiona called out cheerfully.

The constable jerked upright, nearly dropping the crime scene clipboard.

Fiona's elephant-like memory never ceased to impress Ryan. Even back when they were starting out, she'd recalled the names and faces of most people who crossed their path. Bobby, an unfortunate name for a policeman, was from one of the nearby Safer Neighbourhood Policing teams, so not someone she'd have crossed paths with often.

The constable's face brightened when he saw Fiona. "She's still scratching my couch to bits."

"Matilda's a cat," Fiona whispered as they approached the gate.

"Did you try the organic spray I recommended?"

Bobby looked sheepish. "Not yet."

"Give it a go. It's got the DS Bennett guarantee."

Ryan cleared his throat. "What have you got for us?"

He knew Fiona was only trying to help Bobby get out of his own head, but a woman lay murdered less than fifty yards away. Organic pet repellent could wait.

Bobby looked past Fiona as if spotting Ryan for the first time.

"My new boss DI Hale," Fiona said, waving a hand in his direction. "Not one for small talk." She gave Bobby a look that said What can you do? before glancing over at Ryan.

Ryan met her gaze with a look of his own he hoped implied I'm standing right here.

Bobby straightened. His Adam's apple bobbed as he swallowed. "Yes, Sir. Sorry, Sir. I'm PC Matthews." He pointed across the small front lawn to where a scrawny man talked to a female officer. "The husband found her. He's over there with PC Thorne. We were the first responders and secured the scene."

The constable's voice faltered. "I checked her pulse... Her eyes..."

He trailed off as he folded in on himself.

Fiona patted him on the shoulder. "This job can be a real bitch. The things we can't unsee, eh? If you ever need to talk about it, you know where to find me."

Bobby nodded gratefully.

He recorded their names and the time on the log while Ryan and Fiona pulled blue plastic slippers over their shoes. They ducked under the police tape and headed for the house.

"I don't know PC Thorne," Fiona said. "She must be new."

The Norris house was an imposing double-fronted detached property, all rendered walls and large bay windows that spoke of tasteful renovation rather than original features. A gravelled drive swept around to a double garage, and Ryan could see a conservatory extension jutting out at the back. The lawn needed mowing but wasn't quite overgrown enough to draw disapproving looks from the neighbours. The kind of substantial, upper-middle-class home that whispered of bonuses and pension contributions, of having made it but not wanting to shout about it.

A far cry from the modest semi-detached bungalow he and Jaime had owned together, with its massive mortgage and postage-stamp garden.

Being back in Chesterfield was bringing thoughts about Jaime to the top of his mind with increasing frequency. He shoved them aside and refocused on the task at hand.

PC Thorne hurried to meet them, her professional mask in place despite looking barely out of high school.

Ryan flashed his warrant card. "I'm DI Hale from Major Crimes. I'll be the SIO for this case. This is my colleague, DS Bennett."

"Yes, Sir. The husband, William Norris, found Mrs Norris when he came home for lunch. Says he didn't stay in the house last night. He and his wife had a row, so he went and stayed with his sister in Buxton. Decided to pop home on his lunch break and found his wife dead in the bedroom. Says he called 999 immediately." She glanced at her notes. "Her car is still inside the garage. They have a thirteen-year-old son, Carter. I rang the school. The boy's there, safe. They're keeping him in the office."

Ryan nodded, relieved. At least there was one piece of good news today. "Good work, Constable. Has Mr Norris given a formal statement yet?"

"Not yet, Sir. I kept it brief, given the circumstances."

A silver Vauxhall Corsa pulled up, and Cal and Sheri climbed out. Ryan waited for the pair to register with Bobby on the gate and join them.

"Stop for a coffee and a Cornish, did you?" Ryan asked as the pair drew closer.

He noticed Cal had removed the waistcoat from his three-piece suit.

"Sorry, boss," Cal called out. "The new navigator was giving dodgy directions."

Ryan saw Sheri open her mouth to protest, then close it again and press her lips together.

"Cal," Ryan said, "check the back of the property for any signs of forced entry or disturbance. If you find anything, get a tech to secure the evidence before you touch it."

"Sure thing, boss," Cal replied, his usual cockiness tempered by the gravity of the situation.

Ryan pointed to the row of houses lining the lane. "Sheri, see if any of the neighbours are in, and ask them if they saw or heard anything suspicious last night or this morning."

With tasks allocated, Ryan and Fiona approached Mr Norris. The man sat hunched on the front step, head bowed. Behind him, a skeleton wearing a jaunty top hat and covered in fake cobwebs was propped by the front door.

"Mr Norris, I'm DI Hale, and this is DS Bennett," Ryan said, his voice gentle but firm. "I understand PC Thorne has already taken some basic information from you. I'm very sorry for your loss, and I know this is difficult, but we'll need to ask you some more questions shortly. For now, is there somewhere you can wait while we examine the scene? Perhaps with PC Thorne?"

Norris looked up, his washed-out blue eyes rimmed with red. For a moment, he stared at them blankly, as if they'd spoken in an alien tongue. Then, with visible effort, he shook himself and blinked.

"Yes, yes, of course," Norris said hoarsely. "Carter, my son, is he really...?"

"He's safe at school," Fiona assured him. "They're looking after him."

"Would Amanda normally help Carter get ready in the morning?" Ryan asked.

"I usually leave for work before he gets up. Most of the time, Amanda drops him off on her way to the Job Centre, but occasionally she'll head to the gym before work and he'll make his own breakfast and take the bus." His fingers shook as he ran them through his hair. "That has to be what happened," he finished with emphasis, as if the more conviction he showed, the more likely it would be true.

Norris's shoulders sagged, but almost immediately tensed again.

"How do I tell him about his...?" He buried his face in his hands.

"We'll have someone from family services help with that," Fiona said softly. "One step at a time, Mr Norris."

PC Thorne guided the bereaved husband back towards the gate, murmuring something reassuring.

They headed for the door. The animatronic skeleton jerked to life by the entrance as Ryan passed. "Happy Halloween," it croaked, its arm swinging forward. Plastic fingers brushed his shoulder. He leapt back, almost banging into Fiona, hand dropping to the baton on his hip. "Christ!"

"Want me to check the rest of the house for ghosts while you catch your breath?" Fiona asked.

As they passed through the hallway, Ryan could hear Dr Gates's distinctive voice directing the forensics team from a room upstairs.

"Time to see what Odd Bod's found," Ryan said, steeling himself.

They climbed the wide staircase; the steps creaking under their weight. At the top, a white-suited figure stood in the bedroom doorway. The hood pulled tight around his face made him look like a budget astronaut on Halloween.

Amazingly, a name popped into Ryan's head, along with an image of the same guy, years younger, shuffling around crime scenes with a nervous grin, camera in one hand and an inhaler in the other.

"Paul, isn't it?" Ryan said, recognising the tech despite the forensic suit.

"DI Hale!" The man's face lit up. "Great that you're back."

Ryan looked for any sign of sarcasm, but the man seemed genuinely pleased.

"Ah... thanks. Who's the CSM today?"

He gave a self-deprecating smile. "That'd be me, for my sins."

"Okay, can we go in?"

Paul's expression sobered. "Fair warning. It's a bad one. Dr Gates is with her now." He gestured towards the bedroom. "We're still photographing and collecting evidence, so please stay by the door."

Ryan nodded.

Whatever had happened to Amanda Norris in the sanctity of her own home, they were about to find out.

"Ready?" he asked Fiona.

She took a breath and nodded. "Ready."

They stepped forward to meet the dead.

CHAPTER SIXTEEN

Ryan and Fiona followed Paul into the bedroom. Odd Bod, the pathologist, and a woman in a tech suit with a camera stood next to a queen-sized bed, blocking Ryan's view of the body. The photographer leaned over, capturing a series of close-ups of the victim's face.

She checked the photos on the screen, nodded, and stepped back.

Ryan moved further into the room until he had a clear line of sight. He saw immediately why Bobby had been fixated on the victim's eyes.

Or lack thereof.

Amanda's dark hair was tucked demurely to one side, though a hint of grey at the roots suggested the richness came from a bottle. Her bare arms lay at her sides, and her high-necked lace nightgown lay primly around her knees. A glass of water and a Valley of the Dolls paperback with a bookmark placed close to the halfway mark sat on the bedside table. She could have been sleeping peacefully if it weren't for the gaping red holes where her eyes should have been.

"Jesus," Ryan muttered.

He glanced around the room. Nothing looked disturbed. There were no visible defensive injuries on the victim's arms or scratches on her face.

Paul, using a pair of surgical tweezers, removed a thin shiny disc from one of the victim's eye sockets. He dropped it into an evidence bag and repeated the process on the other side. Once he'd finished, Odd Bod swapped places with the SOCO and shone a pen torch into the bloody sockets, inspecting the wounds with the morbid intensity of an artist scrutinising a masterpiece.

"Hi Odd Bod," Ryan said when the pathologist straightened.

Odd Bod looked up. "Ah, Ryan, there you are." Like it had been a couple of days since he'd last seen him, not twelve years. The short bald man waved Ryan over and shone the penlight back into Amanda's right eye socket. "Note that the ocular excision sites show a lack of perimortem haemorrhaging."

"So the eyes were removed postmortem?"

"The minimal coagulation patterns would suggest so, but I won't know for certain until the autopsy when I can compare the eyeballs you discovered this morning to our victim."

"Pretty grisly, but I've seen worse." Images of past cases flashed through his mind. He'd never cease to be amazed by what people could do to each other. "Any idea of the cause of death?"

"No obvious signs of blunt force trauma or stab wounds, but there is a minor cut on her right palm that could be a defensive wound and a bruise on her upper left arm, possibly where she was grabbed. If you look at her neck, there are light curvilinear contusions. If she still had her eyes, I suspect we'd see definitive petechial haemorrhages."

Ryan's brain sorted Odd Bod's words into layman's terms. "Strangled?"

"It seems you learnt some tricks down in the big smoke. That's the most likely scenario at this point. I'll know more once I get her back to the lab."

"Any idea about the time of death?"

"She is nearing full rigor mortis, so I'd hazard a guess at between 11:00 pm and 2:00 am."

"Strange there aren't more signs of a struggle." Ryan turned to Fiona. "I find it hard to believe she lay there while someone strangled her to death."

"They could have tidied up the scene afterward," Fiona replied. "Or threatened to kill Carter if she fought back. He would have been in his room at the time."

"Maybe." Ryan mulled over the possibilities. "What did you pull out of her eye sockets?" he asked Paul.

"A pair of 50p coins."

"Anything special about them we could trace?" If the killer had used rare coins, they might be able to trace them to a buyer.

Paul shrugged and held up the two evidence bags. "They look like everyday fifty-pence pieces to me. If the killer handled them without gloves, we might get a partial print, but otherwise, I doubt they'll offer any leads."

Ryan waved the photographer over. "Can I see the photos of the coins in place?"

The photographer pulled up an image on her screen and zoomed in. Ryan flinched at the stark close-up, with every gory detail on display. A few droplets of blood had dried on the skin around the sockets, probably from when the eyes had been removed. He studied the screen for a moment, then nodded his thanks.

Something nagged at the back of his mind. "Isn't there a

myth about this sort of thing? Something about using coins to pay to cross a river?"

Fiona's forehead furrowed. "It sort of rings a bell."

"A payment to Charon, the ferryman," Odd Bod said, his eyes lit with scholarly interest. "To cross the river Styx and enter Hades, the underworld."

Ryan wasn't surprised he knew the story. The man was a walking encyclopaedia of quirky and obscure things related to death.

"Of course, literature and heroic tales popularised the idea of two coins." Odd Bod gestured expansively. "One coin for the hero to pay their way in and one coin to pay their way out. The souls of the dead, on the other hand, had no need to leave. One coin under the tongue is more historically accurate of Ancient Greek practice. No ties to the practice in Wicca that I know of."

"Why would someone leave coins in modern times?"

Odd Bod shook his head. "That would be your job. It probably ties in with the tarot card over there."

Odd Bod pointed to a small clear evidence bag containing a red, black and gold tarot card, then went back to studying the eye sockets.

Ryan leaned closer and read the small lettering at the bottom of the card. "The Hanged Man."

The design was disturbing. A skeleton in tattered rags hung from a tree by one foot. Vines from the tree wrapped around the torso like snakes. From the centre of the tree, a wide eye stared out.

"The twelfth Major Arcana card," Odd Bod said without looking up.

"Any idea what it means?"

Odd Bod raised his head and locked eyes with Ryan. "Limbo. Sacrifice. Seeing from a new perspective. Surrender."

More occult paraphernalia. All they needed now was a Ouija board. Ryan looked down at Amanda, making her a silent promise to find out who did this to her.

Fiona snapped a shot of the tarot card on her phone. Her fingers flew over the screen. "I'll get Digit to dig into any further meanings for the card and the coins and compare it to Wicca and other occult practices."

Ryan turned to Odd Bod. "What time can you conduct the postmortem?"

"It's a quiet day in the office, so I should be able to get to her as soon as we finish here. I've already begun my analysis of the human remains recovered from the stone circle."

"I'll come by; see if you find anything once she's back at the morgue."

Odd Bod nodded in approval.

Ryan stepped back into the hallway and took a moment to clear his head. The image of those empty sockets would haunt him for a while yet. He needed to walk through the rest of the house and get a feel for the scene beyond the bedroom.

Downstairs, fragments of glass glittered on the stone hearth and in the carpet's deep pile. The remains of what had been a flower vase, based on the limp chrysanthemums scattered across the floor. Otherwise, the living room looked neat and normal.

Ryan studied a mark on the wall above the fireplace. The likely point of impact. It looked like things had got physical during the Norris's argument last night.

The kitchen was tidy apart from the bench top. Toast crumbs littered the surface, and a knife covered in peanut butter sat on a tub of margarine. Signs of Carter's breakfast?

A female tech in a white suit dusted the back door handle for prints with methodical movements.

"Anything?" Ryan asked.

She shook her head. "The door was locked when we arrived." Her frustration mirrored his own.

Ryan walked around the open door and scanned every inch, searching for telltale signs. No visible scratches around the lock. He ran a gloved finger along the frame, feeling for any irregularities. Unlikely anyone had forced entry this way.

He made a mental note to check with Mr Norris whether the front door was locked.

Back outside, Fiona was finishing up a phone call. The look of relief on her face said it all.

"Carter's none the wiser about his mum," she said. "Sounds like he thought she'd left for work early, so he made his own way to school."

Ryan felt the tightness in his chest release. "Good."

"I've also arranged for Mr Norris's sister to pick Carter up and take him back to her house in Buxton. A family liaison officer will meet Mr Norris and Carter there to help him explain to the boy what's happened and gently probe Carter to see if he heard or saw anything last night."

Ryan nodded, impressed by her efficiency. He'd forgotten that in a small team, any good sergeant would anticipate basic orders. "Right. Let's go ask Mr Norris some questions about that broken vase in the living room."

CHAPTER SEVENTEEN

Ryan and Fiona found Amanda's husband still hunched on the front steps, arms wrapped tight around his body as he stared vacantly across the overgrown grass.

Fiona took the lead, as she often did when they spoke to victims of serious crimes. She could instantly put witnesses and colleagues at ease. A fine chisel compared to Ryan's hammer.

"Mr Norris, may we ask you a few questions while everything's still fresh in your mind?"

Mr Norris didn't move. Ryan wondered if the full weight of his loss had pushed him into shock until the man nodded slowly and stood. "Please call me Will. I'll answer anything if it helps you catch whoever murdered Amanda." His voice wobbled at the end, but his red-rimmed eyes stayed dry.

"Here." Fiona handed him a thick wool coat Ryan recognised from the hooks by the front door. He hadn't even seen her grab it. "We can't go back inside yet, so I got the technicians to process it."

Will stared at the coat blankly before pulling it on. Fiona led him to a small round patio table with a pair of white wrought-iron chairs nestled under a large oak. The leaves rustled in the chilly breeze. Ryan trailed behind, wanting to stay out of the way but close enough to listen. He leaned against the oak trunk, ignoring the chill from the frozen bark leeching through his coat.

"What time did you arrive at the house?" Fiona asked, taking out her notebook and turning to a fresh page.

"I got here around one..." His voice trailed off.

"You told PC Thorne you stayed at your sister's last night because you and Amanda had a fight?"

Will grimaced. "I'm sure the busybody next door will tell you all about it." He nodded towards the closest cottage. "The nosy old git had his nose pressed to his window when I stormed out."

"What time was this?"

"About eight, I think?" Will frowned.

"What was the fight about?"

Will sighed. "Money. Like it always is with us. I found three new blouses hanging in our wardrobe with the tags still on. Eighty pounds each." He paused, looking down at his hands. "I took stress leave from my job as a CFO earlier this year, and I couldn't face going back. I'd been working fifteen-hour days, I never saw my family, and then I started having panic attacks." He picked at his fingernails. "I found a position as a retail manager at a furniture store in Chesterfield, but it doesn't pay as well. Amanda... she's been struggling to adjust. She just keeps spending money we don't have." He looked up at Fiona as if pleading with her to see his side, then dropped his eyes back to his hands. His whole body deflated. "It all seems so petty and pointless now."

"Did the fight get physical?" Fiona asked gently.

Will's cheeks coloured. "Amanda threw a vase at me. I

ducked, and it hit the fireplace and smashed everywhere. But I didn't touch her, I swear."

"The broken vase in the living room?"

"Yeah. I guess so... I haven't looked." He screwed his eyes shut. "After that, I left. I was just so angry, and I knew she'd sulk all night. She holds onto a grudge when she wants to. Wanted to, I mean. She could be a silly old cow, but I loved her. Now the last words I ever said to her will be in anger." A strangled wail tore out of him. He dropped his head onto his arms and sobbed onto the table.

Ryan bit back a rush of impatience as Fiona patted the man on the back. While he sympathised, Will had yet to give them anything to run with, and every minute they spent consoling him was a minute not spent hunting down Amanda's killer.

Finally, Mr Norris sat up again, his face blotchy and his eyes swollen.

"Did Amanda have any enemies?" Fiona asked.

He scoffed. "Enemies? She worked at the Job Centre in Chesterfield, not MI5. She might've pissed off the odd dole bludger, but nothing worth murdering her for."

"Did she get along well with her colleagues?"

Ryan noticed a flash of something that might've been guilt cross Will's face.

"She worked with a lady called Rebecca. They weren't close, and Amanda sometimes bitched about her, but they got on fine as far as I could tell."

"Did she mention anything unusual recently, or did she act differently?"

"Come to think of it, she came home rattled about something a week ago. I asked her about it, but she just laughed and said something about her overactive imagination. I was going to try to get her to open up, but then I saw the shopping bags. A bunch of Xbox games and some clothes. She'd gone and spent over three hundred quid on all this crap for Carter's birthday after we agreed a hundred pounds was the absolute limit! We got into it again, and I forgot to ask her any more about it."

"What day was this?" Fiona asked, her pen scratching across the page.

Will shrugged. "Sorry, I can't remember, but all the stuff she bought will be on the credit card statement."

"Any close friends or extended family of Amanda we could talk to?"

"She didn't really have any. Her sister was the only person she was close to, but she died a couple of years ago." He sat up straighter and hurriedly added, "Nothing suspicious. She died of a brain aneurysm." His forehead wrinkled. "Wait! She went to some book club every couple of weeks. On a Wednesday. She never missed it. Even went with the flu once."

"Do you know where the book club's held or who any of the other members are?"

He shook his head. "Sorry. She never talked about what they were reading or any of the members. I just assumed they held the meetings at one of their houses." His shoulders sagged. "I should've taken more of an interest." He turned to Fiona, eyes pleading. "Was I a terrible husband?"

"I'm sure you did the best you could."

Ryan's thoughts drifted to the strange details of the murder scene. "Did Amanda have an interest in religion or the occult?"

Will started as if he'd forgotten Ryan was there. He looked over at him leaning against the tree, his eyes drifting to the scars on Ryan's cheek before dropping to his lap. He gave a slight shake of his head. "No. We're not the churchgoing types, and Amanda's only hobbies are shopping and reading. Were I mean." He looked back up. "Is this because of the eyes?" His face crumpled. "Oh God, her eyes."

"Was the front door locked when you got home?" Ryan asked.

Will thought for a moment. "I... think so."

Fiona glanced over at Ryan, who motioned towards the gate.

"Will, thank you for your time. We'll have more questions as the investigation continues, but we'll leave it there for now. If you think of anything else, you can always call me." She gave him her card. "Can I arrange for a constable to take you to join your son at your sister's?"

Will nodded weakly. Fiona waved over PC Thorne and left him in her capable hands.

As Ryan and Fiona stepped outside the cordon, Sheri hurried over, eyes gleaming with excitement.

"Sir, a neighbour has information that might help." Her words tumbled over each other.

Ryan glanced over her head at the closest cottage. The curtain twitched as someone pulled back out of sight.

"The old man in that cottage heard the Norrises arguing and smashing things last night."

Sheri's excitement faded. "Um, yeah... I mean, yes, Sir."

"The husband admitted they argued, but I still want a word with the—" He looked at Fiona. "What did Mr Norris call him?"

She tapped her chin. "The nosy old twat. Or was it git?"

"Git, I believe. Sheri, come with me. Let's see if the nosy old git has any other interesting nuggets to share about the Norrises."

CHAPTER EIGHTEEN

RYAN LOVED NOSY NEIGHBOURS WITH TOO MUCH TIME ON their hands.

He approached the cottage next door, noting the pruned roses standing like sentries in a spiky row waiting for spring to revive them. A large vegetable patch ran the length of the stone wall separating the properties, planted with what Ryan assumed were winter vegetables but could well be weeds for all he knew about gardening. The neat rows spoke of dedication bordering on obsession. A watering can sat on the stone path with a pair of gardening gloves lying beside it.

Ryan rapped his knuckles against the weathered wood of the front door, the sound echoing in the quiet street. Beside him, Sheri fidgeted.

An elderly man answered. He had wispy white hair and mottled skin, but his sunken eyes were sharp.

"Mr Barclay, I'm DI Hale." Ryan held up his warrant card. "My colleague DC Dewan tells me you have some information for us?"

"I told the wee Indian lassie to bring me the guy in charge." His eyes narrowed. "Are you the boss, sonny?"

Ryan sighed. He was tempted to say his boss was a woman, and it wasn't a great idea these days to call a grown police-woman a wee lassie. Especially one who could have you on the ground and in cuffs in three seconds flat. But from experience, he knew the words would fall on deaf ears, and he wanted to hurry this along.

"I'm the senior investigating officer on site." Not a lie.

"Well, what are you waiting for? I guess you'd better come in."

A wave of heat and eau de old person hit Ryan's nostrils as the door opened wider. The heady scent of stale urine and overcooked vegetables mixed together at a temperature that would have a camel breaking out in a sweat.

Ryan and Sheri followed the man along a dark hallway and through into the sitting room. Every chair had a brightly coloured crocheted cover that didn't match its neighbour. An old-fashioned wedding photo hung in pride of place above the roaring fire, the source of the uncomfortable heat. In the far corner sat a large desk with a magnifying light clipped to the edge. It illuminated what looked like a seventies radio in the process of either being rebuilt or dismantled. The radio squatted in the middle of a pile of metal pieces and jumbled coloured wires with little colour-coded labels marked with letters.

Mr Barclay noticed Ryan looking over at the desk.

"I like to see how things work. Just my little hobby." He took the seat closest to the fireplace and lowered himself down.

"Tea?" He pointed to a tea tray laid out with a silver teapot, milk and sugar, and a trio of chipped porcelain cups. "Lizzy would haunt me from the grave if I didn't offer."

A row of plain digestives lay arranged around the pot. Mr Barclay had been busy while Sheri had been filling them in.

"Thank you," Ryan replied. He and Sheri sat side by side on a stiff-backed sofa. Ryan wasn't much of a tea drinker, but he found the elderly were often more at ease if you accepted their hospitality. "Mind if I pour?"

Mr Barclay nodded. "Milk, two sugars, son."

Ryan looked at Sheri.

"None for me, Sir, thank you," she said, taking out her notepad and pen.

"Is that your wife?" She gestured at the wedding photo as Ryan poured the tea.

"My Lizzy. She died in 2010. Made the best sponge cake."

Ryan was more interested in the woman who'd died last night than the one who'd been dead for over a decade. He handed the old man his tea.

"Mr Barclay, can you tell us what you saw last night?"

"I saw that weedy wimp next door stomp off in a huff yesterday evening." The corner of his lip curled up in disdain.

"And what time was that?" Ryan asked, dunking his digestive in his tea.

"Round eight? A rerun of Gardener's World had started on the telly."

"And did you see anything this morning?"

"I saw their snot-nosed kid slope off to school while I was weeding round the cabbages, then about an hour ago that idiot husband turned up. Not long after that, he was running around the lawn yelling 'Amanda' like a chicken with its head cut off." He took a loud slurp of his tea and followed it with a bite of his biscuit.

"Do you spend a lot of time staring into your neighbour's yard, Mr Barclay?" Ryan asked, his face schooled to a picture of innocence as he sipped.

"I do no such thing," the old man sputtered, biscuit crumbs flying. He put down his cup and folded his arms.

Ryan was about to point out his previous words showed the exact opposite when Sheri jumped in. "Your vegetable garden is very impressive. The cabbages are huge. It must be a full-time job keeping the snails off them." *A mini DS Bennett in the making,* Ryan thought.

"Yes, well." The little man puffed up and picked up his cup. "I grow all my own vegetables. I have since the seventies. It's a lost art if you ask me. Kids these days think a tomato appears magically inside a packet on the supermarket shelf."

"Do you know what time you saw Mr Norris return?" Ryan asked, not invested in the state of the UK education system.

"Killed her, did he?" Mr Barclay asked, ignoring the question.

"I didn't say anyone was dead," Sheri blurted out, then cringed.

Mr Barclay reached over and patted her arm in a condescending manner. "You didn't have to, lassie. I don't imagine the three-ring circus next door is because he gave his lady wife a black eye." He jerked his head towards the front window where they could see the end of the white EMSOU van.

"I'm sorry, Mr Barclay; we can't give out details of an active investigation," Ryan interrupted. "Now, did you notice the time Mr Norris returned?"

"I'm not sure, but he hadn't been home over five minutes before the screaming started. The two police officers turned up about ten minutes later."

Ryan nodded, noting the timeline. He knew he could use the logs from dispatch to establish a rough sequence of events.

"Did you ever see Mr Norris getting physical with Mrs Norris or see her with any signs of injury?"

"Well, I can't say for sure, but she'd be more likely to wallop the weedy little twerp than the other way around. There's nothing wrong with my hearing, though. They were hollering something fierce at each other last night." He leaned forward with a conspiratorial look in his eyes. "Money troubles."

Ryan abandoned his pretence at drinking tea and checked to make sure Sheri was jotting everything down.

"Do you know whether Mr Norris returned at any point during the night or earlier this morning?"

"No, he didn't come back. I know the sound of his car. Noisy bloody thing. Especially given how much he paid for it." His nose wrinkled, as if paying too much for a BMW was the biggest crime.

"You seem certain. Could you have been asleep?"

"Sleep!" he scoffed. "Who sleeps at my age? I'm lucky if I get three hours a night."

"Well, thank you for your time, Mr Barclay." Ryan stood and shook the old man's hand. "As an important witness, we'd appreciate if you could keep our discussion to yourself for the time being."

Fat chance of that. It'll be all around Bakewell in an hour.

"If you think of anything else, please call me." Ryan pulled out a card and handed it to Mr Barclay.

Mr Barkley's eyes narrowed. "This says the Met?"

Christ, they were a suspicious bunch in Derbyshire. "Yes, I've just transferred, but my number's the same."

Satisfied, Mr Barkley placed the card next to his radio wires.

Relief washed over Ryan as they made their way to the door. The oppressive warmth and smell of the cottage was giving him a headache.

"There was something strange," Mr Barclay said as they reached the door. "Round eleven. I know because I glanced at my watch when I saw the lights."

Ryan's pulse quickened. "What lights?"

"The headlights. From the car that pulled up outside the Norrises."

———

THE MYSTERIOUS CAR was a red 1999 Ford Fiesta according to Mr Barkley, who'd got a good look at it with his glasses on. His eyes had gleamed with excitement as he recounted the details, relishing his role as a key witness. The same make and model as the car his late wife used to drive, though hers was blue.

"I know every car on this street," he'd declared, tapping his temple. "It doesn't belong to anyone locally, but I think I've seen it before, not recently, mind you."

Despite his continued assertions that he never slept, he'd been asleep when the vehicle had left and hadn't seen the occupant.

Ryan and Sheri met Fiona and Cal at the front door and recapped what Mr Barkley had seen.

"It's something, I suppose," Fiona said. "I'll find out if any of the other neighbours saw the car and get Digit to pull any CCTV and ANPR logs in the area around that time."

Ryan nodded. "Good. Let me know what you find."

As they turned to leave, a black Toyota Corolla pulled up behind his Range Rover, blocking him in. Ryan frowned. The angle of the light on the windscreen made it impossible to see the inconsiderate knob inside.

The body removal team wheeled Amanda's body past on a gurney, the black body bag stark against the white sheet tucked around it. Ryan watched them load her into the back of the mortuary van. The doors slammed shut with a hollow finality.

"I'll drop you at the station so you can liaise with Digit,

then I'll head to the morgue," Ryan told Fiona, then he turned to Cal and Sheri. "I need the two of you to go to the Job Centre in Chesterfield and speak to Amanda's colleague, Rebecca."

Cal's eyebrows shot up. "You want us to take an interview?"

Ryan fixed him with a steady look. "What, you don't think you're capable?"

"What? No, I just—" Cal cleared his throat. "Right. We're on it."

The pair hurried off towards the side gate closest to their car, Cal's longer strides forcing Sheri to almost jog to keep up.

Ryan's phone rang. He didn't recognise the number. "DCI Hale."

"DCI, huh?" A gruff voice said on the other end.

Ryan could hear people talking in the background.

"Are you the owner of... Maureen, what's the name on the mutt's tag?"

"Winifred," Ryan heard a woman's voice say. "No, sorry, Winston."

"Ginger, big ears, sausage-stealing little bastard. Ring any bells?"

Ryan grimaced. "It does."

The man gave him the details.

"I'll be there in twenty." He hung up and glanced back at the Corolla blocking his Range Rover, but the driver's seat was empty. Where had they gone?

He scanned the area and froze.

A blonde woman stood by the front gate with Bobby, gesturing with her hands. Winston forgotten, Ryan's heart hammered against his ribs so hard he thought it might burst from his chest.

Jaime.

The woman faced away from him as she spoke with the

constable, so he could only see a sliver of her profile past her shoulder-length bob, but her slender build and the way she held herself were achingly familiar. The world tilted.

"Ryan, are you okay?" Fiona's voice sounded distant.

He didn't answer, his feet already carrying him up the path. His gaze fixed on the woman, terrified she'd vanish if he looked away.

"Jaime," he said as he came up behind her.

It came out barely louder than a whisper, but she heard him. She swung around, shock flashing across her face.

The face of his missing wife.

CHAPTER NINETEEN

A moment later, the shock passed. With a detective's eye for detail, Ryan noticed unwelcome discrepancies.

The woman before him bore a striking resemblance to Jaime. If she'd been frozen in time. She looked to be in her late twenties, the same age Jaime had been twelve years ago when she'd blown a kiss from across the kitchen and walked out the front door to drive to work. That memory, so vivid and painfully sweet, twisted Ryan's gut.

There were other subtle differences. A small mole visible on her left cheek. The absence of a faint crescent-shaped scar on her chin. A scar Jaime had received at age eleven after she'd tripped over the family Labrador.

"Ryan?" the woman said, her face screwed up in confusion.

Realisation flooded through him. Not Jaime, but close. "Sophie?"

Jaime's kid sister. She'd been a teenager when he'd last seen her. Hair down to her waist, dyed a rich mahogany brown, and eyes rimmed in too much dark eyeliner. Even knowing it was

Sophie, the sight of her, older and so similar in appearance to Jaime, brought a maelstrom of emotions he kept buried churning to the surface.

Part of him wanted to drink in every detail, eager to pretend for a heartbeat that it was Jaime standing before him. Another equal part of him wanted to let out a primal scream as he faced a living, breathing reminder of what he'd lost.

"I heard you were coming back to Chesterfield as DI," Sophie said, shifting uneasily, "but I didn't know you'd already started."

She even sounded like Jaime. Ryan fought the urge to shut his eyes and pretend it was his wife talking to him.

Instead, he swallowed. "Today's my first day. How's Ruth? I planned to call her once I'd settled in."

Ryan couldn't have asked for a lovelier mother-in-law than Ruth Byrne. Warm and generous with a kind heart and a no-nonsense streak, Ruth had made him feel more loved than his own mother ever had.

His mother had married young and sacrificed her career for what she considered the tedium of full-time motherhood, particularly during the extended periods when their dad had travelled overseas for work. The bitterness she'd nurtured from those years was something she hadn't concealed from Ryan and his brother.

"Mum's okay. She's been following your career at the Met. Every time I'd visit, she'd show me another article mentioning you from the London papers. She cut them out and saved them in a scrapbook. When the kidnapping story broke, she was beside herself. Did you get the card and chocolates she sent you?"

Ryan nodded. She'd sent him three family bags of Boost Bars. Even a decade later, she'd remembered they were his favourite.

Sophie closed her eyes and took a deep breath. *Here it comes.* Jaime had done the same thing right before she gave him an earful.

"Would it have killed you to visit Mum now and again?" Sophie straightened, her hands rising to her hips. "First Jaime disappears, then you skulk off to London. It was like she'd lost a son as well as a daughter."

The accusation in her voice was clear and justified.

Ryan nodded. He looked away, shoulders hunched, and noticed Sheri and Cal watching with interest from inside the Vauxhall. "You're right. I was a coward."

His honest answer took the wind out of her sails.

"Well, make sure you visit her soon, not just a phone call."

"I will."

Bobby cleared his throat, looking like he wanted to be anywhere but here. "I was just explaining to Mrs Ryder that we aren't making any statements to the press regarding our presence here and that she can direct any questions she might have to our Media Office."

"You're one of them?" Ryan snapped. He winced. He hadn't meant it to come out sounding like he was accusing her of baking kittens into pies.

Ever since the media had turned its unforgiving glare on him during Jaime's disappearance, his relationship with the press had skewed closer to hate than love. In London he'd become more savvy about dealing with reporters, but he still found them about as welcome during an investigation as a bout of the shits.

"If you mean a journalist, then yes. Senior reporter for the Derby Observer. Going on four years now. Care to comment on what happened here today, DI Hale? I assume, given you're the new detective inspector of the Chesterfield Major Crimes

Unit, that you're the senior investigating officer on whatever this is?" Her gaze followed the mortuary van as it pulled away.

Ryan ignored her question. "Care to tell me how you knew we were here?"

"I got a call from a local citizen concerned with the sudden police presence in the area."

"A concerned citizen, ah?" Ryan replied. His eyes flicked over to Mr Barkley's house and caught the curtains moving. He wouldn't have put it past the old sod to have called the press. Or she had an illegal police scanner in her car.

"As PC Matthews said, please contact the Northern Division Media Office for any information."

Sophie huffed but didn't argue.

"Anyway… nice to see you," Ryan said.

They stood there awkwardly, staring at each other.

"What?" Sophie barked.

"I need you to move your car." Ryan pointed to the black Corolla blocking in his Range Rover. "Important police work I need to get on with and all that." *After I collect my delinquent dog,* he silently added.

Sophie blinked. "Oh, sorry."

Ryan walked back over to Fiona, who'd observed the exchange but wisely stayed back.

She grimaced as he approached. "Shit. I should have warned you. I didn't even think about how much she resembles Jaime these days."

"She's a crime reporter, huh?"

She nodded. "And an absolute pain in the department's collective backside."

"Sounds about right." Ryan sighed. She was Jaime's sister, after all.

CHAPTER TWENTY

Ryan checked his watch as he hurried along Market Place, scanning the stalls with their green and cream awnings for the Artisanal Sausage Company.

His gaze fell on the furry culprit, tethered to the side of a stall by a cord looped through his collar. The dog's tongue lolled from the side of his mouth in a self-satisfied grin.

Winston turned towards him.

At the sight of his owner, the corgi yipped excitedly, front paws pawing the air as he strained against the makeshift lead.

A man with a bushy white horseshoe moustache emerged from the stall, scowling. His black T-shirt advertised an obscure heavy metal band and stonewashed black jeans completed the biker look. The tough-guy image was undercut by a pinstripe apron emblazoned with 'I season with love... and maybe too much salt'.

"Took your sweet time coming to get the little bugger," the man said as Ryan reached the stall, its counter lined with trays of sausages. Quite high for the corgi to reach, but then he could perform amazing feats when motivated.

Ryan ignored the man, giving Winston a pat on the head.

A thin woman with frizzy, salt-and-pepper hair and deep smile lines appeared beside the man. Maureen, Ryan assumed. "Oh, leave off, Billy. The man's a detective. He's probably busy working on an important case. Isn't that right, love?"

"I am," Ryan replied. "How much do I owe you for the sausages?"

Billy produced an old calculator and began punching in numbers with excruciating slowness.

Ryan resisted the urge to tell him to speed up because he had to get to the morgue. The man could have called the dog warden instead.

Finally, Billy looked up. "Twenty-four pounds."

"Twenty-four? Were they made with gold flakes?"

Billy's scowl deepened. "He stole a kilo and a half of the veal, porcini, and thyme." He gestured at a pile of brown sausages flecked with green at the corner of the display. The sign read Veal, Porcini and Thyme £16 per Kg. "I prefer good old beef myself, but they're popular with the posh wankers visiting from the city."

"We don't refer to our paying customers as wankers, Billy," Maureen called from inside the stall.

Billy huffed. "Sorry, I mean city toffs."

Maureen poked her head out, rolling her eyes.

Ryan looked down at the corgi. "You couldn't have stolen a link of the pork?"

Winston gave an unrepentant whine.

Without the time to argue, Ryan pulled out his wallet and reluctantly handed over the cash.

"Let me wrap the rest so you can take them," Maureen offered. "He only got a couple down him before Gavin from the chutney stall caught him for us. Lovely young man, Gavin, so quick on his feet." She beamed at the adjacent stall, though

Gavin was absent. She showed Ryan an open package of sausages, now coated in dust and bits of grit. One sausage end was slightly mangled, likely from a tug-of-war with Gavin. How the man had wrestled the sausages from Winston without losing a finger, Ryan couldn't say.

"No, it's fine," he said. He didn't want to reward Winston's criminal behaviour, and he was eager to get going.

"Please," she insisted. "I'll throw in a few pork ones as well. Wrapped separately, of course."

Billy grunted in objection but fell silent at the look Maureen gave him.

Ryan checked his watch again. The prospect of recouping some of the expense won out.

He thanked the woman, took the paper bag containing the two packages, and headed back to the car.

He bundled Winston into the back seat. The corgi would have to stay in the car while he attended the autopsy. He didn't have time to detour home and figure out how the little Houdini had escaped from the enclosed garden.

Winston balanced his front paws on the centre console between the seats as Fiona ruffled his fur.

"Sorry for the detour," Ryan said, pulling into traffic. "I'll drop you at the station."

"Who's a handsome boy?" she cooed. Winston leaned into her scratches, tongue lolling.

"I hear the beef ones are good," Fiona said, eyeing the branded paper bag.

"Winston prefers veal, porcini, and thyme, apparently," Ryan replied, stuffing the sausages in the glovebox out of reach of greedy paws. "Whatever the hell porcini is."

CHAPTER TWENTY-ONE

Cal navigated the pool car through Chesterfield's narrow streets, eyes flicking between the road and Sheri's restless fingers drumming against her thighs. He'd spent an extra few minutes when he'd gone home to change out of his wet clothes, selecting his navy Ted Baker blazer and tan chinos. The kind of sharp coordination that stated, "I've got my shit together," even when he didn't. The housing estate where he'd grown up hadn't exactly been a fashion mecca, but he'd learned early that looking the part could get you places attitude alone couldn't.

The Job Centre slid past, but the heavy lunchtime traffic forced him to keep searching for a parking spot.

"Bit nervous about your first interview?" he asked.

Sheri's head snapped around. "What? No." She sighed. "Okay, maybe a little. It's not like I didn't work cases while I was in training, but they kept me in the office."

Her face told him what she'd thought of that arrangement. She rubbed the ruby amulet around her neck, a nervous habit Cal had already clocked.

"My mum keeps asking when I'm going to get a proper office job with regular hours. She made me promise to text her later to let her know I'm safe."

"Safe from what? The only injury I've had in a year is a staple puncture."

"You joke, but she reads the crime statistics." Sheri rolled her eyes. "She's convinced I'll get stabbed every time I leave the station."

Distracted, he almost missed the vacant parking space between a minivan and an old sedan. He hit the brake, and the car jerked to a stop, throwing Sheri against her seatbelt.

"Hey!"

"Sorry, nearly drove past it." He gestured over his shoulder, then expertly reversed into the tight spot, ignoring the horn from the car behind them.

Cal pulled out his phone to check his notifications. 547 likes on this morning's post about being "on the job." He'd captioned it with a coffee cup emoji and "Real detective work ≠ Netflix," which his followers seemed to love.

Detectiveman2000 was trending in Derby's local hashtags. He should post something soon. Keep the engagement up.

He flashed Sheri a grin, cocky confidence masking his own nerves at being put in charge of the interview. "Follow my lead and stay in the background. I'm like kryptonite to a certain type of woman."

"And what type of woman is that?"

"Any still breathing."

Sheri studied his deadpan face, no doubt trying to figure out if he was joking.

Which he was... mostly.

She laughed, but her fingers continued their drumming. "So what's your take on the new boss?"

"He's not a pushover like Dobby, that's for sure. Word is

he's tight with old Cliffy. Could mean more interesting cases come our way." He paused for dramatic effect. "Then there's the whole 'maybe he murdered his wife and got away with it' thing."

Sheri's jaw dropped. "What?"

Cal lowered his voice as if someone might overhear them. "His wife vanished twelve years back. He was CID's prime suspect, but they couldn't nail him for it. Next thing you know, he's taken off to London. Hasn't shown his face round here since, till now."

"So it's still unsolved?"

"According to DS Moore."

Sheri looked sceptical. "So you're saying our new boss could be a murderer?"

Cal raised his hands defensively. "Hey, I don't think he did it, but I didn't want you to be the only one on the team who didn't know."

"I wonder if we could get a look at the case files," Sheri mused.

"Bit of an invasion of privacy, that," Cal replied, blatantly ignoring the fact he'd done exactly that about a minute after he heard and then been stupid enough to tell the new boss all about it.

"Not if we solve it," Sheri countered.

Cal laughed. "A twelve-year-old cold case? Good luck." Looking through the files, he quickly realised he had as much chance of solving Jaime Hale's disappearance as Tottenham had of winning the Premier League. Better to focus on the team's current and much more solvable cases if he wanted to get promoted to DS.

They strode down the street, Cal's long legs outpacing Sheri. He pointed across the road to the Job Centre, wedged between a hairdresser and a kebab shop. "Ready, Robin?"

"What?"

"You know, Batman and Robin."

Sheri looked confused. "Who?"

"The caped crusaders? The dynamic duo?"

She shrugged.

"Come on," Cal muttered under his breath before he noticed the smile that had appeared on her face.

Sheri laughed and darted between the slow-moving cars. "I prefer Hawkeye and Black Widow myself."

Cal grinned and followed. He touched the small tattoo of a bee on his wrist for luck, then he pulled open the shop door and ushered Sheri inside.

The Job Centre was empty except for a woman in her thirties with a short blonde bob that framed her round face. She sat at one of the two large desks at the back of the reception area. She looked up as they entered and gave them a watery smile that didn't reach her eyes. Cal could see she had been crying. Used tissues sat piled next to her keyboard.

"Rebecca Boyle?" Cal asked.

The woman gave a sniff and nodded. "Yes, that's me." She dabbed at her cheeks with a tissue. "Please excuse me. My boss just rang with some bad news, and I'm still processing it."

"That's what we're here for. I'm Detective Constable Pine, and this is Detective Constable Dewan. We hoped you might answer some questions about Amanda Norris?"

"Ah, we weren't all that close." She blew her nose. "Only work colleagues."

"That's fine. These are routine questions."

"Okay." She got up and walked to the door. She flicked the lock and turned over the sign saying 'Back in ten minutes' to face the street.

Cal gestured to Sheri to take Rebecca's seat for clients and pulled over the other chair from the other empty desk he assumed had been Amanda's. Sheri took out her notebook and a pen. Cal appreciated the initiative.

"How long did you work with Amanda?" he asked.

"I started here about two years ago," Rebecca replied. "Amanda's been here much longer, though. At least seven or eight years, I think? She said she started here part time when Carter started school. Tessa, the HR manager at DWP, would know."

"DWP?" Sheri asked.

"The Department of Work and Pensions. They run all the job centres."

"Was she a good manager?" Cal said.

Rebecca paused, as if picking her words carefully. "She was nice enough. So long as we got through our quota, she was happy. She wasn't big on taking any initiative, though. I came to her with a couple of ideas of how we could improve our processes, but she didn't want to know. She was allergic to anything that might increase her workload."

"So she was lazy?" Cal said.

Rebecca's face flushed. It was clear that was what she thought, but she hadn't meant for it to come out of her mouth. "Umm, not lazy, really. The job was more like a hobby for her." She leaned forward and lowered her voice. "Well, at least until recently. Did you know her husband, Will, was let go from his finance job? Sounds like they shafted him, from what Amanda was saying. It's disgusting, given how long he worked there." She sighed. "There's no loyalty these days."

Cal saw Sheri circle something in her notebook.

"She always looked immaculate," Rebecca continued. "The beautiful clothes she wore weren't appreciated by the clientele round here. She was so lucky, especially given her background." She looked down at her patterned blouse, and Cal noticed a faint stain on one lapel.

Odd to say someone was lucky when they'd been murdered, Cal thought, but he pushed on. "Her background?"

"She didn't like to talk about it, but one night she got drunk at a staff party and told me some of the details. How she grew up on a housing estate with no dad and her mum in and out of prison. Sounded like she was in with a rough crowd, but then she sorted herself out after high school and escaped that life. It made me feel pretty grateful for my boring old upbringing here in Chesterfield."

The words hit Cal harder than he expected. Housing estate. Rough crowd. He adjusted his blazer, aware of the expensive fabric against his skin. His own proof that he'd made it out. Except, had Amanda escaped? She had a husband, a kid, a respectable life. And look where that got her. Strangled in bed.

Maybe you couldn't outrun where you came from.

He consulted the notes app on his phone, reading through the bullet points Fiona had messaged him. His thumb hovered over the Instagram icon for a second, pure muscle memory, before he forced himself to focus.

"Will said Amanda was upset about something a week ago. Did she mention anything to you?"

"No, like I said, we weren't very close."

Cal read the next bullet point. "Do you know anything about the book club she attended every second Wednesday?"

Rebecca's lips pressed together. "I only know about it because she used to leave half an hour early to get there. I quite enjoy reading, so I asked her once if I could join. She said it was exclusive, and they didn't have any spots available. That's why I was annoyed when she invited this random client."

"What client?"

"Some guy. Kyle something. Good-looking but on the

smarmy side," Rebecca said. "All fake-tanned muscles and white teeth. Not my type at all."

"Yeah, they're not for everyone." Sheri turned to grin at Cal as his earlier comment from the car came back to bite him in the arse. He ignored her as Rebecca continued.

"Amanda was quite taken with him when she did his initial interview. Not sure why when she had a gorgeous and successful husband at home."

Cal exchanged another look with Sheri. From what he'd seen of Will Norris, 'gorgeous' wasn't the adjective most people would use.

"So why did she invite him to her book club if it was a private group?" Sheri asked.

"She kept saying he wasn't the usual deadbeat trying to dodge work and stay on the dole. They spoke longer than usual. I remember he was still here when I got back from my lunch break. Then after he left, she told me he was going to go with her. Said they needed more male representation. She was giggling like a schoolgirl. It was embarrassing."

"Is there any way to check through Amanda's clients for Kyle's full name?" Sheri asked. "We're trying to track down Amanda's book club members to talk to them."

"Sure." Rebecca opened a database on her computer and tapped a few keys on the keyboard to open up a search tab. "Kyle... Kyle. Here we go. Amanda was the work coach for two Kyles, but only one in the last year. A Kyle Mathers."

The name rang a faint bell in Cal's head, but he couldn't think why. Had he come across Kyle Mathers during another case?

"Did he get placed?" Cal asked, wondering if they could visit his workplace.

She glanced at the screen. "No. It looks like Amanda made a note on his file during their second meeting in June that he'd decided to do a course on project management to increase his prospects. That's when I was away for a week in Greece. That was their last official meeting."

"Do you know whether Amanda had any interest in the occult?"

"What? Like witches and demon worship?"

Cal nodded.

Rebecca snorted, then looked mortified. "Sorry, was that disrespectful? There wasn't a mystical bone in Amanda's body. If anything, she was the opposite. Last year she fired Carter's afternoon sitter because she thought she was filling Carter's head with woo-woo nonsense. Though I think the fact the sitter was a young, beautiful blonde and Will was suddenly getting home from work on time had more to do with it."

"Do you know the sitter's name?"

"We called her the dippy hippie," she replied with a shrug.

Cal got the vibe that Rebecca also disliked Will's interest in the sitter.

"Did Amanda mention any altercations with clients or anything off in her personal life?"

"I always got the impression she was content with her lot in life, and she didn't seem big on confrontation. Why would anyone want to kill her?"

"Where were you last night, Miss Boyle?" Sheri asked, pen poised.

Rebecca's eyes widened. "Am I a suspect?"

"Procedure for anyone close to Amanda," Cal said, giving her his signature roguish grin. It seemed to help as Rebecca relaxed back into her seat.

"I was at a friend's Halloween party until about 2:00 am, then I got an Uber home. I was dressed as Maid Marion." She blushed. "There were plenty of people there taking videos, so I will be in some."

"Would it be all right if we contacted your friend and the Uber driver?" Sheri asked.

Rebecca nodded. She jotted the details down for them on a piece of paper and handed it over.

Cal pushed back his chair, and Sheri followed. "Thanks for your time, Rebecca." He slid a business card across the table. "If you think of anything, please ring us."

Back on the street, Cal shook his head. "That woman has it bad for Will Norris."

Sheri squinted against the afternoon sun. "One step away from boiling Amanda's rabbit, if you ask me."

"What?"

"From Fatal Attraction? It's a classic film about a female stalker. You haven't seen it?"

Cal shrugged. "I only watch TikTok videos."

"Wow, okay. Think Rebecca Boyle belongs on our suspect list?"

"Maybe." Cal unlocked the car with the key fob. "Let's see what the party-goers and the Uber driver say first."

"At least we got the name of a possible book club member," Sheri said as she opened the passenger door. "Though I'll need to tell my parents I'll be late for dinner if we're tracking him down today. My mum's making aloo gobi, and she gets upset if I miss family meals."

"Sounds better than my usual Tesco meal deal," Cal said, sliding into the driver's seat. He took his phone out, already composing a post in his head. No details, of course; he wasn't an idiot. Just vibes. But he couldn't concentrate.

Kyle Mathers.

Why did that name sound familiar?

CHAPTER TWENTY-TWO

Ryan reached the double doors of the mortuary unit in the basement of the Royal Derby Hospital.

"DI Hale here to see Dr Gates," he said into the intercom.

"Come through." The door buzzed.

As they entered, Marley, the mortuary manager, poked her head out of her office. She broke into a smile. "Ryan Hale. I heard you were back in town and DI now, from all accounts. Give me a sec."

The tall black woman emerged moments later, pulling Ryan into a hug before stepping back to study him.

"You look well." Despite the scars on his face and the injuries to his hands, Ryan could tell she meant it. It was amazing someone with such a sunny disposition had ended up running a morgue.

"You too," Ryan replied honestly. The manager didn't look like she'd aged a day since he'd last seen her. He noticed she still wore her red, yellow, and green Rasta bracelet.

Once, as he'd waited for Odd Bod in Marley's office, she'd revealed that her father had named her after Bob Marley. She'd shown him a photograph of her father, a producer for the Wailers, who had died when she was a teenager. In the photo, he stood next to the renowned musician, holding baby Marley and smiling down at her. Ryan wondered if the framed picture was still on her desk.

"Odd Bod asked me to bring you straight to him when you arrived. There are a couple of things he's already found that he wants to show you."

Ryan appreciated Odd Bod preferred the traditional approach.

During his first autopsy as a young DC, the smell of decay and the raw reality of the procedure had overwhelmed him. He had suggested to Odd Bod that he observe from the viewing gallery instead. The pathologist had paused the autopsy and gently pulled him aside, explaining that death offered clues invisible through glass and that it was a disservice to the deceased to distance oneself from their stark reality.

The lesson had sunk in. When he joined the Met, he found that, unlike Odd Bod, most London pathologists preferred using a handheld camera to record points of interest for the investigating detectives.

Ryan's determination to be present in the room was an unwelcome disruption and an intrusion into their domain. Some came around, appreciating the detective's attention to detail and probing questions, while others had joined his growing list of detractors. Ryan hadn't cared either way.

Marley led Ryan over to the PPE area and waited while he put on a face mask, a pair of gloves, a plastic apron and a hair-net. Once he was ready, she swiped him into the pathology suite but didn't follow him inside.

Inside the main autopsy room, the walls were now a lighter shade of grey, but everything else looked the same as he remembered. The deep-lipped stainless-steel tables gleamed under the fluorescents. Sinks flanked each station next to scales waiting for use.

A sheet-covered body occupied the nearest autopsy table. On a separate table, the eyeballs floated inside individual jars filled with clear fluid on a sterilised metal tray beside a row of surgical instruments. The remaining tables in the other bays stood empty.

Odd Bod perched on a wheeled stool behind the table, cradling an eyeball in his gloved hand. He scrutinised it through a magnifying glass. As he rotated it, the hole from the stake became visible, somehow more grotesque than the eyeball itself.

Beneath his lab coat, Odd Bod sported an indigo shirt adorned with vibrant planets and constellations. Ryan wondered about the source of Odd Bod's shirt collection. Was it a local shop in Derby or an online retailer specialising in eccentric designs?

"Wouldn't be fun," Odd Bod said, still studying the eyeball. "Having your eyes gouged out with a blunt instrument." He looked up at Ryan. "At least they were already dead."

"You can tell that without the remaining bodies?"

"There's some light petechial haemorrhaging here." Odd Bod pointed to a spot close to the iris. "If this eyeball had been removed when the victim was still alive, the blood vessels would have been under pressure, leading to more obvious ruptures and a bloodier surface appearance. Also, the extraocular muscles are relaxed." He rotated the eye in his hand and showed Ryan the fleshy bit at the back. "I would expect to see these more contracted if the victim had been alive during extraction."

He gestured to the body covered by a sheet. "It was a post-mortem event for Amanda. No blood pooling in the eye sockets or swelling around the area. The killer probably used a spoon to pop them out and then tore them free."

Odd Bod mimicked the action as he spoke, and Ryan tried to wipe away the graphic image it invoked from his mind.

"I'll take your word for it. So the eyeballs with the green irises belong to Amanda?"

"Yes. The tearing pattern of the connective tissue matches up, so I can say with certainty these are Amanda's eyes."

Ryan had a thought. "Any chance of a fingerprint if the killer handled the eyes without gloves?"

"A long shot, but I checked. This was the last one." Odd Bod placed the eyeball back in a jar. "Unfortunately, the killer was wearing gloves or didn't handle the eyeballs in a way that left any signs of a print. It's a shame. I've been looking for any excuse to contact the lab at Loughborough University to try out their new latent fingerprint technique."

Odd Bod studied Ryan's scarred face. "The plastic surgeon did a good job," he said. "Immaculate stitching considering the damage."

"I'll be sure to pass on your compliments if I see her again. What about Amanda?"

"The lividity of the body suggests she either died in the location and pose she was found or was moved there shortly after death. Her liver temperature is consistent with the window between eleven and two."

Ryan nodded. "That fits with what the son said to the family liaison officer. According to Carter, she stuck her head into his room sometime around ten to say goodnight. Is cause of death confirmed as strangulation?"

Odd Bod moved towards the table with Amanda's body. "As I pointed out at the crime scene, the substantial petechial haemorrhaging on the eyelids and on the pinna of the ear suggested cerebral hypoxia through compression, but there was another, more obvious sign." He pulled the sheet down below Amanda's shoulders, revealing her face and neck.

Ryan could see what Odd Bod was talking about. Amanda's neck was bruised in a V pattern with indentations at the sides. The high neck of her lacy nightgown had hidden the bruising.

"Manual strangulation and the thyroid bone is broken. This takes some force, suggesting a strong assailant. Note the fingernail marks. I found a minuscule amount of a blue plastic substance embedded in one. I believe it came from blue disposable gloves."

Ryan fought down his disappointment. Manual strangulation could leave recoverable prints when natural oils transferred from the killer's hands to the victim's skin, but given the meticulous planning behind this murder, the killer had probably been too careful for that.

"No sign of sexual assault, but there were two things of note I found during my initial search of the body."

He pulled a penlight out of his pocket and waved Ryan forward. Rotating Amanda's head gently, he shone the light on the side of her neck. "Here."

Ryan could just make out a tiny red spot.

"I believe it's an injection mark, and the placement's too far back for it to be self-inflicted."

"So she could have been injected with something that incapacitated her. That would explain the lack of any defensive wounds."

Odd Bod nodded. "There was nothing under her fingernails. I've sent a blood sample to toxicology and requested a rush, but without specific parameters, it will still be a few days before we get the results."

"You said two things. What was the other one?"

"This." Odd Bod shifted down the table to Amanda's feet and folded the sheet up to her knees. One thing Ryan had always respected about Odd Bod was the way he worked hard to preserve the modesty of the victims, even in death.

The pathologist directed his penlight between Amanda's toes. "There's extensive scarring from track marks here, and some scar popping on her legs. All are historic. Nothing recent." He showed Ryan a few faded circular scars that resembled pockmarks.

"Any marks on her arms or neck?"

Odd Bod shook his head. "There was no indication in her medical records of any condition requiring frequent injections. The location suggests she was concealing her usage from those around her."

Ryan nodded. "How historic are we talking?"

He shrugged. "It's hard to say. She could have stopped in her thirties or as far back as her early twenties."

Will Norris either knew a lot more about his wife's past than he was letting on or Amanda had kept her misspent youth a secret from her husband. She must have turned her life around at some point. Ryan had to admire Amanda for not only escaping a rough upbringing but also a drug addiction.

"Anything else?"

"I'll let you know once I've finished the autopsy."

"Anything you can tell me about the other eyes?"

"There's not much more I can deduce without having the bodies. All the eyes were removed in the same manner as Amanda's. One set likely belonged to an elderly person because of the cataracts. The second pair has a flattened cornea and calcific deposits, so probably came from someone middle-aged. The third pair shows no signs of disease and good eye health, making it harder to determine the age."

"Any more insights?"

"No, whatever these eyes saw, they're holding on to their secrets. You need to find their owners."

CHAPTER TWENTY-THREE

"LISTEN UP, TEAM." RYAN PERCHED ON THE EDGE OF HIS desk. "We have four sets of eyeballs but only one body. Odd Bod says all the eyes were removed post-mortem, which means we're looking for three more victims."

"Shit," Cal muttered, leaning back in his chair.

"So one pair of eyes matched Amanda's?" Sheri asked.

Ryan nodded. He outlined the details Odd Bod had shared during the autopsy, finishing with the injection mark found on Amanda's neck and Odd Bod's theory that the killer had incapacitated Amanda by injecting her with an unknown drug before killing her. "What does drugging the victim tell us about the killer?"

Cal and Sheri stared back blankly.

"It suggests our perpetrator is cautious and methodical," Digit said. "They wanted Amanda incapacitated and Carter unaware whilst they staged their scene. The ability to inject the drug with precision might indicate a medical background, or previous experience."

"Exactly," Ryan replied.

Sheri frowned. "Why not just use chloroform?"

Fiona snorted as she emerged from the break room, two cups in hand. "Don't believe everything you see on TV."

Ryan accepted his coffee with a nod. "Fiona's right. Chloroform doesn't knock someone out instantly. A rag soaked in the stuff takes about five minutes on average."

"I'm thinking midazolam," Fiona said.

"My money's on succinylcholine," Ryan replied. "Care to wager a pint?"

Fiona grinned. "Sure. But I'm changing my guess to ketamine."

"What about the possibility that the other eyeballs came from cadavers?" Sheri asked.

It impressed Ryan the rookie had thought of it. He'd asked Odd Bod the same question at the morgue.

"Odd Bod thinks it's unlikely, but we should still rule it out. Digit, first thing tomorrow, run a search of HOLMES 2 for any recent reports from mortuaries or teaching hospitals about mutilated corpses." He took a slow sip of his espresso, savouring the robust flavour.

"Yes, Sir. I can also confirm with 97.6% accuracy that no imagery from the Nine Ladies Stone Circle was posted online."

"That's something at least. How did you get on with Amanda's workmate?" Ryan asked Cal and Sheri.

"Rebecca Boyle." Cal swivelled his chair. "Didn't know much about Amanda outside the office, but she came across as obsessed with Will Norris."

"Think they're having an affair?"

"Not currently," Sheri supplied. "But either something happened between them in the past or Rebecca desperately wanted it to. She gave us an alibi, though. Halloween party. I'm waiting for the host to return my call. The Uber driver confirmed he picked her up at 2:11 am."

"You agree?" Ryan said to Cal.

"There was something off. She also made it sound like Will Norris didn't leave his CFO job willingly."

"But who's lying? Will or Rebecca?" Fiona said.

"There was the overdue mortgage repayment letter on the hallway table," Cal added.

Ryan looked at him.

"I went looking for the SOCO about dusting the back gate when you were interviewing the husband, and I saw it. Looks like they're deep in a hole. Repayments on that place aren't cheap."

Looking for Eloise, Ryan guessed, but he let it slide given what Cal had uncovered.

"Good catch."

Cal puffed out his chest.

"Your reward is to dig into whether Will Norris profits from his wife's death and to speak to his former employer."

Cal deflated.

"Rebecca gave us a promising lead on the book club," Sheri added. "She told us Amanda invited a client called Kyle Mathers to join. I'm about to run the name through the system."

"Don't bother. He's dead," Fiona said.

All eyes turned to her.

She winced. "Sorry, that sounded harsh. He hanged himself from the rafters in his mother's boatshed a month ago. DI Abbas from Derby CID was the SIO, but the rest of his team were working a new assault case with multiple assailants, so Lee volunteered me to help with the scene. It wasn't pleasant."

"Did his mother find him?" Sheri asked. Ryan could see the

horror in her eyes at the thought of a family member discovering the body of a loved one.

"No, she'd died a couple of years before," Fiona replied. "According to Abbas, Kyle and his brother inherited her property, but Kyle was the only one living at the farmhouse. It was a lovely spot with a pretty garden and a small lake. If his girlfriend hadn't discovered him, it could have been a while before he was found. I think the brother lives in Derby."

Digit tapped on his keyboard. "The report says his girlfriend turned up at the house to pick him up for a date because he'd lost his license drink-driving. She saw a light on in the boat shed and found him there. According to the pathologist's report, he'd already been dead for twenty-four hours."

More rapid finger tapping.

"The only next of kin was his brother, Todd Mathers, who was out of town, so Kyle was identified by dental records and a tattoo on his shoulder blade that his brother described. The brother made a formal identification at the Royal Derby two days later."

"Was it definitely suicide?" Ryan asked Fiona.

Fiona looked thoughtful. "There were no obvious signs of foul play at the scene. It was peaceful and out of the way." She shrugged. "From memory, the case was pretty straightforward, but I didn't keep up with it after the first few days."

"Looks like Dr Surrey was the pathologist," Digit said, reading from the screen. "She listed asphyxial death due to suspension by ligature on the autopsy report."

Ryan didn't know Dr Surrey. He turned to Fiona.

"She does good work," Fiona said without him having to ask.

"Did DI Abbas find anything suspicious?" Ryan asked Digit.

"Nothing of significant evidentiary value," he replied. "The case file contains interview notes with three former coworkers, all of whom stated the deceased would be—and I'm quoting here—'the last person to commit suicide'. Their statements suggest they found him narcissistic and disagreeable. One colleague used the term 'complete tool'. Interview transcript number four documents a conversation with the deceased's brother, Todd, who reported the deceased exhibited depressive symptoms during adolescence. When DS Abbas queried whether formal psychiatric diagnosis occurred, Todd confirmed their mother declined to pursue medical evaluation. The investigation was officially closed forty-eight hours after Dr Surrey submitted her post-mortem findings."

"Anything in the autopsy report about injection marks?" Ryan asked, acting on a hunch.

Digit scanned the report. "Yes, but Mr Mathers was a known drug user." He looked up. "There's also a note from Dr Surrey about mild hyperopia and possible carpal tunnel syndrome."

"Is the toxicology report in there?" Ryan knew the odds were that Dr Surrey had ordered a basic toxicology screen.

Digit hit a few keys. "Yes." He sat back. "Interesting. According to the toxicology report, Kyle had a cocktail of diazepam and alcohol in his system. Both at elevated levels."

"Working up the courage?" Fiona asked.

"Could you send the report through to me?" Ryan asked Digit.

The tech nodded.

Ryan pulled out his phone and called Odd Bod.

"Dr Gates speaking."

"Odd Bod, it's Ryan. If a male had diazepam and alcohol in his system, would he be able to hang himself from a rafter?"

"Why, hello to you too, Detective. Is he tall, short, fat, thin? How high a dose are we talking?"

"Wait a moment." Ryan opened the email that had appeared in his inbox. "Slightly above average weight and average height. Three times the driving limit for blood alcohol and 90 mg/L for the diazepam."

"Hmmm. It would depend on his tolerance level to both drugs. Taking twenty to forty milligrams of diazepam would knock someone like you or me on our bottoms, but it might only have a slight dulling effect on a long-time user. Same with throwing alcohol in the mix. He would have been impaired, but without knowing the patient's pharmacological history, it's impossible to say to what extent."

Ryan mulled over Odd Bod's words. "So you're saying it's not impossible?"

"Not for a prepared and determined individual. Trying to add a new murder case to your already busy plate?"

"Working through some vague connections. There's a high chance the suicide has nothing to do with our murder. Thanks for your help."

"Anytime."

Ryan ended the call.

"Sheri, what did the Greymoor staff have to say about Lawrence and the rest of the Broomstick Brigade?"

Sheri gave a wry smile. "They remembered him. Lawrence kicked up a fuss at the front desk around eleven that the chips on the late-night room service menu were cooked in the same oil as the flesh of animals."

"Any chance he could have snuck off during the night and driven back before the rest of them woke up?"

"Hotel security is sending me a link to their cloud storage of the CCTV coverage for the car park. The system's old, so they said it would take a couple of hours."

Ryan nodded. "Let me know if you find anything tomorrow."

"Anything on Emily?" Ryan asked Digit.

Digit furrowed his brow. "Regrettably, no progress. Attractive, fair-haired young ladies in their twenties with a penchant for spirituality and well-being are rather abundant on Instagram." He shrugged. "It's possible she doesn't utilise 'Emily' as part of her online moniker. I've created an AI algorithm to sift through hashtags and comments on Instagram posts geotagged within a forty-mile radius, correlating certain keywords pertaining to Wiccan and holistic subjects along with the name Emily. Alas, all the leads we've encountered thus far have been fruitless."

"Next time, a simple no will do."

"Wait," Sheri said, flicking back through her notes. "Rebecca Boyle mentioned Amanda fired their afternoon babysitter because, in Rebecca's words, she was into 'woo-woo' stuff. She described the babysitter as young, blonde and beautiful. She didn't give us a name, but they called her the dippy hippie. Any chance it's the same girl?"

Ryan looked at Fiona. "Call the family liaison and get them to ask Will about the babysitter. See if her name was Emily and if he knows anything about her."

"What about this Robbie character?" Ryan asked Cal.

"Nah, got nothing," Cal confessed, glancing down at his scribbled notes. "Had a chat with the head of East Midlands Railway's HR department. They don't have anyone called Robbie, Robert, Bobby, or anything close to Lawrence's description in the right age group. But she said he might work for one of their contractors. In that case, he won't show up in their records. She gave me a list of all the companies they've been working with in the last year, but it's long."

"Okay, leave it for now. Tomorrow, we'll dig deeper into Amanda's background. The old needle scars between her toes suggest at one point she had a troubled past. Maybe it's caught up with her."

He downed the dregs of his coffee. "It's been a long day, and I know it's frustrating to clock off while we're missing three bodies, but until we find something that points us in the right direction or the victims turn up, there isn't much we can do. Go home, get some rest, and I'll see you all back here at seven."

CHAPTER TWENTY-FOUR

Ryan studied the fence in the backyard behind the flat, searching for any spot big enough for Winston to squeeze through. Nothing obvious presented itself. The back gate had been latched when he'd returned, and despite his knowledge of Winston's jumping abilities, the corgi couldn't fly.

He gave up and went into the house.

Ryan opened the fridge to search for something to eat besides the sausages he'd retrieved from the glovebox.

Someone knocked on the front door.

Winston belly-flopped off the couch and rushed over to it, barking furiously.

"Ryan?" A voice called out over the racket. "It's Fiona. I come bearing gifts."

Ryan grabbed Winston's collar as the corgi continued with his best Rottweiler impression and opened the door. Fiona stood framed in the doorway, holding up a large brown paper bag like an offering from the takeaway gods. The heady scent of Indian curry hit his nose.

"Hope you still like chicken tikka masala and garlic naan."

She looked down at Winston, who was still half-heartedly growling but had already been won over by the delicious aroma. A blob of slobber hit the linoleum. "Aren't you a fierce guard dog?"

"He talks a big game, but he's got no follow through," Ryan said. "The minute you step inside, you'll be in more danger of being licked to death."

He gestured for Fiona to come in and shut the door behind her.

She put the paper bag down on the coffee table and surveyed the living room. Her gaze flicked from the faded wallpaper to the sagging couch. "I like what you've done with the place."

Ryan shrugged. "I'm still unpacking."

Another knock sounded at the door. Winston ignored it, far too busy trying to work his snout inside the takeaway bag to deal with any additional intruders.

Fiona waved a hand at the door. "That's my other housewarming gift."

Ryan swung open the door to find Digit standing there with his laptop slung over one shoulder.

He looked back at Fiona, who was rummaging in the cutlery drawer. "I'm not sure I need one of these. They tend to cost too much to keep and make a mess around the place."

Digit blinked. "DS Bennett mentioned you were having trouble setting up your Wi-Fi and connecting it to your TV?"

"Actually, what I said is your new boss is a complete Luddite who can barely send an email, and if you want to get on his good side, turn up at this address at this time." She put two dinner plates and some cutlery on the table.

Ryan turned back to Digit. "I appreciate the offer, but you don't need to waste your evening. I can pay a technician to come and hook it up during the week."

Digit looked affronted. "It isn't a waste, Sir. I prefer to be useful to society." He pulled out his laptop and placed it next to the router. "I calculated I've cost myself approximately £847,000 in potential lifetime earnings by joining the force instead of accepting the Google offer." He adjusted his gold-rimmed glasses, not meeting Ryan's eyes. "Though I'm still determining the formula for measuring fulfilment."

He started tapping keys. "It'll take me nine minutes, approximately. Please don't time me. I also brought a few things to improve your connection and add some extra channels, legally of course." He held up a clear bag containing a white box with a short aerial and a black box with a small remote. "I upgraded our system at home, so they were going spare."

Ryan thought about sitting in front of a black screen again at four in the morning. "Okay, thanks, Digit. Want us to plate up some Indian for you?"

Digit wrinkled his nose. "No, thank you, DI Hale. I've already eaten. Gastric distension impairs fine-motor accuracy." He noticed Ryan's frown. "Apologies, Sir. I mean overeating. DS Bennett has asked me to work on the accessibility of my language with the team when offering explanations or insights. Also, I underperform at small talk while chewing."

"I asked him if he wanted me to order him something," Fiona piped up from the kitchen, "but he started going on about fat content and cholesterol, and it all turned into white noise."

"A balanced gut microbiome is the secret to my intestinal health," Digit said.

"La la la..." Fiona sang out with her fingers in her ears.

"A cup of tea?" Ryan asked.

"A green tea would be beneficial for my digestion."

"Ah, I only have black."

"I'm fine. I had a kombucha on the way here that should contribute to my upper bowel production."

Digit set up his laptop and was soon surrounded by gadgets with little blinking lights.

Ryan sank into the sofa and ordered Winston to his dog bed. The corgi gave an exaggerated leap onto the flat cushion and perched with one arse cheek on the fabric and his front paws on the ground. Technically on his bed, but barely.

Fiona handed Ryan a steaming plate of curry with a generous side of garlic naan. The scent of tangy tomatoes and earthy spices swirled up invitingly.

"So rough first day," Fiona said as Ryan shovelled in his first mouthful.

"I've had better," Ryan agreed once he'd swallowed. "It would have been good to spend more time getting to know the team before someone got murdered, but criminals seldom get the memo."

"Does Winston fit through that?" Fiona asked, pointing to the cat flap on the back door.

"He can squeeze his fluffy butt through, but it's not a pretty sight." He took another mouthful of curry.

"Did you figure out how he got loose today?" she asked, cradling a piece of naan bread filled with butter chicken curry.

"No idea. I can't see any holes in the fence. He's the Houdini of corgis."

They ate in companionable silence, accompanied by the patter of laptop keys. A few minutes later, Digit turned on the TV with the remote and flicked through a multitude of channels.

"Here are the passwords for the new Wi-Fi and some instructions if the signal goes down." He gave Ryan a piece of paper covered in neat handwriting. Ryan glanced at words like router reset and WPS button and knew if it went wrong, there was a hundred percent chance he'd be sitting looking at a dark TV again.

"Thanks, Digit."

"I also set it up to be voice-activated through Echo using the Alexa app. You can change channels or play music," he said. "Though I changed the wake-up word to Morgan."

"Morgan? Wake-up word?"

"For example. Morgan, continue playing Spotify."

"*Playing Ryan's Favourites on Spotify.*" The dulcet tones of Morgan Freeman spoke out of the speakers before a lively country tune from Garth Brooks started playing.

"Still got the musical tastes of an Irish mammy?" Fiona said with a smirk.

"This coming from a forty-year-old who worships the Sex Pistols. Digit, care to comment?" Ryan asked.

"Statistically, hip-hop and R&B have higher audio consumption worldwide than country music or classic UK punk rock."

"Is that what you listen to?"

"No, I primarily consume binaural beats."

"Ah, okay." Ryan nodded. "Well, thanks again."

"You're welcome, DI Hale."

Digit packed up his laptop and headed out the door.

Ryan carried their empty plates to the kitchen and put them in the sink. He turned around and leaned against the bench. "Thank you for the meal, but why are you here?"

Fiona looked up at him. Instead of answering, she asked, "Why did you come back, Ryan?"

Ryan knew she wouldn't buy the bullshit he'd fed DCI Lee.

"I need to find out what happened to her." He didn't need to say who 'her' was.

"DCI Lee asked me to spy on you, you know. Find out if

you're investigating Jaime's disappearance. If you are, I'm supposed to go straight to her."

"And will you?"

She gave him a wounded look, as if the fact he'd even asked cut. She fished around in the pocket of her jacket.

"Here." She laid a USB stick on the table. "It's got copies of all the files and reports from her case on it."

Ryan stared at the USB, unable to respond as a cascade of emotions ran through him.

"I reviewed the case while I was making the copy. There's not much there, Ryan. I know how you feel about Lampton, but the team was thorough in investigating the few leads they had."

"You could get fired for this."

"Despite what I said this morning in the car, I owe you. You could have been fired for what you did for me. Now we're even."

"I didn't do it for a quid pro quo down the line."

"I know, just like I know you wouldn't have asked me to do this now, but I wanted to."

"Thank you."

"I hope you find the answers you're looking for."

CHAPTER TWENTY-FIVE

"TALK ME THROUGH WHERE WE'RE AT," DCI LEE SAID.

Ryan wasn't surprised to find her already at her desk when he knocked on her door.

He rubbed a hand over his face. He'd spent half the night pouring through the files on the USB and found... nothing. Not even a hint of a direction to look in.

He took a seat and updated her on what the team had discovered so far. She listened, stopping him only twice to ask for more details. Her questions were probing but insightful, leaving him reassured his immediate boss had a good grasp on the situation and wouldn't hamper the direction of their investigation.

"Digit's requested Amanda's phone records from the provider," he continued. "We're unlikely to get them in a hurry, but the killer must have taken her phone for a reason."

"Let me see if I can hurry it along from my end. I have a guy."

"There's one more thing." Ryan drew a deep breath. "The press knows I'm heading up the case. A journalist for one of the local papers was outside the Norrises yesterday, and she recognised me." He decided not to mention that the journalist in question was his sister-in-law.

"I know." Lee placed a copy of the Derby Observer in front of him. Ryan skimmed down the front page until he found a single-column article about the return of the infamous Detective Inspector Hale, a detective still under a cloud of suspicion for his wife's disappearance twelve years ago. He was relieved Sophie's name wasn't on the byline.

"Not the headline story, at least."

"It will be after the press conference." She sighed. "I wanted to give you more time to settle in before the media discovered your role on the team, but with a suburban wife murdered in a ritualistic fashion, if it's a slow news week this case will attract national attention. Your team's exploring all avenues and, of course, DCC Cliffe and I have full confidence in your ability to lead this investigation and catch whoever's responsible." She paused. "But prepare yourself for your past to be rehashed as part of the coverage. With this in mind, do you want to continue as SIO?"

Ryan felt a stab of disappointment, insulted she felt she had to even bring it up, though he knew she was only following procedure regarding the well-being of staff under her.

"Yes, Ma'am. I want to continue."

She gave a wide smile. "Good. I never thought you'd say anything different."

Ryan nodded and stood.

As he reached the door, Lee called out. "And don't forget your appointment with the psychologist at nine."

He turned, frowning. "Can't it wait? Solving a homicide is more important than lying on a couch rehashing my childhood."

"DI Hale, there will always be a case or something else

more important. If you want your team to stay on this case, keeping that appointment is non-negotiable. Dr Hope is one of the best psychologists in the country, and Derbyshire police are lucky to have her as a consultant."

Ryan straightened. "Alexis Hope?"

Lee nodded.

He bit back a groan, but his face gave away his thoughts.

"Dr Hope raised your personal history with me, but she's the only psychologist based in Chesterfield qualified for this assignment. I don't care if she was your high school girlfriend or the head of the cricket club, I expect you to keep that appointment."

Ryan gritted his teeth and nodded.

———

RYAN FORCED his jaw to unclench as he walked back into the incident room.

Cal, once again dressed like a posh financial wanker who'd got lost on his way to the city, had updated the boards with their findings in his neat handwriting. He'd also added the notes from Odd Bod's report. Not as useless as he looked.

Fiona was dunking a teabag in her mug in the break room. Before Ryan could reach the espresso machine, Digit intercepted him, bouncing on his toes.

"Five months ago, William and Amanda Norris took out substantial life insurance policies on each other."

"How substantial?"

"Half a million pounds per policy."

"Sounds like enough money to sort out William Norris's current money problems," Fiona said.

"And a powerful motive to kill her."

Ryan went back out into the main room. "When are you visiting William Norris's old workplace?" he asked Cal.

The DC looked up from his phone, which was open on some stupid social media app. "Ah..."

Ryan continued to stare at him.

"Now?"

"Take Sheri with you."

Sheri put her screen to sleep and gathered up her things.

"Ah...where'd he work again?" Cal asked the room in general.

"Bolton Financial Investments," Sheri replied, pulling on her puffer jacket.

"I'll send you the pin," Digit piped up from across the desks as his computer gave a high-pitched beep. His eyes scanned the message on screen.

"It's an alert from my crawl bot. A Sarah Astley filed a Misper report for an Emily Astley half an hour ago at St Mary's." Digit read through the file. "Emily's twenty-six years old and blonde. Sarah Astley is her mother."

"Could be our Emily," Fiona said. "The family liaison officer confirmed that was the sitter's name, but Will didn't know her surname. A parent at Carter's school recommended her to Amanda."

Digit's fingers flew over the keyboard. "Her Facebook is linked to her Instagram profile @derbysunshinegirl. She calls herself Sunshine in her posts, which is why she wasn't flagged by my tracer. Lots of wellness and spiritual stuff on her profile." He kept scrolling. "Here's a mention of the triple goddess. I think there's an 82 percent chance she could be the woman Lawrence mentioned."

"When did she go missing?" Ryan asked.

"According to the file notes, her mother hasn't had contact with her since Thursday afternoon, and she hasn't posted on her social media channels since Thursday lunchtime. She normally posts daily."

"The timing's right for her to have missed the coven's ritual on Sunday night," Fiona said.

"Call Mrs Astley and get an address for Emily," Ryan said to Fiona. "See if she'll meet us there later this morning. For now, tell her it's regarding the missing person's report she filed rather than related to another case."

"Later?"

"After ten-thirty if possible." He sighed. "There's something I need to do first."

Ryan could hear Fiona's question in the silence, but thankfully she didn't push.

She picked up the phone. "On it."

CHAPTER TWENTY-SIX

Time lost its shape in the cellar. The constant drip from the tap behind her served as her only clock, each drop a tiny hammer that proved she was still alive.

Stupid, naïve Emily. His words echoed her own negative thoughts. How long had she been here? Hours? Days?

The minute he'd left the cellar, she'd freed her eyes again. The tape's glue had weakened, and peeling it off had been easier the second time. She felt better now she could see.

Now that the drugs had worn off, her mind was painfully clear.

The water bottle lay somewhere on the floor where she'd kicked it. Now her tongue stuck to the roof of her mouth. The drip from the tap was torture. Water. Right there. Just out of reach.

She'd tried to call out during what she thought was morning. When the quality of light filtered through the tiny window had shifted from weak yellow to a brighter shade.

"Hello?" Her voice emerged as a croak. "Please. I need water."

Nothing.

The freezer motor hummed its response, clicking on and off in its own mindless rhythm. She'd started counting the cycles to pass the time. Seventy drips between each click. Or was it eighty? The numbers slipped away.

Why hasn't he come back?

Part of her dreaded his return. That voice. The scorn in every word. But another part, the part dying of thirst, wished he'd appear with more water.

Emily twisted her wrist inside the metal cuff. Felt the sting as broken skin pulled against the dried blood. She'd rubbed it raw trying to slip free, but her hand was too big, the cuff too tight. All she'd managed was to make everything hurt worse.

She shifted on the lumpy mattress. Tried to find a position that didn't send shooting pain through her arm. The hospital bed creaked beneath her weight, and the bedrail shifted.

She froze, then leaned back with all her weight and pulled against the handcuffs. The rail rattled, a slight give that sent a spark of hope through her chest.

Was it looser?

Emily pulled harder. She fought through the pain that shot through her wrist. The rail groaned. Then held.

She flopped back against the mattress, breathing hard. Her shoulder screamed from the awkward position.

Think, Emily. Use your bloody brain for once.

What would her mum do? Actually, her mum would tell her this was all her fault for being too trusting. For letting dangerous people into her life. For thinking she could fix everyone.

Not helpful right now, thanks, Mum.

What would Bren do? Her NA sponsor. Practical, no-nonsense Bren, who'd kicked heroin and rebuilt her entire life from scratch.

Bren would assess the situation methodically. Break it down into manageable steps.

Step one. Some kind of bracket or bolts attached the rail to the bed frame, but it was loose.

Step two. If she could break that connection, she could detach the rail from the bed.

Step three. Figure out step three after she'd completed step two.

Emily leaned over the rail as far as the handcuffs allowed and ran the fingers of her free hand over the connection point. She felt the rough edge.

The bracket felt old, the cold metal corroded under her touch.

She pulled straight up. The rail lifted but caught on something. She tried to twist it. A grinding sound made her freeze.

Silence. Just the drip, drip, drip behind her head.

Emily resumed her work, more carefully now. She rocked the rail back and forth, feeling for any weakness in the connection. The metal groaned. Her wrist burned. Sweat trickled down her spine despite the cellar's chill.

She braced her feet against the bed rail. She ignored how her bare soles chafed on the rough metal, and pushed with everything she had. The handcuff chain bit into her wrist. Her shoulder felt like it was tearing out of its socket.

The bracket screeched.

Emily froze again, heart pounding. Had he heard that? Was he up there, listening? Waiting to see what she'd do?

The seconds crawled past. No footsteps. No door opened. Just the endless drip.

She went back to work with renewed desperation. The thirst clawed at her throat. Her head pounded. But it was loose now. She could feel it.

Just a bit more.

Emily rocked the rail. She pulled and pushed in rhythm. Metal ground against metal. The sound was deafening in the quiet cellar, but she couldn't stop now.

The bracket gave with a sudden crack. Emily tumbled backwards onto the mattress, the rail still attached to her hand-cuffs but free from the bed frame.

She lay there in disbelief, breathing hard. The metal rail dangled from her bound wrist, cumbersome, but she was no longer tethered to the bed.

Emily sat up and tested her new range of movement. The rail was about a metre long and heavy, but she could lift it. Could stand.

She swung her legs off the bed. Bare feet touched the cold stones. Her legs wobbled as she stood. How long had she been lying down? Everything felt weak, disconnected.

She turned to the sink. The beautiful, dripping tap behind the bed.

Emily shuffled towards it, the rail dragging behind her. Her legs threatened to give out, but she forced them to keep moving.

She reached the sink and thrust her face towards the tap, tongue out. The water tasted metallic and strange, but it was water. Infuriatingly slow, but water.

She pulled back and gasped. Her eyes caught her warped reflection in the old mirror above the sink. She tried to turn the tap to increase the flow. It spun, but wouldn't catch. So she hunched over the sink for what felt like hours, and lapped at the drips like a cat, until she could think clearly again.

Right. What now? The window was too small and too high to reach.

The door at the top of the stairs. That was the only way out.

Emily turned towards them, the end of the rail scraping across the stone floor. Fifteen steps, maybe. She could make it.

She took one step. Two. Her legs shook but held.

The rail caught on the bottom step. Emily tugged, but it was wedged in. She pulled harder. The metal shrieked.

Emily froze. Was he up there? Did he hear that?

Silence.

By the time she reached the top, her legs trembled and her breath came in ragged gasps.

She pushed against the door with her shoulder. Solid wood, thick and unyielding. She tried again, harder, putting her weight into it. Nothing.

She found the handle. Locked, of course. Through the tiny gap between the door and the frame, she glimpsed heavy bolts. There would be no way to pick the lock even if she'd known how. She rattled the handle, then pounded the door with her fist. "Please," she whispered. "Please."

Emily's legs gave out. She crumpled onto the top step, the metal rail clattering beside her, and let the tears come. Great heaving sobs shook her whole body as the reality of her situation crashed down. The weeping turned to choking gasps as her still-parched throat seized.

He was right. Stupid, naïve Emily.

She pressed her forehead against the door, the timber solid and cold.

No.

She'd freed herself from the bed and made it up the stairs.

Maybe I'm too trusting, but I'm not stupid, and I'm not going to give up.

CHAPTER TWENTY-SEVEN

Ryan stood outside Dr Alexis Hope's office, hand hovering above the doorknob. He could leave, orders be damned, but that meant he could kiss his DI role goodbye. And without that, he'd never get answers. He took a deep breath.

The door swung open before he could turn the knob. It left him awkwardly poised with his hand outstretched.

"Argh!" A tall woman with dark hair pulled up short to avoid colliding with him. She glanced at his face, then down at her watch. "Ryan. Shit. Is that the time?" She turned back and beckoned him inside. "Come in, come in."

"We could do this another time if now isn't convenient," Ryan said, spotting an escape route and grasping for it with both hands.

"No, now's good." Alexis marched up the stairs two at a time without checking if he followed. "You've saved me from myself. I was heading out in search of a sugary snack to keep me going through the morning slog." She froze at the top of the stairs. "Not that talking to you will be a slog." She glanced back at him. "Actually, it will be if you're still as full of stubborn male pride as you used to be." She flashed her trademark lopsided grin and studied his face.

Before he could open his mouth to argue, her grin widened. "Slog then. Good, I love a challenge."

He followed her into the office. She hadn't changed much. Still striking, even with her long hair pulled back into a practical ponytail. Not conventionally beautiful like Jaime or Sophie, but there was something about her features that drew the eye. Ryan had always thought she looked like the real Cleopatra might have, though a rumpled version.

Her silk blouse was creased, and her trousers hung loose, held up by a thin black leather belt. Scuffed ballet flats peeked out from below the hems. At close to his own six feet, she didn't need heels. Her appearance suggested someone who'd received a memo on how a clinical psychologist should dress, but had stopped caring halfway through the process.

She caught him appraising her and gave him a wry smile. "I know. When we were at uni, Jaime always said I'd leave our flat in a bin bag if she wasn't there to stop me."

Working in PR, Jaime had understood the importance of appearances. His throat tightened as he remembered the time, a few months into their relationship, when she'd gone through his wardrobe and made a large pile of clothes she declared he needed to mourn before she donated them to the 'big clothes recycling bin in the sky'. Then she'd taken him shopping. He'd complained the whole time but secretly enjoyed it. As she'd brought him increasingly absurd outfits to try on, her infectious laugh had rung through the changing room.

"God, I miss her," Alexis whispered.

"Me too." Ryan looked around the room to avoid meeting her eyes.

The office was airy, with a series of soothing abstract watercolours on the walls. At one end sat an unassuming desk with an ergonomic chair. At the other, a pair of padded chairs with a low coffee table between them. A crystal jug of water with two glasses sat on the table.

"No couch?" Ryan asked.

Alexis raised an eyebrow. "My clients aren't the type who want to lie down, but if you fancy it, there's always the floor."

Ryan's lips twitched. Alexis's take-no-prisoners attitude hadn't softened over the years. He sat in the nearest padded chair. "This is fine."

She didn't sit opposite him. Instead, Alexis headed over to a combi boiler hung above a small cabinet with an extensive selection of canisters.

"Still doing your thing with the herbal tea, then?" Ryan asked.

"Everyone needs a party trick."

In her early days of clinical psychology, Alexis had explained how she used her love of herbal tea and her knowledge of herbs' properties to create a personal infusion for each client. A soothing blend if they arrived unsettled, or an invigorating brew if they seemed drained. She professed to having a talent for perceiving what tea they needed to help them have a productive session. Despite her insistence it worked, Ryan had remained sceptical.

"Hold the tea. I have a case to get back to."

"Humour an old friend." She gave him another lopsided smile and placed down a tray with two mugs and a teapot with a colourful knitted tea cosy between them. Steam curled from the teapot's spout. "We'll give it a moment to steep."

She settled into her chair. "How have you been?" Her expression was sincere.

"Getting on with it," Ryan replied.

"And what does that mean?" Alexis leaned back, and the

left sleeve of her blouse rode up. Ryan noticed a dark purple bruise on her forearm.

Alexis followed his gaze and laughed. "No need to open an investigation, Detective. This was me versus a challenging roof overhang at the weekend. You should see the overhang..." She paused. "It looks the same, damn it. Still impossible to climb over."

"Climb?" Ryan blinked. "Like rock climbing?" The Alexis he knew hadn't been a lover of the great outdoors.

"Don't look so shocked." Her smile disappeared. "I took up climbing after Jaime vanished. I needed to switch my thoughts off. Hard to wallow when you're thirty feet up in the air, dangling by one hand."

Ryan closed his eyes. Seeing Alexis, someone who'd been a big part of Jaime's life, dredged up memories of happier times.

"Would you prefer I didn't talk about her?" Alexis asked softly.

Ryan thought for a moment, then opened his eyes. "There were times when all I wanted was to talk about her, but everyone had moved on or thought I'd killed her. It's nice to speak about Jaime with someone who doesn't think I did it."

Twelve years ago, when Alexis had said she knew in her heart Ryan had nothing to do with Jaime's disappearance, he'd believed her.

She nodded and reached for the teapot. "I want you to know that when DCI Lee approached me to do some sessions with you, I told her about our history. She thought my personal knowledge of you before Jaime went missing might be useful, not a hindrance. I believe enough time has passed that we can work together, but if you don't want to talk to me, there are psychologists in Derby I can refer you to."

She handed him a mug of tea. A fragrant scent he couldn't identify enveloped him.

"Honestly, Lexi, I don't care who I speak to. We've just started a case that's turning into a multiple murder investigation, and I haven't got time to traipse between here and Derby." He looked at the mug in his hand. "Or drink tea. Can we get on with it?"

"All right then. I'd like to start with the case that led to your abduction. I've read the police report and Dr Rubin's assessment that you were fit to return to duty, but please tell me about it in your own words."

"What sort of person gouges out someone's eyeballs with a spoon?" Ryan asked.

"Is that what they threatened while they held you captive? To gouge out your eyes?" She swirled her mug without drinking.

He waved his hand. "Not London. It's a new case I'm working on here in Derbyshire. The killer gouged out a woman's eyes to use them in a pagan ritual in the middle of a stone circle. Dr Gates thinks she was already dead, but it was brutal." Normally, Ryan would never disclose information about an active investigation to someone outside the force, but Lee had already mentioned Alexis's status as a paid consultant for the department, and he trusted her discretion.

Alexis gave him a look that said she knew what he was doing, but answered anyway.

"From a psychological viewpoint, removing a victim's eyes is disturbing. This type of mutilation is often associated with a desire to assert power and control, even after death. By removing them, the killer is symbolically stripping away the victim's identity and humanity."

Ryan nodded. "Go on."

Alexis paused. "I'd say this person has difficulty making genuine connections with people. They may have a history of antisocial behaviour and a lack of empathy. It's also possible they are obsessed with eyes, or it could be related to an event they witnessed and couldn't process in childhood."

"Could there be a religious element?" Ryan took a sip. The tea tasted better than it smelled. Chamomile with a hint of lemon.

"In some ancient religions, the removal of eyes demonstrated commitment to the gods or a way to earn their favour. In others, it was a means of protection from spiritual harm." She shrugged. "Or it could be as simple as the killer trying to say the person saw too much." She took a sip from her own mug. "Now, tell me about London."

"We were working a homicide of a twenty-nine-year-old male found stabbed in his vehicle on Tottenham Court Road. The connection wasn't obvious as the victim was born in Glasgow, but we eventually linked him to a human trafficking operation run by the London branch of the Solntsevskaya Bratva crime group."

Ryan realised his foot tapped and stopped. He felt his heart race as he recalled how easily he'd fallen into the trap they'd set for him. A trap that ended with him tied to a chair and tortured in a riverside warehouse in Charlton.

"My team had pulled the various threads together, and it all led to something bigger than a single homicide." He stared into the green and blue strokes of the nearest watercolour painting. "That's when I got a tip-off. It came from an informer I'd worked with before, so I took it as genuine. The informer told me that the Bratva group's hitman, who was supposedly the one who'd taken out my victim, would be part of a group meeting a shipment of women arriving from Russia via the river. The only catch was the meeting was in just over half an hour. I wasn't far from the location, but there wasn't time to coordinate a full raid with the Organised Crime Unit at the

National Crime Agency. Turns out that was all part of their plan."

"It was a set-up?"

"Met Ops wasn't sure they'd be in position in time for a takedown. I went anyway just to observe. Thought if I could follow the women after the handover, I could call in a team to rescue them. But when I got to the location, someone was lying in wait. I never even saw them. They knocked me out from behind. I still don't know whether the shipment was real. Next thing, I'd woken up sliding around in the back of a panel van with a cracked skull and my hands and legs tied."

Ryan paused and cleared his throat. The longer he spoke, the tighter his windpipe seemed to close around the words. "May I?" He pointed to the jug of water.

"Help yourself," Alexis replied.

Ryan poured a glass and offered it to Alexis. She declined, so he took a couple of sips and placed the glass on the table.

"How did you feel once you knew you'd been deceived?"

"Stupid. Terrified. The knowledge of what these guys would do to me had me close to pissing myself. A fingernail might be all anyone would find once they finished. My eagerness for a break in the case had blinded me to all the red flags."

He took another sip.

"My informant told me she'd found out about the meeting through a Russian guy she'd been seeing for a couple of months. Said she'd overheard him on the phone going over the details that afternoon when he thought she was asleep. It was flimsy, but I bought it. Turns out the Bratva had discovered she was snitching and threatened to harm her son if she didn't pass me the false intel."

He held his left hand in front of him, displaying his bent fingers, letting Alexis see the extensive damage and the still fresh scars. He remembered how the desperate need to free those captured women had consumed any rational thought. Most agreed to leave Russia willingly, too naïve to understand they'd become slaves, not employees. Others the gang snatched from quiet streets in forgotten towns.

"I was lucky they slipped up. One of my team uncovered where they were holding me. I got shot in the shoulder by friendly fire during the raid, but overall I got off lightly."

"I don't know about that, Ryan." She drank her tea and let the silence lengthen. "It sounds like they'd researched you." Her voice was gentle but probing.

"Those families not knowing if their daughters were alive or dead. The sleepless nights, the unanswered questions." Ryan swallowed. "Just like Jaime."

Alexis leaned forward. "When you thought of those stolen women, you saw Jaime. The case you couldn't solve."

Ryan nodded, unable to speak.

"So you ignored protocol."

"Yeah. I played right into their hands."

CHAPTER TWENTY-EIGHT

CAL AND SHERI FOLLOWED THE SECRETARY INTO MR Bolton's empty office and took the seats set out for visitors.

The traffic had been heavy on the short drive to Sheffield, but the current view made up for it.

Cal watched the secretary's fitted skirt follow the lines of her figure, relieved he'd ignored the team's ribbing about his fashion sense and had instead doubled down with his silk waistcoat and most flattering charcoal trousers. DI Hale had rolled his eyes when Cal had walked into the incident room, but thankfully stayed silent.

Aware Sheri was watching, he kept his expression neutral and adjusted his blazer.

The woman turned, flashing a brilliant smile full of whitened teeth. "Mr Bolton will be with you shortly. He's just finishing a conference call. Can I get you some refreshments whilst you wait?"

Cal gave her a wide grin. "Black coffee would be great, thanks."

"Just water for me, please," Sheri said.

The secretary left the room.

"Nice digs," Cal said. Behind the polished teak desk, floor-to-ceiling glass windows revealed a view over Barker's Pool and the War Memorial. A framed photograph of an older man with kind eyes hung on the wall closest to Cal. It was flanked by a pair of expensive-looking abstract oil paintings that suggested someone had sneezed paint onto the canvas. Cal knew nothing about art, but the paintings looked like originals. Probably investment pieces that would be worth more than his flat in a few years.

Sheri's fingers worried at her amulet. "My mum would be over the moon if I worked somewhere like this. You certainly look the part." She glanced down at her rumpled navy skirt and practical low heels.

"Honestly, I'd rather stare at a wall. Numbers aren't it for me. Mum was so hyped when I joined the police. My uncle put the idea in my head. He's a paramedic. At least we get a pension, yeah? Mum stopped stressing I'd end up back on the estate on the dole after I wrecked my knee."

"Sorry to hear you got injured."

Cal shrugged. "That's life, innit."

Taking the hint, Sheri gave him a small smile and pulled out her notebook, flipping to a fresh page. "It's a bit of a step down from CFO of this place to managing a furniture store in Chesterfield."

Her pen hovered over the paper. Preparing to document everything, Cal guessed. Worried she'd miss something crucial.

A few moments later, the secretary returned with their drinks on a silver tray. A man strode in behind her without bothering to hold the door open. He was tall, with a receding hairline and pinched lips. His Armani suit cost more than Cal's monthly rent.

The secretary laid out a porcelain cup of black coffee in

front of Cal and a small bottle of still mineral water with a crystal tumbler in front of Sheri.

"Anything for you, Mr Bolton?"

"No. That will be all, Eva." He didn't look at her as he dismissed her with a wave of his hand. Turning to the detectives, he glanced at his watch.

A TAG Heuer, Cal noted.

"Sebastian Bolton. You have ten minutes. I have a conference call with my analyst at Goldman Sachs in twenty."

He didn't offer to shake their hands. Instead, he took his seat behind the desk and leaned back as though holding court.

"We wanted to ask you about William Norris," Cal said. "He was the chief financial officer here until earlier this year?"

Sebastian's lip curled. "I might have known this would be about Norris. What's he done now? Gambled away that pathetic little bungalow? Held up a corner shop?"

Sheri sat up in her seat. "Mr Bolton, we're from the East Midlands Major Crimes Unit. This is a serious matter. Could you tell us about Mr Norris's departure from the company?"

Sebastian's eyebrows shot up. "Major Crimes?" He checked his watch again. "Norris was terminated after an audit uncovered substantial discrepancies in the company spending accounts. He'd been embezzling funds for eighteen months. Small amounts at first, thought he was clever, but they added up to over eighty thousand pounds. Online poker—not that I cared why. My father hired him fifteen years ago. Trusted him completely. Norris cried when I confronted him."

"Your father?" Cal asked.

"Reginald Bolton. He's retired now." Sebastian's tone was dismissive. "I took over as CEO six months ago and ordered a comprehensive audit. That's when we discovered Norris's sticky fingers." Sebastian examined his nails. "To preserve the company's reputation, we allowed him to resign quietly rather than involving the police. A mercy he didn't deserve, frankly. But I made it clear he'd never work in finance again. Not with any firm that values its reputation, anyway."

"That seems generous," Sheri said, then looked down at her notebook, as if worried she'd overstepped.

Sebastian laughed, a sharp, unpleasant sound. "Generous? It was pragmatic. The last thing I needed was negative press during the transition. But generous? No, I made certain every financial firm in the Midlands knew why he left. Blackballed him completely." He said it with obvious pride.

"Do you know if William Norris and his wife Amanda were having problems in their marriage?" Sheri asked, her pen poised over her notebook.

"I don't make it my business to insert myself into employees' personal lives. Though I imagine stealing eighty thousand pounds to piss away on online poker wouldn't strengthen a marriage, would it?" His tone was condescending, as if explaining something obvious to a child.

Cal noticed Sheri's jaw tighten, but she kept her voice level. "Would you consider him capable of violence?"

Sebastian leaned forward, interest flickering across his features for the first time. "Violence? Has he hurt someone?"

"We're just gathering information, that's all," Cal said.

Sebastian considered the question. "Norris? The man's pathetic. All that crying when I confronted him. He knocked over a chair then threatened to sue us for defamation. Can you imagine? We had him dead to rights, and he still tried to bluff his way out." He shook his head. "But physically violent? I don't know. Desperate people do desperate things, don't they? And he was very, very desperate."

"How desperate?" Cal asked.

"He begged. Got down on his knees and begged my father and me not to sack him. Said something about his wife not understanding, that she'd leave him if she found out." Sebastian's expression was disturbingly gleeful at the memory. "My father felt sorry for him. I didn't. The man stole from us."

"Must've been awkward," Cal said. "Your dad bringing him in, you having to chuck him out."

Bolton's eyes went cold. "My father's judgement in recent years has been questionable. William wasn't the only poor decision he made." He glanced at his watch. "Six minutes."

Cal and Sheri exchanged glances.

"Did his wife know about the embezzling?" Sheri asked.

"Who knows? Norris has always played his cards close to his chest. I once saw him take a call that upset him. He went white as a sheet. When I asked if everything was all right, he smiled and said it was nothing. Two minutes later, I saw him from this very window, down in the square, screaming into his phone like a madman." Sebastian gestured towards the expansive windows. "The contrast was fascinating. Two different people."

He checked his watch again. "There was a woman who called here a month ago asking about him. Rachel or something similar. Somehow she'd got hold of my direct dial line. Said she worked with his wife. Amelia, was it? Wanted to know if I'd reconsider giving Norris a reference."

Sheri looked up from her notes. "Rebecca Boyle?"

"If you say so. Maybe from India as well, if I recall correctly from her accent. Sounded like you."

Cal saw Sheri's hand pause mid-sentence. A flush crept up her neck.

"I was born fifty minutes from here," Sheri said firmly. "I'm British."

Sebastian waved a hand dismissively. "Whatever. The

point is she was pleading with me to help him. Going on about his 'potential' and what a 'wonderful man' he was." He smirked. "Sounded like she had quite the crush. Probably why she was so invested in helping him. Women can be irrational about these things."

Cal was amazed the temperature in the room could drop any further. Sheri's knuckles whitened around her pen. Before she could respond, he jumped in.

"When was the last time you saw or spoke to William Norris?"

Sebastian shifted in his chair, sighing. "The day we terminated him. March fifteenth. I had security escort him from the building. I haven't thought about him since. Time is money, Detective, and Norris isn't worth either of mine."

"We'll probably need to speak with you again," Cal said, standing. *Though I won't bring Sheri.* She'd probably punch him in the face if she spent another five minutes in his company.

"You'll need to go through my secretary. And next time, I'd appreciate over twenty minutes' notice." Sebastian didn't stand. "Eva will show you out."

Sheri's jaw was clenched tight as they left the office, her notebook clutched against her chest.

"What a bellend," Cal muttered once they were in the lift. "Rebecca calling to plead for a reference is dodgy as hell. She told us she barely knew Amanda."

Sheri was quiet for a moment, her fingers still gripping her notebook. "A woman going to bat for a man she barely knows? It's worth asking why."

"Yeah, we might need another chat with Rebecca." Cal jabbed the lift button. "But Bolton made Will sound proper desperate to keep his job. All that begging."

Sheri nodded, but Cal could see her mind working, replaying every detail of the interview in her head.

"Desperate enough to kill?" she asked.

Cal shrugged. "That's what we need to find out."

CHAPTER TWENTY-NINE

Ryan turned onto Daisy Lane, a quiet country road barely wide enough for two cars to pass. Emily Astley's cottage sat at the dead end, a quaint whitewashed building with climbing roses framing the door. Across the road, Flowerbank Woods loomed dark and dense even in the weak sunlight. According to Digit, Emily had tagged the location in many of her Instagram posts during the warmer months.

"There they are," Fiona said. "The search party for Emily."

A crowd of about twenty people milled about near the woods' entrance. Most wore walking boots and waterproof jackets, clutching torches despite the daylight. A man with straggly brown hair and round glasses stood at the centre, gesticulating as he organised them into groups.

Ryan pulled up behind a late-model Audi.

They approached the gathering just as the man in glasses clapped his hands together. Up close, Ryan noted his pudgy build and the sweat-stained T-shirt peeking out from his open anorak. The logo across his chest read 'Masters of Combat Tournament 2024 - Finalist'.

"Right, so Group A take the western path, Group B head east. Keep your phones on, yeah? If you find anything, call the police straightaway." The man scratched his head, tugging at his lank hair. "And, um, thanks for coming. Emily would... she'd appreciate it."

An older woman with Emily's features and the same straight blonde hair pulled into a tidy chignon pushed through the crowd, holding her blue woollen coat close to her body. "Thank you all for giving up your time to help look for my precious girl. God bless you all."

"Mrs Astley?" Ryan held up his warrant card. "DI Hale, this is DS Bennett, who spoke to you on the phone."

Emily's mother turned. "Thank you for coming, officers." She shook both of their hands weakly. "Truthfully, I'm surprised you responded so quickly. I expected to have to call Karen to get any movement. We went to school together."

Ryan assumed she meant the Chief Constable of the Derbyshire Police Force, Karen Woodward.

"We're treating Emily's disappearance seriously," Fiona said.

Luckily, Mrs Astley didn't question why two high-ranking detectives had been rapidly dispatched so soon after her report had been filed. She wouldn't like the answer if she knew.

"At least people are looking for her now. This young man has organised twenty people to search the woods because Emily often walks there." She beamed in the man's direction.

The man in glasses shuffled forward, pushing his frames up his nose. "Todd Mathers. I, uh, I saw Felicity's post on Facebook about Emily being missing and thought I could help."

Ryan studied him. "What's your connection to Emily?"

Todd rubbed his head, leaving his hair even more dishevelled. "My brother Kyle knew her. They dated for a bit. Didn't work out, and he died recently, but he cared about her, you know? So when I came across her sister's post asking for help, I thought… I don't know. Felt like the right thing to do. Organise something. For Kyle's memory."

"I'm sorry for your loss," Fiona said.

Mrs Astley's expression softened. "Kyle was a charming boy, but he and Emily weren't a good fit."

Todd looked over at her as she continued. "At least his brother's doing something useful."

Ryan scanned the assembled volunteers. Most looked like locals, wrapped in North Face jackets and carrying National Trust memberships in their back pockets. One man stood apart from the group, younger than the rest, with a wiry build and heavy black eyeliner. He wore a black tie-dyed T-shirt despite the cold and shuffled from foot to foot in heavy black boots.

The description Lawrence had given them flashed through Ryan's mind. Early twenties, skinny, with long dark brown hair and an Emo vibe.

"Todd," Ryan said, keeping his voice casual. "The young guy over there in the Metallica t-shirt. Is he a mate of Emily's?"

Todd squinted in that direction. "Never met him before, but then I don't know most of these people. He just showed up when I was organising everyone. Said he knew Emily through some group or something."

Ryan's pulse quickened. He moved towards the young man, Fiona falling into step beside him.

Robbie's head snapped up as they approached. His eyes darted between them.

"Robbie?" Ryan called.

The young man bolted.

He crashed through the tree line before Ryan could close the distance, branches snapping as he ploughed into the undergrowth.

"Bloody hell." Ryan sprinted after him, but Robbie had a

head start and the advantage of youth. Within seconds, he'd disappeared into the dense woodland, leaving only the crack of breaking twigs in his wake.

Ryan stopped a short way into the woods, breathing hard. The shadows turned the forest into a maze of brown and grey. Pursuing him would be pointless.

Fiona appeared at his elbow. "Well, that's not suspicious at all."

"Get Digit to dig deeper into Robbie. We need a last name."

"On it." Fiona pulled out her phone.

Ryan walked back to the group, where Todd stood with Mrs Astley, both staring at him with open confusion.

"What was that about?" Todd asked.

"Just wanted a word with him. Did you collect any contact details from the volunteers?"

"Nah, most just DM'ed me on Facebook."

"Can you check if any of them are called Robbie?"

Todd looked hesitant. "Do you need a warrant for that?"

Ryan fixed him with a flat stare.

"Ummm, sure."

Todd pulled his phone from his anorak pocket and scrolled through his messages. "Ah, nothing from a Robbie. He might have just seen the community post, you know? But I'll have a dig around when I'm back at my flat. See if I can track him down. I'm handy with a computer."

He certainly looked the type, Ryan thought. He pulled out one of his cards and handed it to Todd. "If your search party finds anything, call me."

Todd took the card, studying it. "You don't think we'll find anything, do you?"

"I think Emily's disappearance is more complicated than her taking a walk and getting lost in the woods." Ryan turned to

Mrs Astley. "Would you mind showing us Emily's cottage? We need to understand her state of mind before she went missing."

Mrs Astley's shoulders sagged. The fight seemed to drain out of her, replaced by a mother's worry. "Of course. Though I'm not sure what you'll find. Emily's always been... flighty. But she's never disappeared without telling anyone where she was going."

They left Todd organising his volunteers into search groups and followed Mrs Astley across the narrow road towards the cottage. Ryan flexed his left hand against the cold. The building looked even more picturesque up close, the path to the cottage lined with cheerful clumps of winter-flowering pansies and the silvery mounds of a plant Ryan didn't recognise.

"Emily's lived here for a year now," Mrs Astley said, pulling keys from her handbag. "Her father and I bought it as an investment property, but we let her live here rent-free. The deal was she had to check in with us twice a week."

"When did you last hear from her?" Fiona asked.

"Thursday afternoon. She rang to tell me about a babysitting job she had that evening. Said she'd call Sunday, but..." Mrs Astley's voice cracked. She cleared her throat. "She never did."

"Did you know whether she went to the job?"

She shook her head. "I don't know who she was child minding for."

Ryan's phone buzzed. He pulled it out to see Digit's name flashing across the screen.

"Excuse me for a moment."

"I'll unlock the cottage," Mrs Astley replied.

Ryan stepped away, answering the call. "What've you got, Digit?"

"I've cross-referenced William Norris's family members with the ANPR database as you requested," Digit said, rapid-fire. "His sister, Jenna Norris, owns a 1999 red Ford Fiesta, registration M—"

"Skip the registration. And?"

"It was captured on the ANPR camera on Haddon Road at 10:45 pm on Sunday night. That's two point seven miles from the Norris residence and fifteen minutes before Mr Barclay reported seeing mystery headlights outside their house."

Ryan felt pieces clicking into place. "You're certain?"

"You can't make out the driver in the image capture, but the registration matches. I've sent the image to your phone for verification, but I'm ninety-seven percent confident in the match."

Fiona caught his expression and moved closer.

"Good work, Digit. Keep digging."

"Yes, Sir. The station also received an anonymous call. According to the caller, William Norris is up to his eyeballs in debt, some owed to Jack Stalker."

Ryan winced. Even twelve years ago, Jack Stalker had been a boil on the force's backside. The loan shark had a reputation for breaking kneecaps first and asking questions later. If Will was behind on his repayments, he was in serious trouble.

"DCI Lee is having Mr Norris brought in for formal questioning. She wants you to conduct the interview."

"Right. Thanks, Digit."

Ryan ended the call and filled in Fiona.

Fiona's eyebrows rose. "Owing money to Jack Stalker. Not a great position to be in."

"It's not looking good for Will Norris."

"Do we have enough for an arrest?"

Ryan considered it. "Not yet. But we have enough to sweat him properly in an interview room."

Mrs Astley appeared in the cottage doorway, keys jangling in her shaking hand. "Are you coming or not? I thought you wanted to see Emily's place."

Ryan exchanged a glance with Fiona. There was a possibility Emily's disappearance was connected to their murders, but William Norris and his sister's car had just jumped to the top of their priority list.

Still, they were here now. Might as well take a look.

177

CHAPTER THIRTY

RYAN AND FIONA FOLLOWED MRS ASTLEY INTO A SMALL living room dominated by a blue sofa decorated with plump, squashy cushions in pinks and purples. A row of prisms hung from the window, casting rainbows around the room.

Ryan sat on the sofa and almost got swallowed by it. He hauled himself out, pointedly ignoring Fiona's grin as she perched on the edge next to him.

Mrs Astley settled herself in an armchair and looked at them expectantly.

Ryan cleared his throat. "Walk us through the timeline of your last contact with Emily."

"Like I said," she began. "She didn't call. She always calls on Sunday mornings and Thursday evenings. It's our arrangement." She bit her lip. "Her phone went straight to voicemail all day Sunday, so I came round early this morning. When Felicity said she hadn't heard from her either, I filed the report at the station." The woman's composure faltered.

"This arrangement. Is it usual for Emily to miss contact?" Fiona asked.

"Emily got into trouble in London a couple of years ago. Drugs." Mrs Astley's eyes narrowed. "The charges were dropped. A misunderstanding. I blame Georgina's daughter. That girl has always been wild. Introduced Emily to a crowd of trust fund kids who partied day and night. Emily's lovely, but she's quick to embrace whatever new shiny thing takes her fancy. Makes her easy to lead astray."

Ryan noted the defensive edge in her tone. The mention of drugs and dropped charges suggested a more complicated history than a simple misunderstanding.

"We helped her get straightened out," Mrs Astley continued. "She lives in the cottage rent-free, but she has to check in twice a week."

"In the report you said her car is missing? A green Peugeot 106?" Fiona asked.

"Yes, I thought it could be at my cousin's garage. But it's not. The blasted thing is always breaking down."

"Boyfriend? Friends she might stay with?"

"No boyfriend that I know of since she and Kyle broke up four months ago. My other daughter, Felicity, might know. She's flying back from Bangkok tomorrow. Emily and she are close."

"We'd like to speak to her when she gets back," Ryan said.

His phone buzzed. DCI Lee. He silenced it without answering, filing the call away as something requiring immediate attention. Just not this second.

"What about your husband?" Fiona asked. "Does he have any idea where Emily might be?"

"James is working on a bridge project in Yorkshire. He's rarely home."

A similar situation to Ryan's own upbringing, with an absent father working away. He knew the particular flavour of that absence. How it shaped the space around a family.

"Emily's shifted to more of a holistic lifestyle here?" he asked.

Mrs Astley looked to the heavens. "My daughter, the new-age hippy. For now, at least."

"Did Emily ever talk about Wicca or spiritual practices?" Fiona said.

"It might have come up in passing, but I didn't pay it much mind. She's always chasing Instagram likes and TikTok views." Mrs Astley snorted. "Such a vapid use of her time, but it made her happy."

Fiona's expression remained neutral, but Ryan caught the slight change in her posture.

"Is Emily prone to heading off for a few days with no contact?"

"No, since we made our deal, she's stuck to it and always told us her whereabouts."

"Do you mind if we look around the rest of the cottage?"

"Not at all." Mrs Astley stood. "Follow me."

As they walked through the kitchen door, the scent of disinfectant filled the air.

Ryan took in the clean oak benches and the stack of dishes drying on a rack. He frowned at the freshly wiped surfaces. Even the fridge doors gleamed.

"Mrs Astley, did you clean up inside the cottage this morning?"

Mrs Astley looked guilty. "I may have tidied up a little. I couldn't have strangers seeing the place in the state it was in."

A little. The smell of cleaner was so thick Ryan could taste it. He gritted his teeth. She'd scrubbed the entire house from top to bottom, obliterating evidence in the process.

"Was anything disturbed when you first arrived?" Ryan kept his tone level.

Mrs Astley frowned. "Just Emily's usual mess. Margarine and marmalade on the bench top. Half-eaten toast." She paused. "There were two nearly full teacups on the table. One was green tea, and the other was tea with milk. Though Emily doesn't drink black tea anymore."

Ryan fought down the sharp edge of frustration. The teacups suggested company. Possibly the last person to see Emily before she disappeared. The fact the tea was unfinished could point to something happening before they'd finished. An argument. A sudden departure.

Or something worse.

"Does Emily have a job?" he asked.

"Casual shifts at a local daycare. 'Early Ways', I think? And the odd babysitting job." Her expression suggested what she thought of Emily's career choices.

"May we conduct a quick search of Emily's belongings?"

Mrs Astley looked torn, no doubt thinking what her daughter might say when she found out her mother had let strangers paw through her things, but in the end she nodded. "I'll wait on the porch swing until you are done."

Ryan pulled on a pair of disposable gloves and checked the kitchen bin. At least she hadn't emptied it. He pulled out a paper bag from a local Chinese takeaway shop, fished a receipt out of the bag, and read it.

Chicken chow mein and spring rolls for one. Thursday night.

The contents of the bin yielded nothing else useful. No convenient evidence with timestamps.

Ryan leaned closer to the wall calendar, his fingers flipping between October and November. Sunday, the 31st, bore two words. 'Twelve Apostles'. So Emily Astley was Lawrence's missing maiden. Wednesday evening displayed 'Book Club'.

He traced back through the months. 'Book Club' appeared every fortnight without fail, each entry marked with the same playful smiley face.

Was Emily also a member of Amanda's mysterious book club?

Friday's square contained one word. 'Work.' The daycare centre would know if Emily had been scheduled that day, and more importantly, if she'd shown up.

The shopping list pad on the fridge contained nothing of interest. Bread, apples, milk, butter.

He moved to the bedroom to help Fiona search. Airy and spacious, the room featured soft pale green painted walls. Delicate rose patterns on the curtains and duvet combined with a floaty white net canopy over the bed, giving everything a Laura Ashley vibe. The room was tidy for someone Mrs Astley had described as messy. The only items out of place were a few clothes thrown over a padded chair in the corner and makeup scattered across a white dressing table. Though Mrs Astley could have tidied in here as well.

He told Fiona about the receipt and the book club entries.

"Look at this." Fiona held up her gloved hand. In it was a bundle of ripped-up photographs wrapped in ribbon with a dried posy of flowers and herbs. An earthy scent tickled his nose. Lavender and sage. The same herbs used in the Nine Ladies ritual. He stepped closer. At the top of the pile was half of a photo. A guy wearing aviator sunglasses and a cocky grin, his arm around someone Ryan was guessing was Emily. The photo had been torn through the middle of the couple.

"The Top Gun wannabe is Kyle Mathers?"

"What gave it away?" Fiona replied.

"This suggests a messier breakup than Todd implied."

"I'll see if there's a way for forensics to match these herbs to the ones from the crime scene," Fiona said, slipping the bundle into an evidence bag. "And there are these." She stepped away from the tall chest of drawers and gestured to the books on top.

Ryan read the titles.

The Tradition of Alexandrian Wicca and *Circles of Power: Advanced Spellcraft and Energy Work.*

"She's Lawrence's girl. What's your theory?" He was interested to see if they were thinking along the same track.

"The two cups of tea suggest she might have been interrupted, but it's not definitive proof she was taken," Fiona said. "She or her guest could have just changed their minds about a hot drink, and then she left later in the day of her own accord. Her mother did paint her as flaky and unreliable, but I think the complete social media silence is out of character."

"Lawrence said she was excited about Sunday's ritual." Ryan counted off on his maimed fingers. "She's into the occult. Babysat for Carter Norris. Possibly a regular attendee of the same book club as Amanda, who also shares some connection with Emily's ex-boyfriend."

"Yeah, I don't think she wandered off."

Fiona looked up from photographing the Wiccan books. "I'll talk to Mrs Astley about getting forensics in here. Document everything before the trail goes any colder."

Ryan nodded, already running through the logistics. His gaze fell on the torn photographs and their ribbon binding. "What we need to work out is whether Emily is a victim, or..."

"If she's our murderer," Fiona finished for him.

Ryan's phone vibrated a second time. DCI Lee again. He pulled it out.

"The three missing bodies have been discovered."

Ryan's grip on the phone tightened. Was one of them Emily? "Where?"

"A house near Holymoorside. The housekeeper found

them. All three victims are from the same family." She gave him more details.

So not Emily then.

"We'll head there now." Ryan ended the call. "The missing bodies have turned up," he said to Fiona in a low voice. "And one of the victims is William Norris's old boss."

CHAPTER THIRTY-ONE

Ryan pulled into a wide circular driveway, the space crowded with squad cars and forensic vehicles.

Fiona whistled. "Nice place. Imagine trying to clean all those windows."

"I'd say that's the least of the housekeeper's problems today."

Rows of large decorative windows lined the symmetrical facade of the stately Edwardian manor house, surrounded by manicured lawns and landscaped gardens. To the right stood a converted carriage house, now a four-car garage with an apartment above. Not a tacky Halloween decoration in sight.

A familiar nasal voice carried across the drive. "That's Chief Inspector Lampton to you, Constable."

Ryan gritted his teeth. Of course Lampton would be here. Nothing drew him more than a high-profile case and a chance to claim the credit.

The man himself stood near the entrance, his receding hairline catching the light. He directed two constables with sharp, economical gestures, a wet sniff punctuating each command.

The officer running the crime scene log met them at the front door and introduced himself as Sergeant Combes. He recorded their names and handed them each a pair of paper booties.

"DI Hale." Lampton's voice dripped with something between acknowledgment and challenge. He approached with measured steps, hands clasped behind his back. "Sergeant Bennett."

"Inspector," Ryan replied, enjoying Lampton's wince at the incorrect title. Lampton opened his mouth, but Ryan beat him to it. "Sorry, Chief Inspector, wasn't it?"

"Three bodies," Lampton said, producing a damp sniff. "Elderly male, older female, young female. All missing their eyeballs, apparently. My officers have secured the scene." He paused, his pinched features sharpening. "Under my leadership, naturally."

More like unnaturally, Ryan thought. The man looked like a walking Halloween costume.

Fiona stepped forward. "We appreciate the uniformed response. Perhaps Sergeant Combes can brief us on the specifics?"

Lampton's bulging forehead creased. "I've just given you the specifics, Sergeant. Though I suppose Major Crimes needs everything spelled out these days. Particularly given the calibre of detective we're working with."

Ryan kept his voice flat. "The victims have been identified?"

Lampton pulled a notebook from his pocket, opening it with deliberate slowness. "Reginald Bolton, his wife Isabel Bolton, and her daughter Lottie Garrett. The cleaner found them. Made the nine-nine-nine call. My officers took her statement."

"Where is she now?" Ryan asked.

"Guest apartment." Lampton gestured towards the garage. "One of my constables is with her. Though I imagine you'll want to re-interview her yourself. Can't trust anyone else's work, can you, Hale?"

Ryan studied Lampton's pinched face, noting the smug satisfaction of a man who'd held a grudge for over a decade.

"We'll need access to the scene," Fiona interjected. "And copies of the initial statements your officers have taken."

Lampton's wet sniff was pronounced. "Yes. Well, my uniformed officers have done the hard work securing the perimeter. I suppose the detectives can stumble about inside." His gaze fixed on Ryan. "Try not to contaminate anything. Some of us take procedure seriously."

Ryan's scarred fingers flexed. He forced them still.

He moved past Lampton towards the entrance, Fiona falling into step beside him. Behind them, Lampton's voice carried, "Do try to solve this one, Detective Inspector. Wouldn't want another unsolved case on the team's record."

Ryan didn't turn around. Three people were dead inside. Lampton could keep whistling into the wind for all he cared.

"The housekeeper, Esme Banks, found them about an hour ago," Sergeant Combes said once they were out of Lampton's earshot, his voice dropping. "She seemed surprisingly unflustered by the whole thing. Maybe they were difficult employers?"

Ryan glanced at his watch. "Doesn't she work every day?" The family had to have been killed on Halloween night at the latest for their eyes to have appeared at the Nine Ladies Stone Circle in the early hours of the following morning.

"She said the family were supposed to leave for Portugal on Sunday morning. On the 9:30 flight from Heathrow. They go every year about this time. She agreed to come in and do a tidy-up after they left." He read his notes. "She normally cleans during working hours on Mondays, Wednesdays and Fridays, but she was in Nottingham visiting her mother over the week-end. Since the family were away, she stayed a day longer and came in today instead."

"We'll look at the victims first, then speak to her," Ryan said. "Can you make sure she stays put?"

Combes nodded. "The responding constable's making tea."

Inside the entrance foyer, the interior matched the grandeur of the exterior. Intricate plasterwork adorned the high ceilings. A crystal chandelier cast a warm glow over the marble floors. A sweeping staircase with wrought-iron banisters led up to the first floor. In the corner, antique furniture formed a small seating area.

"Ah, detectives, so nice of you to join us," Odd Bod called down from the first-floor railing. Today the pathologist wore a pale green shirt with a banana pattern. "Come on up."

Odd Bod led them into what had to be the master bedroom. The cloying sweet-sour smell immediately caught in the back of Ryan's throat. Rich gold-leaf wallpaper covered the walls. Heavy velvet curtains were pulled across large sash windows, making the room dim despite the daylight outside. A crime scene tech dusted the mantel of an ornate fireplace for fingerprints.

Ryan's eyes were drawn to an enormous oil portrait hung on the far wall over the carved headboard of a four-poster bed. He immediately wished they hadn't been. The painting depicted an elderly man and a middle-aged woman, both with angel wings and stark naked, locked in a passionate embrace on a cloud.

"Wow, that's a conversation starter," Fiona said. She tilted her head, assessing. "Think it's anatomically correct. It's very detailed." She glanced down at the bed, then back up at the painting.

"Too detailed," Ryan replied with a grimace. His gaze shifted deliberately away, landing first on a pile of paperbacks on the bedside table, then past them to the two bodies on the bed. Luckily, both were clothed in sleepwear.

The way the pair lay under the red and gold silk duvet made them appear to be sleeping, as if he and the crime scene techs were intruding on their rest.

"Detectives, meet Isabel and Reginald Bolton," Odd Bod said. "Manual strangulation. Same as Mrs Norris." He pulled back Isabel's dark hair, revealing dark bruising across her throat. "No defensive wounds, no signs of a struggle. Tucked up in bed as if for a nap but, as your nose is probably telling you, they have been here for a while."

He gestured towards the door. "And that's not all. Come this way."

Ryan and Fiona followed the pathologist down the hallway. Odd Bod stopped at the door two down from the master suite and pushed it open.

This room was smaller, but no less opulent. Silk wallpaper shimmered in the light from a small crystal chandelier. In the centre of the room, a woman with dark hair lay propped against a mound of pillows in a carved mahogany bed. She was larger than her mother, her face soft and round in death.

"This is Lottie Garrett. Only thirty-four, according to the housekeeper," Odd Bod said softly. "Also strangled. Also tucked in for the night."

"Inspecteur." A cool voice cut through from the doorway.

Eloise Durrant stood with her forensic case, her expression unreadable. She moved into the room with a dancer's grace, even in the rustling scene suit.

"Did you find the victims' phones?" Ryan asked her.

"The young woman and the man's were on their bedside tables and have been bagged, but Mrs Bolton's phone has yet to be found." She held up two evidence bags. "I believe you will want to see these."

She passed the bags to Ryan. One contained a fifty-pence piece, identical to the ones from Amanda's eyes. The other held a tarot card. This one depicted a large wheel inscribed with symbols and surrounded by four winged creatures.

Fiona pulled out her phone, her thumb already moving across the screen.

"There was a coin placed in each of the eye sockets, as with the previous victim," Eloise stated. "The card was placed on the older female victim's chest, beneath her folded hands. I will process it for fingerprints, though I suspect our killer is too careful for such mistakes."

Ryan stared at the card. "What does this one mean?"

"The Wheel of Fortune." Fiona read from her phone. "It represents change, cycles, fate. Forces beyond personal control." She looked up. "It can also symbolise karma. A sense of cosmic justice."

"So what goes around, comes around?" Ryan said.

"The scenes feel theatrical," Fiona agreed. "Like a statement."

"Hell of a statement."

Ryan turned the evidence bag, the chandelier's light catching the card's surface. Four bodies. Two scenes. Both carefully arranged. "Has our killer finished dispensing justice, or are they just beginning?"

CHAPTER THIRTY-TWO

"Mrs Banks, I'm Detective Inspector Hale, the senior investigating officer in this case. This is Detective Sergeant Bennett. We need to ask you some questions about the family."

The housekeeper gripped the edge of the table, her knuckles white, but as the sergeant had mentioned, for a woman who'd just discovered her employer and his family maimed and murdered, she seemed remarkably composed.

"Please call me Esme. I still can't believe it. I was here on Friday, and now..." She pressed a hand to her chest. "Anything I can do to help. I've watched every episode of Midsomer Murders, so I understand even the smallest detail can crack a case wide open."

Ryan opened his mouth to reply that they weren't going to solve this in ninety minutes, including ad breaks, but Fiona cut him off with a subtle touch to his arm. "I'm sure your insight will be invaluable, Esme. How long have you worked for the Bolton family?"

"Over ten years for Mr Bolton, long before those two

arrived." Her voice caught. "He brought me some expensive port last October to celebrate the milestone. Very thoughtful of him."

"Before those two arrived?" Fiona let the words hang.

"Isabel and that piece-of-work daughter of hers, Lottie. Isabel is Reginald's second wife." She gave a series of little tuts. "She was his late wife's nurse after she had a stroke three years ago. Took advantage of a grieving old man, if you ask me."

Nobody had, Ryan thought, but Esme clearly intended to share her opinion, regardless.

"The family was supposed to leave for their holiday home in Portugal yesterday morning?"

"They've gone the last two years around this time. Well, not Sebastian, but the rest of them. Isabel was born in Spain. Can't stand English winters. The cold gives her awful grief with her hip." Esme shifted in her chair. "She was in a terrible car crash just a couple of months after they married. Her pelvis got crushed on impact. The crash was her fault, according to the papers. She's had half a dozen surgeries, but is still in constant pain. Just goes to show, money can't buy everything."

She sounded as if she thought Isabel had received exactly what she deserved.

"Sebastian?" Fiona prompted.

"Mr Bolton's son. He'll be devastated about Reginald." Esme's expression darkened. "But those other two? He hated them with a passion. Called them gold-digging layabouts, whenever his father was out of earshot." She leaned forward. "There was a terrible row here about three weeks ago. I was upstairs changing the linens when I heard shouting from Mr Bolton's study. Sebastian was screaming at Isabel about the will, saying she'd manipulated his father into cutting him out of his rightful inheritance and he wasn't standing for it. Said he'd drag her through every court in England if he had to."

Ryan's attention sharpened. That was more than family drama.

"What did Isabel say?" Fiona kept her tone neutral.

"She told him his father was of sound mind and that Sebastian had only himself to blame for their estrangement, the way he was gutting the company Reginald built. Then she said something about the solicitor assuring her the new will was ironclad. After Sebastian left, Isabel was shaking. Lottie had to fetch her anxiety medication."

"And Mr Bolton's reaction to the argument?"

"He wasn't here. He'd gone to play golf with some of his retired cronies. When he came back and I mentioned Sebastian had stopped by, he just looked tired and changed the subject." She dabbed at her eyes with a tissue. "Poor Reginald. For the last few months, he seemed so worn down by it all."

Ryan filed that away. A contested will, a furious son who felt cheated, and now three convenient deaths.

"Sebastian works hard, though," Esme added, maybe realising she wasn't painting the son in a good light. She glanced around the room. "I suppose he'll inherit the lot now."

"Lottie was going with them to Portugal? Did she get time off work?" Fiona asked.

"In her thirties and that girl's only full-time job was sponging off poor Reginald. She started a stupid company involving edible decorations a couple of years ago. Convinced Mr Bolton to invest a bunch of his money, but it flopped within months and she hasn't lifted a finger since." Esme wrinkled her nose. "Isabel would never have forced her to get a job. They were very close, more like sisters than mother and daughter. Told each other everything. Isabel told me she was only eighteen when she had Lottie."

"Did Isabel or Lottie have many friends in the area?" Fiona asked. Ryan recognised her strategy. The housekeeper clearly had no love for Isabel and Lottie, so a friend's perspective might balance the picture.

"They were forever shopping and going for beauty treatments, but I don't think they socialised much around these parts. The late Mrs Bolton was very popular with the local ladies, and from what I've overheard, Isabel hasn't been too well received at the country club." She paused. "Lottie talked a lot about various girls on Instagram, but I'm not sure if they were friends or just influencers she followed. Isabel went to a book club every second Wednesday, but that's about it."

"Valley of the Dolls," Ryan said from behind them. Both Fiona and Esme turned. "It's at the top of the pile of books in the master bedroom. Isabel was reading it?"

Fiona's eyes widened as she made the connection. The same book that had been on Amanda's bedside table.

The housekeeper shrugged. "Wouldn't have a clue. Not her normal cup of tea. She mostly read trashy bodice rippers. Six months back, the book the club was reading was A Thousand Splendid Suns. It's one of my favourites, but Isabel wasn't interested in chatting about it." She sniffed. "At least not with me."

"Do you know the name of the book club or where it met?"

She shook her head. "They were oddly secretive about it. Lottie always drove her. Isabel wouldn't even let Ralph, that's Mr Bolton's chauffeur, take them. Lovely man, Ralph. Came over from Romania in the eighties as a teenager. He was chronically ill as a child, but he overcame—"

"The book club?" Ryan interrupted before they received the chauffeur's full medical history.

"Oh yes, I got the impression it was very exclusive. They'd be gone for a few hours each time, so I assumed it wasn't held anywhere nearby. Lottie wasn't a reader, but she'd sometimes accompany her mother." She looked thoughtful. "I'm not sure it'll help, but a month ago I overheard Lottie complaining about how some hot guy called Carl had died. She said he was the only thing that made it bearable for her to sit in on the sessions, then Isabel noticed I was in the room and shushed her."

"Could the guy have been Kyle?" Ryan asked.

Esme thought for a moment. "Possibly. I was on the other side of the room, and I tried not to listen to their conversations."

Ryan doubted that was true but held his tongue.

"Have Isabel or Lottie ever shown any interest in the occult? Wicca? Tarot cards?" Fiona asked.

Esme snorted. "That pair's only hobby was running down Reginald's bank balance."

The detectives thanked Esme and headed back towards the main house.

"I don't care what your protocols are. That's my father in there!"

Ryan exchanged a glance with Fiona. Sebastian Bolton. It was as if the housekeeper had conjured him out of thin air. Or more likely texted him.

They rounded the corner of the mansion to find a tall man with thinning temples and deep frown lines squared off against Chief Inspector Lampton at the police cordon. Sebastian's expensive suit was rumpled, his face flushed.

"That's Chief Inspector Lampton to you," Lampton said. "And this is a crime scene. No unauthorised personnel beyond this point."

For once, Ryan thought, Lampton's officiousness was actually useful.

"Unauthorised?" Sebastian's voice rose. "I'm the victim's son. I have every right—"

"You have the right to wait until the SIO clears you to enter. Which he hasn't."

Sebastian's gaze snapped to Ryan and Fiona as they approached. "You're in charge?"

"DI Hale," Ryan said. "DS Bennett. You're Sebastian Bolton?"

"Obviously." Sebastian checked his watch, a gesture so automatic Ryan suspected he barely registered doing it. "How long is this going to take? I have calls to make, arrangements—"

"We'll need to speak with you," Fiona said, her tone modulated to project both sympathy and authority. "Perhaps we could arrange a time tomorrow morning at the station? I know this must be a terrible shock—"

"Tomorrow?" Sebastian's jaw tightened. "My father is dead. I'm not waiting until tomorrow for answers."

"We're in the middle of processing the scene," Ryan said. "DS Bennet here will call you to arrange a time." *And it will give us a chance to dig into your appeal of the will,* he added silently.

Sebastian's lips compressed. He looked like he wanted to argue, but something in Ryan's expression must have convinced him otherwise. "Fine. But I'll have my lawyer present."

Of course he would.

"That's your right," Fiona said. "We just need some background information about your father and the family. Standard procedure for a case like this."

Sebastian's eyes narrowed. "Cases like this. You mean murder investigations where I'm a suspect. What about Norris? Your officers were in my office asking about him only this morning. That isn't a coincidence."

Fiona ignored his comment. "We'll be talking to everyone connected to the family."

"Then you should check the gate cameras. Only someone with the code can get in or out, unless they're buzzed in by someone at the main house," Sebastian said. "It's a digital system, cloud backup. I had it installed last year after some vagrants were spotted on the grounds. I give you permission to view the footage. See who came and went."

Like you could stop us, Ryan thought, but useful information. Was Sebastian's eagerness to direct them towards evidence innocence or calculation? Hard to tell.

"We'll do that," Ryan said.

Sebastian glanced down at his watch again, nodded curtly, and stalked back towards a sleek black Mercedes parked down the driveway.

"Charming fellow," Fiona murmured.

"Three weeks ago, Sebastian and Isabel were fighting about Reginald's will," Ryan said. "Now she's dead along with his father, her daughter, and he inherits everything."

"Convenient."

"Very." Ryan looked back at the house. "Though I can't see how Amanda fits into this. Let's ask forensics about the gate cameras."

CHAPTER THIRTY-THREE

Ryan updated DCI Lee with his notes from the Bolton residence and strode towards the incident room. His phone buzzed. A text from Fiona.

Interview Room 4. Your coffee's getting cold.

Ryan changed direction and headed for the interview rooms. Fiona stood leaning against the wall, one foot propped behind her, scrolling through her phone.

"How is Mr Norris?"

"According to Goody, getting anxious. He's been here for three hours." She held out a cup of coffee. No steam rose from its surface.

Ryan took the mug and pushed open the door to Interview Room Four with his shoulder, Fiona right behind him.

The room was standard station fare. Grey walls, a scarred metal table bolted to the floor, and three uncomfortable plastic chairs that had seen better days. Fluorescent light filled the room with a harsh glare, and a small camera blinked red in the corner.

"Mr Norris, thank you for coming in," Ryan said, settling into the chair across from Will.

"Of course, Detective." Will's fingers were laced together so tightly his knuckles had gone white. The man seemed to have aged twenty years in the last twenty-four hours. "But I don't understand why I'm not allowed to leave?"

"We have some urgent questions." Ryan leaned back, adopting a casual posture. He took a sip of his coffee and grimaced at the temperature. He set the mug aside. "Rebecca, Amanda's colleague, mentioned Amanda had a rough start in life?"

Will nodded, and his shoulders relaxed. "She grew up on an estate in Birmingham. Her mum was in and out of prison throughout her childhood, so she was always being passed around between relatives. She never met her father."

Ryan already knew this, but he wanted to find out how much Amanda had told her husband about her past.

"Any run-ins with the law?" Fiona asked, notepad open, though Ryan knew she rarely needed to check her notes.

"I think she got arrested for shoplifting when she was a teenager?" Will's eyes drifted to the wall behind them, as if searching his memory. "She didn't like to talk about her upbringing, and I didn't press. From the few times it came up, it sounded like she fell in with a dangerous crowd for a while. I got the impression she was proud of herself for shaking off her past and going to college to earn her Diploma in Office Administration."

According to Digit, Amanda had been fifteen when she was picked up by Derbyshire Police for possession of heroin.

"Do you know whether Amanda was ever involved in

anything drug-related?" Ryan asked. He watched Will's face for any telltale flicker of understanding.

Will scoffed. "She wouldn't take as much as a sleeping pill when she was up with insomnia after her sister died. We met in my last year at uni, and I still remember the time we were out clubbing and one of my friends offered her an 'E'. She looked down at his hand like he'd taken a shit in it, then tried to convince me to stop hanging out with him."

Will half-smiled at the memory. "I was more into drinking than taking anything illegal, so it wasn't a hardship to give up the pills." His eyes widened. "Christ, should I have said that? I don't use anything now!"

Ryan waved his words away. Reformed addicts often made the most zealous converts. Like his sister-in-law, who'd quit smoking and now had a coughing fit whenever anyone lit up within fifty feet of her.

Amanda had kept the unsavoury parts of her past a secret from her husband. Odd Bod was certain the scars between Amanda's toes had been track marks. Had Amanda relapsed with the stress of her husband's job loss and turned back to drugs to cope?

"Tell us more about Emily Astley," Fiona said, tilting her head in that way she did when she wanted someone to open up.

"Who?"

"Carter's babysitter, Emily."

"Astley," Will repeated. "I didn't know her last name."

Ryan noticed red creeping up Will's neck. He wondered if it was because of Emily's attractiveness or something more.

"Do you remember when Amanda last used her services?"

"Maybe six months ago? Now that Carter's getting older, he doesn't need a sitter in the afternoon."

"You've had no contact with Emily recently?"

Will blinked. "No. How could Emily have anything to do with what happened to Amanda?"

"Emily's missing. It's possible there's a connection."

"Missing. That's awful." Will's Adam's apple bobbed as he swallowed hard. "She seemed like a lovely girl, but I had little to do with her, sorry."

Ryan looked over at Fiona. Will appeared sincere. She nodded, her fingers drumming once on the table. Her 'let's move on to the good stuff' signal.

"Your sister drives a red Ford Fiesta," Ryan stated.

Will jerked back. "Yes, so?"

"Her car pinged the automatic number plate recognition system two miles from Bakewell. The timestamp is twenty minutes before your neighbour saw the same make and model car outside your house on Sunday night."

Will's chair scraped against the floor as he shifted. "That's ridiculous. I was fast asleep. Crazy Barkley is making it up." He stilled, thinking for a moment, then lifted out of his seat.

"Emily's car was an old Peugeot, similar to my sister's Ford Fiesta. Maybe Barkley saw her car?" A moment later he deflated, slumping forward on his elbows. "But hers was green."

Ryan moved in for the kill.

"Mr Norris, our colleagues also uncovered information that pointed to your being let go from your CFO job at Bolton Financial Investments for siphoning money from the company's spending accounts."

Will's chin dropped to his chest, his whole body seeming to fold in on itself. "I got hooked on online poker. Started innocent enough. I played on my lunch break, evenings on the couch. Then the hole got deeper."

He drew a shaky breath, his fingers tracing invisible patterns on the metal table. "Amanda thought it was harmless fun, and I couldn't disappoint her. So I skimmed money from work accounts to cover what I owed. Small amounts. A drop in the bucket to them. Figured no one would catch on."

A familiar story. Ryan had heard this tune before, different verses but always the same desperate chorus. He wouldn't call £80,000 loose change, but many gambling addicts soon learned small bets could add up.

Will's knuckles whitened as he gripped his hands together. "Then Sebastian took over and demanded an independent audit. It all came out. The company cut me a deal. I had to pay back what I took, resign quietly, and they wouldn't press charges. They didn't want the mess. But I'm getting better. I haven't gambled for the last three months."

Ryan wondered if that was true. In his experience, addicts always rounded down their last slip-up. Three months probably meant three weeks, maybe three days. Gambling wasn't an easy addiction to overcome.

"I couldn't get decent finance work without a reference," Will continued, his voice growing steadier as he talked, "but honestly, I was burned out. Part of me felt relieved that door slammed shut."

He straightened, rolling his shoulders back. "Retail management pays less, but when my shift ends, I'm done. No weekend calls from an unreasonable boss, no late nights at the office. Home every evening for dinner. Amanda makes these incredible meatballs from this authentic recipe she got when we went to Italy for our honeymoon. They have to be fresh..."

His bottom lip wobbled. "Oh God, for a second there I forgot... that she's..."

A wail escaped him.

Fiona handed over a clean tissue from her pocket with the practiced efficiency of a mother with young kids.

Will blew his nose.

"Reginald Bolton was a terrible boss?" Ryan asked.

Will looked up, confused, dabbing at his eyes with the tissue. "What? No, Reg was okay. It's Sebastian who's the ball-breaker. Got handed the company on a plate and treats the profits like Monopoly money."

"So you have no animosity towards Reginald or his family?"

"No, they were right to fire me." Will crumpled the tissue in his fist.

"Does the name Jack Stalker mean anything to you?" Ryan watched Will closely for any sign of recognition.

"No, it doesn't," Will replied, his brows furrowed.

"He's a loan shark with links to organised crime."

"Does he have something to do with Amanda?" The colour drained from his face, leaving him grey as the interview room walls. "You don't think this Jack fellow..."

"No, that's not Mr Stalker's style, but his name has come up in our investigation, and it raises questions about the half-a-million-pound life insurance policy you took out on Amanda a year ago. Your wife dying is turning into a convenient solution to your debt problem."

Will gaped like a fish, but no sound came out. His hands fluttered up to his throat. Eventually, he found his voice.

"The policies were Amanda's idea. After her sister's aneurysm. We both got them." His voice rose higher. "You can ask our insurer. She'll tell you. I don't care about money. I just want my Amanda back."

Will pleaded with the detectives as if they could resurrect the dead.

"Does it ever get easier?"

Will seemed to ask the room a rhetorical question, but Ryan answered him.

"It can take a while. For a long time after my wife was gone, I'd turn to tell her something funny that happened at work or I'd think about asking her opinion, then realise. The pain never goes away, but it becomes easier with time."

Will rubbed his face. "I still don't know why you're holding me here."

"What about Rebecca Boyle?" Ryan asked.

Will gave a weary sigh. "What about her?"

"According to my colleagues, she seems quite taken with you. Anything happening there?"

"No! Leave Rebecca out of this!"

Ryan and Fiona shared a look. Touched a nerve there.

"Mr Norris, Reginald, his wife and his stepdaughter were found dead in their home this morning. Their murders are connected to your wife's."

Ryan saw when the news and its implications sank in. The man's face went through a series of expressions. Confusion. Shock. Fear. Like someone flipping through TV channels.

"I want a lawyer."

Ryan stood, gathering his notes. "Mr Norris, we're holding you for further questioning. You'll be here overnight."

Will's head snapped up. "What? You can't just keep me here. I haven't done anything!"

"We can hold you for up to twenty-four hours without charge," Ryan said evenly. "Given the serious nature of these crimes and the questions that remain unanswered, we believe it's necessary."

"But Carter! My son needs me. He's just lost his mother!"

"Family Liaison is already making arrangements," Fiona said, her tone softer than Ryan's. "Carter will stay with your sister Jenna tonight. They'll explain what's happening in a way he can understand."

"Then what?" Will pleaded. "You charge me with a crime I didn't commit or you let me go?"

"That depends on what the next twenty-four hours reveal," Ryan replied.

CHAPTER THIRTY-FOUR

The conference room at Chesterfield Station smelled of coffee and printer ink. A laminated Derbyshire Constabulary crest was clipped to the front of the podium, two microphones sprouting above it like antennae. Ryan stood to Lee's right, half a pace back. Close enough to show support, far enough back to pretend he didn't exist. He kept his hands clasped behind his back to stop himself strangling the next person who waved their phone camera in his face.

He needed at minimum another cup of espresso before dealing with this bunch of twats first thing in the morning.

DCI Lee stepped up to the podium, the picture of calm authority. She surveyed the room, her gaze sweeping over the assembled reporters before delivering a concise, carefully worded statement. The statement confirmed the multiple homicides, the link between the scenes, and the establishment of a dedicated major incident team. She appealed for public help. Anyone who saw anything unusual in Bakewell or near the Bolton residence over the weekend should come forward. She gave them something to print, but nothing of substance.

And no mention of a suspect in custody.

"Questions?" Lee's voice was crisp.

A forest of hands shot up. She pointed to a familiar face in the front row.

Sophie.

Ryan bit back a groan.

She rose, phone held out with the microphone pointing towards the podium. Her sleek blonde bob caught the light, and for a disorienting second, Ryan saw Jaime standing there.

"DCI Lee, you've mentioned the victims were murdered in their own homes. Can you confirm whether the killer used a substance to incapacitate them before death? And if so, have you identified it?"

The question hit the room like a change in air pressure. A ripple of murmurs spread through the other journalists, pens scratching on notepads. It was specific. And close to the bone.

Ryan locked eyes with Sophie. She met his gaze without flinching, her expression a mask of professional enquiry.

Lee didn't blink. "We are exploring several forensic avenues, but I can't comment on the specifics of an ongoing investigation." She gestured to another reporter, but the seed had been planted. The next few questions were variations on the theme. Sedatives, drugs—all of which Lee stonewalled with practiced ease.

Then a new voice cut through the noise, sharp and grating, with a London accent that felt out of place this early in the case.

"Martin Hodge, Metro Mirror."

Ryan looked up. The man was in his late fifties, with a florid face and a cheap suit that strained at the buttons. Ryan recognised him. A bottom-feeder who haunted press conferences like a vulture circling a carcass.

"Given DI Hale's controversial history—specifically the

unsolved disappearance of his wife and the questions surrounding his own involvement—is he the right choice to lead such a sensitive investigation?"

The room fell silent.

Warmth crept up Ryan's neck, but he kept his focus fixed on a point on the back row. He counted the phones crowding the air.

Lee stepped forward, moving almost imperceptibly to her right as if to shield Ryan from the question.

"DI Hale is a highly decorated officer with an exemplary record of solved cases. He was never charged in connection with his wife's disappearance. He has my full confidence and that of the Derbyshire Constabulary."

Hodge smirked. "A DI with friends in all the right evidence lockers. Were you protecting one of your own twelve years ago, or was it just incompetence that left a woman missing and her husband free to run major investigations? Including a recent botched operation that resulted in him being kidnapped?"

Lee leaned forward, her knuckles white on the podium. "Let me be absolutely clear, Mr Hodge. No one is above the law. Not a member of Parliament, and not a police officer. What you are implying is not only baseless; it borders on slander. This investigation will be conducted with the utmost integrity. If you have a relevant question about the four murders we are here to discuss, I suggest you ask it. Otherwise, this press conference is over."

She held his gaze for a long, silent moment before turning away. "Thank you, everyone."

Lee swept out of the conference room, leaving Ryan to follow in her wake as chaos erupted behind them.

He made it three steps into the back room before Lampton blocked his path.

"Quite a performance Lee had to put on in there for you."

Lampton's voice was loud enough to carry; his face flushed. A few reporters lingering in the doorway craned their necks to watch.

Ryan tried to sidestep him. "Not now."

"When, then? When another investigation goes sideways because you're too busy playing the tragic widower to do actual police work?" Lampton moved with him, maintaining the blockade. "My brother would have solved it in a day, but he's dead, and you're not. There's no justice in that, is there, Hale?"

Lampton's brother had been part of CID before Ryan's time. Shot during a raid on a meth lab in Sheffield, he'd died before the ambulance arrived. But this wasn't about facts.

Ryan's hands clenched at his sides, every muscle coiled tight. He could feel eyes on them. Journalists, uniforms, someone from the media office hovering nearby.

"Move," Ryan said quietly.

Lampton held his ground for another beat, his jaw working, before stepping aside with exaggerated courtesy. "Don't worry. I'll be watching you. Someone has to."

Ryan pushed past him into the main hallway, forcing his breathing to steady. The last stragglers from the press conference were filing out, and that's when he spotted her.

Sophie knelt by the side wall, packing her bag.

"How did you know the victims had been incapacitated?" Ryan kept his voice low. "It hasn't been released."

Sophie finished zipping her bag, the sound loud in the empty corridor. "Maybe it was a lucky guess." She looked up. "A guess you've now confirmed, by the way."

She stood and went to step past him, but he blocked her path.

"Is one of my team feeding you information?" It came out as a flat statement, the anger a cold, hard knot in his stomach.

Betrayal from his own team. Again.

She tucked a strand of blonde hair behind her ear, a gesture so like Jaime's it made his breath catch. "Interesting you'd jump to that conclusion. You've always had trust issues."

"Don't play games, Sophie. Who is it?"

"I'm a reporter, Ryan. I protect my sources. It's the first rule." She slung her bag over her shoulder. "A London detective, of all people, should understand the need for a good-faith relationship with an informant."

"This isn't about a source. This is about my investigation. You could compromise it."

"Or I could help you solve it. A little public pressure never hurts. Keeps everyone honest." Her eyes held his, a challenge in them. "I'm doing my job. You should focus on doing yours."

"Be careful, Soph."

Her expression hardened. "It's Sophie and I'll go wherever the story takes me, DI Hale. If you're in my way, then move."

———

Ryan stalked back into the incident room, his stomach tight. His brain understood it was Sophie he'd been arguing with, but his heart felt like it was Jaime. The team looked up from their workstations as he entered.

"Right," he said, draping his coat over the back of a chair. "Where are we?"

"Sebastian Bolton's lawyers called," Fiona told him. "He's unable to help us with our enquiries until after midday."

"Just keep Bolton away from Sheri or we might have a lawsuit on our hands," Cal joked.

Sheri spun her chair around and gave Cal a dirty look. "He put the capital 'M' in misogynist, but I can handle it." She turned to Ryan. "I've been going through the hotel's security footage, Sir. Mr Potts lied in his statement. He drove out of the hotel parking lot just before midnight on Saturday."

"Did he go back to the hotel?"

"He did." She pulled up the footage on her screen. "The van leaves at 11:44 pm and doesn't return until 4:34 am."

On the monitor, grainy black-and-white footage showed a white transit van with its left headlight smashed, rolling out of the car park. The timestamp glowed in the corner.

"That's enough time to get to Amanda's and back," Fiona said from her desk.

Ryan moved closer to the screen. "Has anyone tried calling him?"

"Three times," Sheri replied. "Straight to voicemail."

"Send uniform to Mystic Wellness Lodge. I want him brought in for questioning."

Digit cleared his throat from his corner fortress of monitors. "There's something else. I've been examining Lawrence's company filings. His profit margins don't line up with his outgoings, and his electrical bill expenses are astronomical for the building."

"Think Lawrence is growing more *herbs* than sage?" Cal suggested.

"It would line up with a weed operation," Ryan said. He thought of the interview with Lawrence in his office, the desperate theatricality of it all. A man performing spirituality while dealing on the side? "Keep digging," Ryan said.

Digit nodded.

"The Bolton gate camera footage came through," Cal said, pulling up a second screen. "Small car passes through at 11:05 pm Saturday night. The same car leaves at 12:40 am on Sunday morning."

Ryan moved to stand behind Cal's chair. Like the hotel CCTV, the footage was poor quality, the car a dark blur against the darker driveway. But there, visible as it passed under the gate light, was a distinctive badge.

"Peugeot," Cal said. "Can't make out the colour or registration in this light, but definitely a Peugeot."

"Emily drives a green Peugeot," Fiona pointed out.

Ryan nodded. "The wires on Mr Barkley's desk were labelled by colour."

Digit caught on. "Deuteranomaly could explain it. It affects one in twelve males, and it can worsen with age."

Fiona looked askance at him. "Dumb it down for the room, please."

"Colour blindness," Ryan replied. "My father had a mild form. If Mr Barkley is colour blind then..."

"He might confuse his greens and reds," Fiona finished.

Digit swung his screen around. "A 1999 Ford Fiesta and a 1998 Peugeot 106 have similar shapes. It would be easy to mix up the two."

"Sheri, call Mr Barkley later and check," Ryan said.

"No problem." Sheri shrank down in her chair. "Sir, we also have a problem with our case against William Norris."

"Go on."

"Uniform retrieved some door cam footage from the neighbour across from Will Norris's sister's residence. Will's sister was the person driving her Ford Fiesta. They questioned her, and she said she was picking up her teenage son from a Halloween party in Bakewell. The friend's father confirmed it. Timings match."

One potential lead evaporating. Ryan rubbed his neck. Only an hour into the day and he could already feel tension knotted there.

"There's more," Fiona said carefully. "Will Norris's lawyer also contacted us this morning. Will wants to amend his statement."

Ryan waited.

"He wasn't sleeping Saturday night when the Boltons were killed. He was on a video call with Rebecca Boyle from the Job Centre. From eleven until two in the morning."

"Rebecca?" Sheri's voice rose.

Fiona nodded. "Will confessed they'd kissed at the Christmas party last year. Been having what he called an 'emotional affair' since then. Mostly phone calls and texts, complaining about Amanda. He said he didn't want to tell us because of how it looked, but with a murder charge hanging over his head..." She trailed off.

"That's convenient," Cal said. "His wife's murdered and suddenly he's got a three-hour alibi with the woman who's obsessed with him."

"His phone records back it up," Digit said. "Three hours and fourteen minutes on Saturday night. Video call to Rebecca's mobile."

"Could be faked," Cal argued. "Set up a call, prop up the phone, go out and commit murder. Rebecca might go along with it so they can be together."

Ryan considered it. "It's possible. But it's looking less likely Will's our man."

He moved to the whiteboards, studying the victim photographs pinned there. Amanda Norris. Reginald Bolton. Isabel Bolton. Lottie Garrett. Four sets of missing eyes. Coins in the sockets. A tarot card.

"What if the fifth empty stake was meant for William Norris?" he said. "The only reason he wasn't in the house Sunday night was because of his fight with Amanda. What if the killer expected him to be there?"

"Do you think he's in danger?" Fiona asked.

"Hard to say. We'll put a watch on him if he's released."

Ryan sat at the desk he'd claimed next to Fiona's. Emily

Astley. Missing since Saturday. Connected to Amanda through babysitting Carter. Connected to Kyle Mathers through their past relationship. Connected to Lawrence through Wicca. And now, potentially at the Bolton residence the night of the murders.

"The book club," he said aloud. "It's the only thing linking all our victims. Emily had it on her calendar. We know Amanda attended a book club. Isabel Bolton attended one as well, according to the housekeeper. We need to know more about it."

He pictured the overlapping circles. Three separate lives, one shaded centre. Was it where the answers lay?

"How do we do that?" Sheri asked.

Ryan grabbed his coat. "Todd Mathers. Emily's ex-boyfriend's brother. Maybe his brother told him about the book club, or he might have some insight into Emily."

Cal jumped up, already reaching for his blazer. "I'll come with you, yeah?"

Ryan opened his mouth to disagree but caught the slight nod from Fiona. He sighed and nodded.

"Where we headed?" Cal asked.

"Digit?"

Digit tapped a few keys. "Derby city centre. DE1 1SA. Pin pushed to DC Pine. My suggested route avoids roadworks on Siddals Road. ETA 53 minutes."

Precision. Digit's comfort zone. Ryan made a mental note to get him out of the office and into the field on future cases.

"Hope you got that, Cal. We'll swing by the morgue after," Ryan added. "Odd Bod should have the preliminary autopsy findings on the Boltons by now."

Cal's enthusiasm dimmed. "Right. Yeah. The morgue."

Ryan caught the shift in his tone.

"Problem, Detective Constable?"

"Nah, boss. No problem at all."

Ryan glanced at Fiona. "I should be back in time for Mr Bolton's interview."

"And if Uniform can't locate Lawrence at the lodge?"

"Put out a BOLO on the van. He couldn't have gone far."

Fiona nodded, reaching for her phone.

"What if Todd doesn't know anything about the book club?" Cal asked as they hurried down the stairwell.

"Then we keep looking until we find someone who does," Ryan replied.

They exited into the station car park, the grey Derbyshire sky pressing down overhead.

Until they spoke to Sebastian Bolton, the book club was the only thread they had to pull.

CHAPTER THIRTY-FIVE

RYAN REACHED FOR THE ENTRANCE DOOR OF TODD Mathers's apartment building when a scrawny man with gold teeth and a buzz cut shoved past him. His companion, same build, same sneer, but with greasy hair to his shoulders and ink crawling up both arms, spat "pigs" as he swaggered by.

Ryan sighed. The cockroaches of Derby had spread from the shadows into the city centre, bringing their trade to doorsteps that once saw nothing worse than parking disputes. He could follow them, get them to turn out their pockets. But a small-time bust wouldn't bring him closer to his killer.

"Which apartment?" Ryan asked Cal.

Cal checked his phone. "Sixteen. Second floor."

When Ryan knocked, Todd Mathers opened the door wearing the same sweat-stained gaming tournament T-shirt from the search party two days ago. His straggly hair looked even greasier as he blinked through his round Harry Potter glasses, noise-cancelling headphones around his neck.

"Oh. You got here fast. DS Bennett just called me."

"Mr Mathers, thank you for agreeing to speak with us," Ryan said.

Todd tugged at his T-shirt. "Sure. Come in, I guess." He left the door open and headed for the couch, scooping clothes off the arms and dumping them on the kitchen table. An empty pizza box followed, then beer bottles from the coffee table. "Sorry, I wasn't expecting company. Got an advance copy of Hellgate Rebellion in the post and lost track of time."

Ryan's gaze tracked to the pro streamer setup dominating one wall. Blue and green LCD lights competed with the abstract screensaver. Large, framed posters of video game releases lined the walls.

"I'm a gaming reviewer," Todd said, following Ryan's look. "Hellgate Rebellion: Urban Uprising. It's going to blow Grand Theft Auto off the charts."

Ryan nodded, though he knew as much about gaming as embroidery.

Cal wandered over to examine a poster depicting a space battle. "Soldiers of the Void, yeah? The nebula trench run's a right bitch."

Todd's forehead wrinkled. "Huh?"

"Zero-gravity combat in the trench. Mate of mine complained about it for weeks."

Todd shrugged. "Didn't have any trouble with it. Barely registered."

Cal pulled out his phone. "Mind if I...? My followers would lose it over this rig."

"Whatever." Todd perched on a high-backed chair across the coffee table, scratching his head.

Ryan brushed crumbs off the couch and sat. Cal remained standing, snapping off photos. His attention drifted between the gaming setup and his phone.

"Did you have any luck tracking down Robbie?"

Todd slapped his head. "Shit, I forgot to look. I'll see what I can find tonight."

"I'm sorry for the loss of your brother," Ryan said.

"Oh, um... thanks, I guess." He scratched his head again.

"You don't live at the farmhouse? DS Bennett said it's a beautiful spot."

"Wi-Fi's crap." Todd gestured vaguely towards his setup. "Can't stream from the middle of nowhere, can I?"

"Your brother's name keeps appearing in our investigation. We're hoping you can help us understand why."

"I'm not sure I'll be much help. Kyle and I weren't close."

Ryan caught the defensive edge. "I'm surprised you organised a search party for his missing girlfriend then."

"Ex-girlfriend. It's ah... complicated." Todd straightened. "Kyle was a complete arsehole to me growing up. He beat me up, bullied me constantly. Moving out of home was the happiest day of my life. But then when he got arrested and lost his job, he called me. We started hanging out. It wasn't all bad after that, and he was still family, you know?"

Ryan found himself nodding. He thought of his own mother, who'd had a love-hate relationship with her sons until cancer had ended the debate. Family was the knot you could never quite untangle, even when you wanted to.

"Were you surprised he killed himself?"

"Yeah. He had everything going for him before the arrest. Good looks, regular Tinder hookups, decent money." Todd scratched his head. "Though there were signs, I guess. As teenagers, he'd bounce between extremes. Sky-high one day, crashing the next."

"Bipolar?"

"He was always being dramatic, and he loved being centre stage, so Mum dismissed it as attention-seeking. She thought he was being difficult, but looking back..."

Cal moved to the rack of hand weights behind the couch, picking one up and testing its heft. Todd's eyes followed the movement.

"You lifting heavy? Cal asked.

"Trying." Todd grimaced, looking down at his paunch. "Kyle gave me those. Spent hours teaching me proper form. Said he'd help me get laid." A nervous laugh escaped. "I've put on twenty pounds of muscle since I started. The nicest thing he ever did for me. Strange, though."

"Strange how?" Ryan asked.

"Kyle lived for the gym. Had since high school. Then he gives me his weights and quits cold turkey. Within a couple of months, you could notice the change. He looked softer, less defined."

Cal set the weight down with a clang that made Todd flinch. "Bro was dealing, yeah? Bit of gym culture goes with that territory."

Todd's face flushed. "I don't think so."

"Do you use anything yourself?"

Todd laughed nervously. "Does Red Bull count?"

Ryan noticed something on the bookshelf and picked up. A framed photo from Brighton Pier. A younger, chubbier Todd with long hair flopping across his eyes stood next to a frail woman. On her other side stood a shirtless man with a banker's haircut and defined abs. Despite their different builds, Ryan could see the family resemblance between the two men.

Todd hurried over. "That's Kyle and me with Mum. Five years ago, just after she first got sick. Kyle paid for the trip. He wanted Majorca, but I don't fly. He got pretty pissed about that."

Ryan studied Kyle's arrogant eyes and overconfident smile as Cal glanced over his shoulder at the photo. "He looks like a bit of a prick."

Takes one to know one, Ryan thought.

Todd's eyes tightened. Still protective of the brother who'd abused him.

Ryan returned the photo to the shelf. "Did he game as well?"

"Not really. He played better than he deserved to, given how little he played. If he'd applied himself, he probably would have been beating me. He was that kind of guy." Todd's gaze flicked to Cal, who was now examining his own reflection in one of the dark monitors, adjusting his hair. "Lucky for me, he was more into the gym and girls than video games."

Cal turned back, catching Todd's look. "What?"

"Nothing."

Ryan sat back on the sofa. "Tell us about Emily."

"I met her only twice, but she seemed like a nice girl. Kyle dated her for a bit, but they broke up about four months ago. Not long after that, he lost his job. I got the vibe that he was still hung up on her. That she could have played a part in his..." He trailed off.

"Kyle had a girlfriend when he died? A dental assistant?"

"Stacey. I think she was new. I'd never met her until the funeral."

"You were in Edinburgh when she found him?"

"Yeah. Digital Realms Gaming Convention. Made the final playoffs of the Masters of Combat Tournament. I was having the best night at the same time Kyle would have been..." He paused. "You know... It's super rare for a reviewer like me to beat so many pros. A couple of them were out after dodgy scrambled eggs at the buffet, but my best result before that was fifteenth in the Legends Cup. Would've got to the grand final if NightfallKing hadn't leaked my build strategy."

Todd seemed to realise how he sounded. "If I'd known Kyle was in a dark place, I wouldn't have competed."

Cal snorted. "Convenient alibi though, innit?"

Todd's lips pressed together. "What's that supposed to mean?"

"Nothing, mate. Just making conversation."

Ryan shot Cal a look. "Did Kyle ever mention being in a book club?"

Todd looked confused. "Nah. He was more of a movie guy."

"Any interest in the occult or Wicca?"

Todd thought for a moment. "He played The Witcher with me once. Does that count?"

Ryan ignored the question. "Anything else strange about your brother's behaviour before he died?"

Todd shrugged. "Aside from being nice to me and getting fatter, nothing jumps to mind."

"Do you still have my card?" Ryan asked.

Todd nodded.

"Call us if you think of anything after we've gone." Ryan stood.

"Will do."

Todd shut the door behind them.

Cal started down the stairs. "Reckon Todd has a thing for Emily, yeah? All that effort organising the search party for his brother's ex. Bit keen, innit? And he got proper defensive when I mentioned the timing. Bloke's living alone in that flat, obsessing over games. Emily probably gave him the time of day once, and he's been nursing it ever since."

Ryan pushed through the exit. Cal saw the world through the lens of attraction and ego. "Or he's trying to be the person his brother never was. Maybe it's not about Emily; maybe it's about proving he's a better man than Kyle."

Cal waited until they were back at the car before speaking. "I still think that bloke's carrying some serious baggage."

"Bullied throughout his entire childhood. Self-loathing doesn't disappear overnight."

"Still think it's convenient he was in Edinburgh when his brother topped himself."

"I looked through the records. Abbas cleared him. Tournament records confirm he was playing from his room at the approximate time of death."

Cal scrolled through the photos he'd taken of Todd's setup. "Yeah, but that doesn't mean he couldn't have—"

"Drop it." Ryan pulled out into traffic. "None of this helps our case. Here's hoping Odd Bod has something for us. Here, you're driving."

Cal pocketed his phone and caught the keys. "Right. Whatever you say, boss."

CHAPTER THIRTY-SIX

Ryan's phone rang mid-text to Fiona; the number was unfamiliar.

Cal glanced over from the driver's seat.

Ryan answered. "Detective Inspector Hale."

"Hello! Is this Winston's fur-daddy?" A loud female voice with a strong American accent blared through the speaker.

Ryan paused. "Sorry?"

"They're such furry bundles of joy, aren't they?"

"I'm not sure I follow." Had he somehow signed up for a pet product survey?

"Corgis. We had a pair when I was growing up. My mum always said I had OCD." She giggled. "Obsessive Corgi Disorder."

"I have a corgi called Winston," Ryan said. "Who is this?" Even as he spoke, dread crept in. Winston was supposed to be snoring on the couch. His collar tag had Ryan's mobile number on it.

The woman didn't seem offended by his tone. "Sorry, Detective. I'm sure you can't be too careful in your line of work.

"

My name is Savannah Calhoun. Fifty-five Clarence Road, Chesterfield. Would you like my National Insurance Number?"

"That won't be necessary," Ryan said quickly. Clarence Road was four blocks from his flat. "Did Winston escape?"

"He was trotting down my street without a care in the world. Sniffing walls, peeing on every gatepost. Reminded me so much of my dear departed Dash that I almost felt bad interrupting him. Then I thought about the poor fellow reaching Saltergate and what might happen. So now he's in the back of my SUV enjoying half my ham sandwich."

Ryan checked his watch. Speaking to Odd Bod and driving back would take at least ninety minutes. "Thanks for picking him up. I'm working on a case outside of Chesterfield, so it might be a couple of hours before I can collect him. Is that all right?"

"I'm heading to my Pilates class, but the girls would love to meet him. Who wouldn't? I could drop him at Chesterfield Station if you're based there. It's on my way home."

He considered asking her to leave Winston in the garden, but given the dog had escaped twice in two days, that seemed pointless.

"That would be great. If you could ask for DC Asare at the front desk, he'll take him off your hands." Ryan wasn't certain he'd be back in time, but Digit should be in the incident room. Hopefully, he didn't share Cal's aversion to dogs.

"It's no trouble at all. Winston's a furry ball of delight, aren't you, fluffy buns? And, Officer, thank you for your service."

Ryan blinked. He couldn't recall a single UK citizen ever thanking him for his service, let alone with such sincerity.

"Not a problem. Thanks again for picking him up." He hung up.

"Your dog escaped?" Cal asked.

"I should rename him Houdini. Apparently he's off to Pilates."

"Downward dog and all that."

"That's yoga."

"Come on, mate. Still a good one."

Ryan abandoned his text and called Digit instead.

"DC Asare speaking."

"Digit, it's DI Hale. How do you feel about dogs?"

"The companionship of a canine can have many health benefits. There are numerous studies showing pet ownership can lower blood pressure and diminish sympathetic responses to stress."

Not my dog, Ryan thought. "You're not allergic or anything?"

"No, but my apartment doesn't allow pets."

"I'm not asking you to adopt one. My dog escaped, and an American woman called Savannah is dropping him at the station in about an hour. I need you to collect him from the front desk and keep him in the incident room until we're back from the morgue."

"Will he need bedding?"

"Just point him at a corner and tell him to lie down."

"Understood, Sir. I've uncovered some information about Sebastian Bolton that could be pertinent to the case. Is now a good time?"

"One second." Ryan pressed the speaker button so Cal could hear. "Right, go ahead."

"Three months ago, Sebastian Bolton challenged an amendment to his father's will, citing coercion by his step-mother and claiming Reginald Bolton had undiagnosed early dementia. He lost. The judge ruled there was insufficient evidence to prove Reginald's mental incompetence."

"Did you find out what amendments he was contesting?"

"Is the square root of negative one an imaginary number?"

Ryan frowned. "Does that mean yes?"

"Correct. In July, Reginald amended his will to split his estate three ways between his son, Sebastian Bolton, his second wife, Isabel Bolton, and his stepdaughter, Charlotte Garrett. Prior to that, everything was left to Sebastian."

"How much money are we talking about?"

"The estate is estimated to be worth thirty-two million pounds. Mr Bolton's lawyers are still in the appeals process."

"Now all three of them are dead, Sebastian inherits everything."

Cal whistled. "That's a lot of motive."

"Court records also indicated the case was time-sensitive, suggesting that besides the dementia, Reginald could have been terminally ill. I can apply for access to his medical records."

"Let's see what Odd Bod has uncovered first."

"I also found an old photograph on Emily's Facebook of her, Sebastian, and another man called Tom Montgomery at a party in London 634 days ago."

Ryan sat straighter. "Go on."

"They all appear intoxicated. The party was celebrating Mr Montgomery's birthday. He posted the photo in an album titled 'Birthday Shenanigans' and tagged them both. They appear in other images from the party, but that's the only one of them together."

"Excellent work, Digit. Send the photo to my phone and make sure Fiona has a copy for our interview with Bolton."

"Immediately, Sir."

CHAPTER THIRTY-SEVEN

R YAN AND C AL WALKED THROUGH THE ENTRANCE OF THE
Royal Derby Hospital. They descended in the lift; the temperature dropping with each floor until they reached the lower level with its sterile white walls and the faint chemical tang of formaldehyde mixed with industrial cleaner.

Cal shifted his weight from foot to foot as they walked down the corridor. His eyes darted towards each closed door they passed, as if expecting a corpse to lurch out at any moment. Ryan had seen that look before on junior detectives. In real life, the mortuary had a way of getting under your skin, no matter how many crime shows you'd watched.

Marley greeted them at the door before Ryan could press the intercom.

"Is Odd Bod ready for us?" he asked.

Marley nodded. "He's in his office."

"Come in," Odd Bod called out at Ryan's knock. He looked up from his laptop and pulled off a pair of black-rimmed glasses. "A new necessity," he said, waving the glasses in their direction. "We're all getting older."

He glanced down at the crime scene photos spread across his desk. "I suppose we should count ourselves lucky."

The glasses were new, but the office remained the same as it had been twelve years ago.

Still an absolute mess.

Forensic specimens sat on display. A preserved hand here, a gnawed leg bone there. Like Marley's office, there were plenty of textbooks, but unlike Marley's tidy space, the books were scattered in piles amongst pieces of paper Ryan hoped weren't important to any current cases.

Cal had gone pale. He stood near the door, hands shoved in his pockets, trying but failing not to look at the preserved hand.

The only thing new was a series of large prints that lined the wall behind Odd Bod's head. Each print showed a Leonardo da Vinci anatomy drawing incorporated into a bright pop art design. Colourful, quirky and oddly disturbing. In many ways, the prints were a perfect reflection of the man himself.

"Did William Norris confess?" Odd Bod asked.

"Unfortunately not," Ryan replied. "He'll likely be released today."

Odd Bod nodded. "Please take a seat, detectives."

Cal remained standing. Ryan caught his eye and jerked his head towards the empty chair. The younger detective sat, though he perched on the edge as if ready to bolt.

Odd Bod pulled the printed report closer, squinted, then gave up and put his glasses back on. "Not that there was any doubt, but I can confirm the eyeballs are a match for our three additional victims. The complete lack of rigor mortis and the discolouration of the abdomen would suggest they were killed at least fifty hours before they were discovered."

Ryan sat up straighter. "So before Mrs Norris?"

"Yes, I'd estimate they were killed sometime between 8:00

pm Saturday night and 8:00 am Sunday morning. I'll have a more exact timeline with more testing."

"Emily's car enters and exits the property within that window."

"All three victims were found in bed, strangled. None had defensive wounds or any signs of sexual assault. All had had their eyes gouged out with a blunt instrument."

"So the same as Amanda," Ryan said.

"Right down to the injection marks on the necks." Odd Bod pushed three photos across the desk.

Ryan studied the photos of the three small pinpricks, each barely discernible.

"Can we put in a rush request with Toxicology?" Ryan asked. "Knowing how the killer incapacitates his victims could be a valuable clue."

Odd Bod shrugged. "I can ask, but no promises." He adjusted his glasses and peered at the report. "Reginald Bolton was a heavy smoker according to the state of his lungs. He was also suffering from advanced stage four adenocarcinoma. It had spread extensively through his bones and his liver."

Odd Bod laid a photograph down. The image showed a pair of lungs that bore little resemblance to the healthy pink organs from medical textbooks. Instead, they were a mottled patchwork of greys and blacks, the tissue heavily carbonised from years of tar deposits.

Cal glanced at the photo, then jerked back. "Christ, I only just had breakfast."

Ryan ignored him. "How long would he have had?"

"Six months at most. Forensics found chemotherapy tablets used to treat metastatic non-small cell lung cancer in the bathroom cabinet of the master ensuite, along with some ibuprofen and paracetamol. He knew about the diagnosis. Whether he'd told anyone, I'm not sure, but it would have been hard to hide."

"What about Lottie?"

Odd Bod deflated. Ryan knew he struggled when the victims were young. "Lottie was overweight for her height and age but otherwise healthy. The techs found a pill bottle of sleeping tablets prescribed to her on her bedside table. I found trace amounts of one in her stomach. She would have been groggy, disoriented and confused when she was attacked."

He paused, shuffling through his notes. "There was something, likely not pertinent to the investigation. Lottie had undergone extensive plastic surgery. Her nose, her chin, her cheekbones. Breast augmentation. Liposuction scarring. Botox injections. The list goes on."

"Sounds expensive." Ryan said.

Odd Bod's usual enthusiasm dimmed. "I've seen a lot of bodies in my time, detectives, but this was troubling. Many procedures, all of them unnecessary from a medical standpoint. Some appeared to have been done recently; others, maybe a year or two ago." He sighed. "I don't think she liked herself very much."

The room went quiet. Cal's earlier discomfort shifted into something else. A mirror held up to the superficial world he embraced?

"Isabel was underweight for her size." Odd Bod's voice was gentler now. "There were signs pointing to an eating disorder in the past, but overall she was a healthy fifty-two-year-old. She had some old injuries consistent with high-impact trauma, including surgery scars on her right knee."

"Mrs Banks, the housekeeper, said she seriously damaged her hip in a car accident four years ago and had tried multiple surgeries since to reduce the pain."

"A car accident would be consistent with the injuries I found." He pulled another photo from the stack. "The lividity patterns suggest that Isabel had been moved. Maybe an hour after her death.”

“Any significance?”

He shrugged. “You’re the detectives.”

“The tarot card was found next to Isabel,” Ryan said. “She could have been the primary target. The one who opened the door to Emily or someone pretending to be Emily.”

Odd Bod continued. “I noticed Reginald had a patch of hair cut off on the side of his head. Both Lottie and Isabel were also missing a lock of hair from the underside of their heads that looked like it had been cut off with a pair of blunt scissors or a sharp knife. That prompted me to check Amanda. A lock of hair had also been taken. It was less obvious as her haircut contained more choppy layers and had recently been cut, so I missed it during the autopsy.”

“So as well as the eyes, the killer took a second trophy from each of the victims,” Ryan said. “Something to hold on to.”

“Jeffrey Dahmer, Ted Bundy, and Ed Gein all sometimes took hair as trophies,” Odd Bod added with scholarly enthusiasm.

“Yeah, if we can prove they’ve got it stashed somewhere, that’ll do nicely in court,” Cal said.

Ryan thanked Odd Bod and stood. “We’ve got to catch them first.”

CHAPTER THIRTY-EIGHT

RYAN STOOD WAITING BY THE COFFEE MACHINE, WATCHING black coffee trickle into his cup when Fiona walked into the station cafeteria. Cal slumped at a nearby table, scrolling through his phone while shovelling crisps into his mouth.

"Ready?" Fiona asked.

"One minute." Ryan pulled out his wallet and dropped a tenner on the table in front of Cal. "You need to pay for your lunch."

Cal looked up, confused. "What? I did already."

"The cashier said your card declined."

Cal's face flushed. "I've got more than a tenner in my account. Must be a bank error."

Fiona's eyebrows rose. "Bank error? That's what we're calling a pair of Yeezy trainers now?"

"They keep flagging my card for suspicious activity," Cal protested.

"Right," Fiona said, smiling. "Suspicious activity. Like spending two hundred quid on the world's ugliest shoes."

"They were limited edition. Investment pieces."

"Perhaps invest in a packed lunch next time," Ryan said.

They left Cal to pay for his late lunch and headed towards the interview rooms.

"Bolton brought Margaret Ashworth," Fiona said as they approached Interview Room Two.

Ryan groaned. "Of course he has." He knew the name. Margaret Ashworth was a London-based criminal defence lawyer who didn't come cheap. She also didn't appear unless there was something worth hiding. "Interesting choice."

"Very."

Ryan's shoulder twinged as he pushed through the door. The pain always seemed worse when he was about to deal with something unpleasant.

Unlike Interview Room Four, the walls of Room Two had been painted in the last decade, the lighter grey less oppressive. The fluorescent lights were also softer. The table was still bolted to the floor but showed fewer scars, and the chairs had thin vinyl cushions that did little for comfort but at least suggested someone had tried.

Sebastian Bolton sat ramrod straight in his chair, expensive suit still crisp despite the journey from Sheffield. His lawyer, the infamous Margaret Ashworth, sat beside him, a sleek leather portfolio open in front of her. Her vintage tortoiseshell frames caught the light as she nodded to the detectives.

Ryan and Fiona took their seats opposite. Ryan started the recording, and then Fiona went through the formalities. While Sebastian checked his watch. Twice.

"We understand there wasn't much love lost between you and your father's second wife, Isabel?" Ryan began.

"Who told you that? It was that nosy old bat who scrubs the toilets, wasn't it?"

Given Esme had been on Sebastian's side, Ryan wasn't sure she'd appreciate being called a nosy old bat by the man she'd defended. Then again, gratitude probably wasn't in Sebastian's vocabulary.

"But it's true?" Fiona asked, her voice gentle.

Sebastian sighed. "It wasn't a secret that I didn't get on with that scheming gold-digger and her leech of a daughter." He paused and crossed his arms, glaring at the two detectives as though they'd contradicted him.

Margaret cleared her throat in warning. Sebastian ignored it.

He stabbed the table with his finger. "I didn't kill them, but that doesn't mean I'm not happy the two vultures are dead. My mother's corpse wasn't even cold when Isabel latched her claws into my father and started sucking him and the estate dry."

Margaret's lips pressed together.

"You thought your stepmother was spending too much of your father's money?" Ryan asked.

"She was like a locust, stripping everything bare." He wrinkled his nose.

Fiona leaned forward, keeping her tone curious rather than accusatory. "Given how you felt about Isabel, you must have been concerned about your father's well-being?"

"Concerned?" Sebastian's laugh was bitter. "I was watching him waste away whilst she redecorated. Again."

"You argued he was mentally incompetent," Ryan said.

"Because she was manipulating him, and he wasn't thinking straight."

Margaret Ashworth touched his arm. "Sebastian."

"Your father had terminal cancer," Fiona said, her voice still gentle. "He had six months left at most."

"I'm aware." Sebastian's jaw tightened. "He told me when he was diagnosed three months ago."

Ryan filed that away. Three months was around the time

Sebastian had filed to have his father declared incompetent. "How did you feel about that?"

"How do you think I felt? He was dying and giving away my inheritance to a parasitic freeloader." His voice cracked on the word 'dying.' He cleared his throat roughly, his hand coming up to cover his mouth for a moment. "Six months. That's all he had left, and he spent it..." He stopped, jaw working. "It doesn't matter now."

Ryan changed tack. "Do you recognise this woman? Her name is Emily." He leaned across the interview table and showed Sebastian a recent photo from Emily's Instagram profile. The photo was a close-up of Emily sitting in a field with a soft smile on her face. There were flowers braided into her hair, which fell in loose waves across a yellow lace top.

Sebastian looked over at his lawyer. She adjusted her glasses and nodded.

His eyes flicked down to Ryan's phone, his lip twisting in disdain. "Pretty, but I've never seen her before in my life. I don't run in the same circles as Woodstock rejects."

"Funny you say that. A couple of years back, you and this woman ran in very similar circles." Ryan swiped his screen to the next photo of Emily and Sebastian with Tom, the party host in London. For a split second there was a flare of recognition then a flash of guilt across Sebastian's face. *Interesting,* Ryan thought. He might not have recognised Emily, the wellness influencer, but he recognised Emily, the London party girl.

"You knew I'd met her. This is entrapment. Showing me a photo of someone out of context. I should leave now." He glanced at his lawyer again to see if she agreed with him. She shook her head.

"This is you," Ryan pointed to Sebastian, "and this is Emily." He pointed to the blonde woman with both arms draped around Sebastian's neck. "Tell me about her."

Sebastian's lip curled. "I don't catalogue every blonde who hangs off me at parties. This was Tom Montgomery's birthday bash at Annabel's. I'd finished half a bottle of Macallan before I walked in. You want me to recall some trust-fund groupie I posed for one photo with two years ago? Good luck."

"This trust-fund groupie has vanished, and we believe her disappearance could be connected to your family's murder. Quite a coincidence that you knew her."

Ryan noticed Sebastian winced every time Ryan referred to Isabel and Lottie as part of his family but not when he said the word murder. That told him something. The deaths themselves didn't bother Sebastian. Referring to these women as family did.

"My client has stated he doesn't know or remember this woman, regardless of whether you think his meeting her once at a party is relevant. Please move on with your questions, Detective," Margaret said.

"It's come to our attention that you lost your civil court case to get your father, Reginald Bolton, declared incompetent. Is this correct?"

Margaret gave Sebastian a pointed look. This was news to her.

"How else would you explain how crazy he's been acting recently? Did you see that disgusting portrait Isabel commissioned in their bedroom? My God." He shuddered and, for the first time, Ryan agreed wholeheartedly with Sebastian. That portrait would haunt him for weeks.

"You also requested that the recent changes he made to his will be voided?"

"I've been his son for forty years, then suddenly he's giving two-thirds of my inheritance away to two bitches he's known for three? I'd call that insanity."

"Do you have any interest in the occult?" Ryan asked.

Sebastian's eyebrows shot up at the abrupt change of topic. "Me? That's absurd. I'm a Christian."

Ryan suspected Sebastian was more familiar with the seven deadly sins than the values of Christianity but kept that to himself. "Amanda," he said. "How well do you know her?"

"Who?"

"Amanda Norris. William Norris's wife. Surely you met her at some point in the last fifteen years in your role as a managing director?"

Sebastian waved a hand dismissively. "I couldn't pick her out of a lineup."

"She was murdered Sunday night. In the same manner as your family."

Sebastian's face darkened. "That thieving bastard William Norris. This has to be him, getting revenge on my father for firing him. Embezzling prick."

"Mr Norris told us you were the one who fired him, and Mr Norris has an alibi for both nights," Fiona said.

"Then he hired someone," Sebastian shot back.

Ryan leaned forward. "We're more interested in where you were Saturday night between eight and two in the morning?"

"At my home in Sheffield."

"Can anyone verify that?"

Sebastian's eyes narrowed. "I was alone."

"And Sunday night? Between eleven and two?"

Sebastian glowered across the table at him. "Also at home. Also alone." He sprang to his feet, scraping his chair legs across the floor. "That's it. I can see where this is going. You think I killed my father and those two cows to get the money."

"Did you?" Ryan asked.

Margaret grabbed Sebastian's arm and pulled him down. She whispered in his ear, but he shook her off.

He turned back to Ryan. "No, I didn't. But I will not pretend that whoever it was didn't do me a big favour."

Margaret held up her hand. "I need to confer with my client."

Ryan ended the recording.

"That went about as well as I thought it would," Ryan said once they were back in the corridor.

"God, he's such an arse. I hope he did it so he doesn't get a cent," Fiona replied.

Ryan sighed. "If wishes were horses, then beggars would ride."

"Shakespeare?"

"My mother. Usually right before she told me life wasn't fair, and I needed to get over it." *Not that she followed her own advice.*

His phone buzzed. He unlocked it and read the message from DCI Lee. "William Norris has been released. His alibis have been confirmed, and Lee doesn't think we have enough to hold him."

"Not surprising," Fiona said. "Lawrence Potts wasn't at the wellness lodge either. Sheri's trying to get hold of his ex-wife in case she might know where he is."

Ryan leaned against the wall, feeling the cold seep through his shirt. Another lead evaporating. Another thread to chase. "Brilliant. So we've got a cheating husband in a gambling hole, a hedge fund son who's far too delighted about three of our four murders, a Wiccan high priest who's lying to us, and a missing woman who could be the fifth victim or the murderer?"

"When you put it like that," Fiona said.

"Yeah." Ryan pushed off the wall. His shoulder complained.

Fiona's phone buzzed. She read the screen and looked up.

"Digit's uncovered some footage of Lawrence with our mysterious friend Robbie."

———

At the sound of Ryan's voice, Winston launched himself off a pile of high-vis jackets in the corner and bounded across the incident room. He slid to a stop at Ryan's feet, his fluffy tail wagging as he gazed up at him. Ryan crouched to give him a pat. Once Winston deemed the greeting sufficient, he trotted over to Fiona for ear scratches.

"I hope Winston behaved himself?" Ryan asked Digit.

"I found myself sitting with him for several minutes. Not analysing anything." He paused. "Just... sitting and stroking his fur. I'm uncertain how to quantify that."

"The best things in life can't be measured."

"I suppose not, Sir," Digit replied. "He mostly slept, except when he stole Sheri's sausage roll."

Sheri looked up. "I was only in the bathroom for a minute. How did he even get up there?" She gestured to the white paper plate from the cafeteria, pastry crumbs scattered across it and then leading to the edge. "My chair was pushed in, and the desk is over three feet off the ground. I still don't know how you didn't see him, Cal."

"Even if he had, I doubt he would have intervened. Given his cynophobia," Digit said.

Cal frowned. "My what now?"

"Cynophobia. Fear of dogs."

"I'm not afraid of dogs. I just don't like the staring."

Sheri snorted. "All he did was sit at your feet and watch every remaining crisp go from the packet into your mouth. And you didn't give him a single one, you miserable sod."

"You shouldn't feed human food to dogs," Cal muttered. "Anyway, he shouldn't be in here."

"I enjoy having a dog in the office," Sheri said.

Ryan grimaced. "I'll try not to make a habit of bringing him in, Cal. And I'm sorry about your sausage roll, Sheri. When food's involved, Winston somehow transforms into the Michael Jordan of corgis. I'll buy everyone sausage rolls for morning tea tomorrow." He turned to Digit. "So what's this about Lawrence and Robbie?"

"I found this on the CCTV footage from the September full moon that the owner of the Forest Sage Inn sent through." Digit showed Ryan a grainy black-and-white clip of Lawrence sitting in his van arguing with a man in the passenger seat. The man's shoulder-length black hair partially obscured his face as he gestured wildly.

"The elusive Robbie," Ryan said. "It doesn't help us identify him, but it confirms Lawrence knows Robbie better than he let on."

"There's more." Digit leaned forward and pulled up a spreadsheet. "I wrote a programme to sift through Emily's Instagram posts. Look at these."

Ryan scanned the comments and timestamps over Digit's shoulder.

Beautiful energy in this photo!

The goddess smiles through you.

Your eyes hold ancient wisdom. We should discuss your true path.

Some connections transcend this physical realm. See you soon.

"What am I looking at?"

"Recent comments by @VidirBlessed on Emily's Instagram feed. Lawrence has liked almost every post she's made for the last six months."

"So he has an interest in her and failed to disclose her social media account when we interviewed him."

"Also, Uniform called while you were out," Sheri said. "They showed Mr Barkley a picture of Emily's Peugeot. He admitted it could be the car he saw, but despite confirming he's colour blind, he's still insisting it was red."

Ryan rubbed his temples. "Right. Thanks, Sheri. Unless anyone has anything to add, I'm off to tell DCI Lee we have sweet bugger all."

"I've got something," Digit called out.

Ryan's phone pinged. A photo of Winston appeared on the screen, surrounded by women in exercise tops and leggings. His tongue lolled in a doggy grin as he basked in the adoration of his fans. Digit's head popped up above his screens. "Savannah wanted you to have that."

CHAPTER THIRTY-NINE

Emily lay on the hospital bed, the rail propped up beside her.

She focused on her breathing. In through the nose, out through the mouth. The exercises her mum called New Age nonsense were the only thing that kept her from spiralling into complete despair.

A sound from above.

Her body went rigid. The scrape of the bolt sliding back, then the groan of the door swinging open at the top of the stairs. Her measured breaths became shallow pants. She squeezed her eyes shut.

Heavy footfalls on the wooden steps. Slow and deliberate. He didn't rush.

The last board creaked as he reached the bottom. Silence stretched, thick and suffocating. Her blood pounded in her ears.

"I know you're awake."

Emily flinched as fingers brushed her cheek.

"Did you miss me?" His voice was a murmur, a mockery of intimacy that made her skin crawl.

"What do you want?" Her voice came out raspier than intended.

A soft laugh. "What do I want? You haven't figured that out?"

The mattress dipped as he sat beside her. She flinched away, an involuntary jerk. The scent of dried lavender filled her nostrils, mixed with something else. Candle wax, perhaps?

She remained silent but turned to face him. Their eyes locked. Anything she said would be twisted, used as fuel for his sick game. She knew that now.

The man ran a rough finger along her jaw, his nail scratching against her skin. "Not talking? That's a shame. I'd rather hoped you'd have some of that positive energy to share. What's the universe sent you today to be grateful for?"

She jerked her head away, the movement made her wrist throb where the handcuffs had rubbed it raw.

He chuckled. "Defiant. I admire that in you. Even now." He shifted his weight. "I brought you a bottle of water. You must be thirsty after your little adventure."

Her blood turned to ice.

"Yes." His voice dropped lower, intimate. "Did you think I wouldn't notice? The rail pulled from the bed frame, your agonising shuffle to the door." He leaned closer, his breath hot against her ear. "I saw every. Single. Pathetic. Step."

Emily's throat constricted. He'd watched her desperate attempt to free herself.

"You'll never escape me, Emily. Not ever." He held the plastic rim of the bottle against her lips. "Now drink. It'll be more satisfying than lapping up a drip at a time."

Her body screamed for water, but her mind rebelled. It could be drugged. She pressed her lips together.

"No? Suit yourself." He screwed the lid on and placed the bottle at the foot of the bed. "It won't matter soon, I suppose." He stood, the mattress springing back. He sauntered to the workbench in the far corner.

A cold knot formed in Emily's stomach. *Soon.* The word hung in the air between them.

"Why am I here?" She kept her voice soft. Not begging. Offering. The way she spoke to someone jittery at an NA meeting. "If you tell me, I can give you what you want. I will. No judgement."

He opened a drawer and rummaged inside, humming a tuneless melody that grated on her nerves. "Promises, promises."

Heat flushed her cheeks. "I mean it."

You never know what someone else is going through. The phrase she'd repeated so often to her NA group now echoed mockingly in her head.

She tried to change tack. "How long have I been here?"

"Long enough for people to miss you." He grinned and slammed the drawer shut. "Not that anyone's looking in the right places. The police searched your cottage and found nothing. I'd already removed what I needed."

Emily's breath caught.

"I've been preparing something special for you." He dropped a heavy rectangle object onto the workbench, but the angle was all wrong for Emily to see what it was. "Candles. Your pagan statues arranged just so on a proper altar." His voice took on an almost dreamy quality. "You'll photograph beautifully if they get to you in time."

"In time?" Her voice strangled on the words.

"My grand finale. Everything's already prepared. I just need the last piece. You." He paused. "What tarot card do you think best represents you? The High Priestess? The Fool?"

Emily kept silent.

He laughed and held up two small shiny circles. "I also have two coins. To replace those pretty blue eyes of yours."

The words hit her like ice water.

He returned to the bed, and the mattress dipped once more. She cowered against the wall. This time, his hand settled on her ankle, his grip firm, possessive. His thumb stroked her skin, a gesture so at odds with the terror of the moment it made bile rise up her throat.

"Do you know what these are?" Something cold and metallic rested against her cheek.

Emily shook her head, the object moving with her.

"Scissors. Very sharp ones." He traced the closed blades down her jaw to her neck. "I'm going to need a lock of your beautiful hair. It goes in the grimoire, you see. Completes the ritual."

She whipped around but had no way to stop him. The scissors snipped, and he stood, apparently satisfied.

A phone message alert sounded, making her jump.

"Hmmm. What do we have here?" He walked to the bottom of the stairs. "Say your prayers, Emily. To whichever gods will listen."

CHAPTER FORTY

"Felicity, thanks for coming in to talk to us, especially straight from such a long flight," Ryan said.

The young woman's shirt was wrinkled. Her jeans bore a food stain on one knee. Bloodshot eyes and greasy sandy blonde hair suggested she hadn't stopped at home for a shower and change of clothes before coming to the station. She seemed less concerned with her appearance than her older sister, which was fortunate given she took after her mother more than Emily did.

Ryan felt more than a little rumpled himself. He'd poured over Jaime's case files again, unable to accept there was nothing to find. He rolled his left shoulder. The bullet track nagged when he sat too long.

The girl gave a solemn nod and swallowed audibly, then took a sip of water from the plastic cup in front of her. Ryan sensed her nerves stemmed more from her sister's disappearance than from talking to the police.

"Can we get you anything else?" Fiona asked. "Coffee or tea? Maybe a fizzy drink?"

"No thanks, water's fine," Felicity said. "Mum said you wanted to speak to me because I'm the closest to Emily out of anyone, so I got her to drive me here straight from Heathrow. What if I can tell you something that helps you find her? She's been missing for over five days now." She shuffled in her chair. "Isn't there a statistic that if you don't find a missing person in the first twenty-four hours, the chance of finding them drops massively?"

She bit her lip, waiting for a reply.

Ryan figured she didn't want to hear the actual figure was ten percent, so instead he assured her they were doing everything they could to find Emily and had not given up hope.

"How long were you overseas?" he asked. He wanted to establish how much recent knowledge she might have.

"About three months. I flew to Vietnam in early August, but I've spoken to Emily at least once or twice a week since I left, and I follow all her posts on social media."

"Your mum touched on it, but if you don't mind my asking, why did your sister move back to Chesterfield from London?" Fiona asked.

Felicity shrugged. "She was open about it. Emily got mixed up with the wrong people when she moved to London. Started with pills at weekend parties. Ecstasy first, then cocaine. Soon she was out every night, ducking into work bathrooms to snort lines to keep her eyes open through meetings."

Her fingers worried the edge of her plastic cup. "Then one night she mixed heroin with the coke. The paramedics had to resuscitate her."

She paused, staring down. "Emily had Mum listed as her emergency contact. When she came around, as soon as they took the tubes out, she told us everything. She agreed to rehab the next day."

"Was there anyone who might want to hurt Emily? An ex or a boyfriend?" Ryan asked.

Felicity thought for a moment. "She was seeing this one guy. It was going well for a couple of months, but he got controlling, so Emily broke up with him and purged him from her socials. He was pissed about it. He sounded like a complete dick in the end."

"Do you know his name?"

"Kyle something. I don't remember his last name. Never met him. I'd gone back to uni when they got together."

"Kyle Mathers?"

"Maybe? She called him Kyle the Penis after they broke up, but I'm pretty sure that wasn't his surname." She smirked. "This was a while ago, though. Do you think this Kyle guy could be involved in her disappearance?"

Only a twenty-year-old would think four months was a long time ago.

"We're trying to establish if there's anyone close to her we should look into," Fiona said. "Your mum mentioned Emily's car is missing. Do you have any idea where it could be? Maybe she lent it to someone?"

"You never know with Emily. It could have broken down, and she left it on the side of the road, or she could have seen a young mother struggling with her groceries and offered to let her borrow it. She was that kind of person."

"What kind?"

"Too trusting. She's always willing to see the best in people and forgive them their faults, especially in the last year since she's embraced an alternative lifestyle. My parents and I have talked about it. We worried someone could take advantage of her."

A saint in a world full of sinners. Ryan had seen how that story ended before.

"Your mum seemed to think it would be uncharacteristic for Emily to leave town for a few days without telling anyone. Did she have a new boyfriend you knew of that she wouldn't have told your mum about?"

Felicity considered the question. "No one since Kyle. A month or so ago, she went on a few dates with an older guy, but she wasn't feeling it. After that, she said she wanted to focus on self-love, whatever that means."

At the mention of an older guy, Lawrence Potts jumped into Ryan's head. Lawrence had said Emily joined the coven in the summer, so the timing would be right. "Did she tell you the older guy's name or how she met him?"

"I think they met at some spring festival when she was with Kyle, but she didn't agree to go out with him for a while. When she first told me about him, I asked if he was a silver fox, and she said he was more of an elderly squirrel, so we called him that."

Ryan made a mental note to ask Lawrence if he appreciated being compared to a rodent.

"Is Emily part of a book club?"

Felicity's mouth fell open. "Yeah, I know all about Emily's book club." She made quotation marks in the air with her fingers.

"Do you know the name of the group or where they meet?"

"It's not really a book club, you know that, right?"

Fiona exchanged a look with Ryan. "We didn't know. Can you enlighten us?" she asked.

"Two of the older rich ladies hated going to the meetings with the riff-raff, so Emily let them meet more informally. She knew it was against the rules, but she's terrible at telling people no, and the ladies kept on at her about it. They liked to refer to the group as The Book Club because they didn't want their husbands to find out. Emily was out in the open, but she went along with it. She was always saying that everyone deals with their issues in their own way and we need to give people grace. I—"

"What was the group really?" Ryan interrupted.

"Narcotics Anonymous. Emily's one of the local coordinators. After rehab, she got into the idea of helping others shake off their addictions in a big way."

The connection between the victims fell into place. Rename the book club 'NA' and the columns line up.

Amanda Norris had endured a rough upbringing and fought her way out of a drug addiction in her youth, according to the track mark scars between her toes.

Isabel Bolton had a debilitating and painful hip injury, yet the bathroom cabinet in the master bedroom had held only supermarket brand ibuprofen and paracetamol. She'd likely been prescribed something stronger in the aftermath of her accident, oxycodone or a similar opioid, many of which were addictive and prone to abuse by patients.

Kyle had been a cokehead according to his colleagues.

And Emily, as the local coordinator for Narcotics Anonymous, was the link between them all. The book club wasn't literary. It was recovery. The problem was, with all the known members either dead or missing, Ryan wasn't sure how the connection would help them. Dead people didn't make good witnesses.

"If you think of anything that might help us find Emily or if she contacts you, please let us know." Fiona handed her a business card.

"I will." Felicity stood. "Please find her, detectives. I don't know what I'll do if..." Her voice cracked.

Fiona slipped an arm around her as Felicity sobbed into her shoulder.

CHAPTER FORTY-ONE

LAWRENCE POTTS SAT IN HIS VAN. HE WIPED THE SWEAT from his forehead as he stared at the text message on his phone. The words blurred together, but the meaning was clear. With the police sniffing around, his secrets were in danger of exposure.

He tried the number for the sixth time in an hour. No answer.

"In desperate need of a sage smudging," he muttered, scanning the peeling paint and boarded-up windows of the run-down house he'd parked outside of. Not that there was enough sage in the UK to do the job. He'd been inside only once before. It hadn't been a pleasant experience. But if turning up on the doorstep was the only way to get this sorted, once and for all, then so be it. He couldn't go on this way.

"You'd better be here, you prick."

Outside the van, wind fluttered his beard plait and whipped at his thin cotton shirt. He searched the interior for a woolly jumper, but the only warm layer in sight was his high priest's robe. He considered putting it on, but the curious gazes of two teenagers loitering against a chain fence across the street made him reconsider. In such unenlightened surroundings, his sacred robes would draw too much attention. He eyed the teenagers again, muttering a quick chant to the god of the forest to protect his van from break-ins or slashed tyres. Satisfied he'd done all he could, he followed a narrow path of crushed weeds down the driveway and around to the back of the house. A patch of dandelions caught his eye. He'd stop and pick them for tea on his way out. After he'd straightened out this nasty business.

The kitchen door stood open despite the cold. The smell of stale food and dampness assaulted his nostrils as he stepped inside. Unwashed dishes filled the sink, and takeaway cartons and pizza boxes were strewn across every surface.

Lawrence crinkled his nose but forced himself to press on, dodging the piles of discarded clothes and empty beer cans that littered the floor. A warm glow came from the room at the end of the hall.

He moved into the lounge, taking in the details of the dimly lit room. Candles sat arranged on a large, old-fashioned dining table. Across the surface, a crude pentagram had been scratched into the varnish.

"Hello?" he called out hesitantly. There was no response, and a shiver ran down his spine. Why was the dodgy prick playing games with him? He knew he should leave, but the setup on the table captured his attention.

The placement of the statues was all wrong, and the pentagram points were crooked. He took a step closer. Was that his stolen grimoire in the middle of the table?

His limbs froze as realisation flooded through him. Photos he'd been shown of another ritual incorrectly laid out but with a gruesome twist.

A floorboard creaked. He started to turn.

"Who's—"

Hands clamped down on his shoulder, yanking him off balance.

Lawrence's instincts kicked in, and he fought against his attacker, trying to break free. As he struggled, he felt a sudden prick in his neck. He reached up to swat it away, but his vision blurred. An arm clamped around his throat.

With one last surge of strength, Lawrence tried to swing his arm, hoping to land a blow on his attacker. But the effort was futile, and his arm fell limply to his side.

The grip around his throat slackened, and his legs gave way, the room spinning as he sank to the floor. His thoughts jumbled together as he tried to stay conscious.

As the darkness crept in, someone leaned down and breathed in his ear. "Time for some scream therapy."

CHAPTER FORTY-TWO

"This is where Lawrence's ex-wife asked us to meet?" Sheri said as she pushed open the door with its flaking paint. An old-fashioned bell rang as they stepped into the second-hand bookstore. Dusty bookshelves with piles of books stacked on top loomed around them. Dust motes swirled in the morning light shining through the store windows. Cal felt if he so much as sneezed they'd be buried in an avalanche of yellowing pages and silverfish.

"Yeah," Cal replied. "She owns the place."

"For twenty years," a voice said.

Cal jumped and spun around as a short, mousy woman in a shapeless blue twinset appeared from behind the nearest shelf.

"Good morning, detectives," she said. "You're early."

"We made good time on the A61," Cal said, recovering his composure. "Mrs Potts?"

"It's Ms Wright now, but call me Mary." She didn't offer a smile, just a sharp look that could have cut glass. "I reverted to my maiden name when we divorced. Never a big fan of the surname Potts."

"Right. I'm DC Pine. I was the one who called you. This is DC Dewan."

Sheri started to wave, then turned it into a nod.

"Follow me," Mary said, already turning away.

Cal caught Sheri's eye and pulled a face. This was going to be fun.

She led them into the bowels of the store, to a small reading nook in the corner.

Sheri settled into one of the large armchairs and was enveloped in a cloud of dust. She broke into a coughing fit and leaned forward. Cal reached over and gave her a helpful thump on the back.

"What are you doing? I'm not choking," Sheri hacked out between coughs.

Cal shrugged and thumped her once more for good measure.

Sheri cleared her throat, cheeks flushed red.

Mary gestured to the setup with pursed lips. "This area doesn't get much use. Patty, my business partner, insisted it's what all the fancy chain stores do, but I don't see the point of it, really. Why read a book in the store when you could be curled up on the couch at home?" She looked at them with the patience of someone who'd rather be anywhere else but was raised better than to show it. "Can I get you anything to drink? I'm in the middle of making tea."

"I'm good, thanks," Cal said. Given the unkempt state of the bookshop, he wasn't sure he'd risk going near Mary's mugs.

"No thank you," Sheri added.

Mary nodded curtly and bustled off into the back.

"She's a fair bit older than Lawrence, isn't she?" Cal said in a stage whisper.

He saw Sheri wince. He heard a cupboard open and could only hope Mary had missed the comment.

"She's not exactly how I pictured a Wiccan high priestess," Sheri replied in a much softer voice.

"Ex-high priestess, dear," Mary said, causing Cal's heart to jump into his throat for the second time in as many minutes. The woman moved like she was the ghost of George Best.

Mary settled herself on a low wooden stool, cradling a steaming mug in her hands.

"So," Cal said, leaning forward with his elbows on his knees, "can you help us out with a few questions about Lawrence?"

Mary's mouth pulled down. "I can try. Though I don't know what use I'll be. We're not on Christmas card terms."

"Fair enough." Cal nodded. "Can I ask if that's why you divorced? Was it the whole Wiccan thing?"

"All the world's a stage, and all the men and women merely players," Mary replied.

"What?" Cal said.

"Shakespeare," Sheri whispered to him.

Mary let out a short, humourless laugh. "What you don't know is that Vidir, the high priest, only appeared maybe six or seven years ago. Back when we first married, he was Lawrence the accountant. Then he discovered crystals and moon circles and decided he was some kind of spiritual guru." She took a sip of her tea. "We became very different people when he embraced his new lifestyle. I tried to give it a go for a while, be supportive, but freezing my bits off chanting in the woods wasn't my thing. And neither was watching him prance at festivals pretending to commune with nature spirits while eyeing up anything in tight jeans."

Cal nearly choked. *Tell us how you really feel.*

Sheri balanced her notebook on her knees. "Based on what you're saying, it sounds like there was more to the separation than lifestyle differences?"

Mary's eyes narrowed. "You could say that. Lawrence's Mystic Wellness Lodge? Wellness, my arse. That outfit hasn't made a cent in the last five years. Ask him about his special greenhouse. 'Medicinal herbs' he calls them. Funny how his cash-only clients all have 'chronic pain' and happen to be under thirty. Not that I care anymore. His 'alternative medicine' paid for my divorce lawyer."

Cal's eyebrows shot up. *Right then,* he thought, vaguely impressed with the former accountant. Walter White in diaper pants.

"Any idea where he's hanging out?" he asked. "We've tried to contact him over the last twenty-four hours, but he hasn't answered, and now his phone's turned off."

"Haven't got a clue, and I can't say I'm losing any sleep over it." Mary set her mug down with a decisive *clunk.* "I hope you find him, Detective. And I hope he hasn't done anything too stupid this time." Then the hardness returned. "But knowing Lawrence, that's too much to ask."

"Do you recognise this man? He recently joined the coven." Sheri showed Mary the blurry photo of Robbie and Lawrence together in Lawrence's van.

Mary's lips compressed as she studied the photo. "Probably one of his hookups, Detective. His type, that one. Young, dumb, and impressed by all that mystical nonsense. That was the main reason we divorced."

Cal sputtered and sat up straighter. "Sorry, what?"

Mary blinked at him like he was slow. "A year ago, Lawrence came out as gay."

CHAPTER FORTY-THREE

Ryan waited in line at the cafe and eyed the golden pastries behind the glass counter. Flakes of buttery puff pastry crowned each roll. The herbed pork filling peeked through deliberate slits in the dough, glistening with rendered fat and black pepper.

A woman in a bright yellow raincoat jabbed her finger at the barista. "This has dairy in it. I ordered oat milk." Her voice rose higher with each word.

Ryan's foot tapped on the polished concrete floor. He'd wanted to treat the team to something better than the cardboard-wrapped slabs of grease that passed for sausage rolls at the station cafeteria, and maybe take Winston home a spare, but the argument showed no signs of ending. The line behind him grew longer.

His phone rang. He looked down at the screen. DC Pine.

"What?"

"Boss, uniform found Lawrence's van." Cal's words tumbled out in a rush. "It's parked outside what looks like a derelict house. They were following up on a tip about some teenage drug dealers in the area and couldn't stop to investigate so they called it in."

Ryan straightened. "How long ago?"

"Five minutes, max. Goody just passed it along."

The woman in the yellow raincoat's voice climbed another octave. Ryan's jaw tightened. He could practically taste the pastry melting on his tongue. "Where?"

"It's local. Over on Burbury Street. Ten minutes from the station."

Ryan threw the sausage rolls a mournful look and then stepped out of the queue. "Swing by and pick me up. Let's see if he's there."

———

"So Lawrence is gay?" Ryan said to Cal.

"Yeah, boss. According to his ex-wife, he came out just over a year ago and has been dating men ever since."

Ryan pondered that for a few seconds. "He's unlikely to have been Emily's silver fox then."

"His ex-wife reckons Robbie might have been a hookup, innit. Said he was just Lawrence's type."

The map app's voice announced they had arrived at their destination. Overhead, grey clouds pressed down like a concrete ceiling.

Ryan pulled the Range Rover to a halt behind Lawrence's white panel van parked crookedly against the kerb. Ryan got out and checked inside. It was empty. The same purple robe still lay on the front seat.

Cal slammed the passenger door and studied the house. "What a shithole."

Ryan couldn't argue that one. Weeds choked the front yard where a garden should have been, their brown stalks reaching knee high through rusted wire fencing. Paint peeled from the weathered boards in long strips, revealing grey wood underneath. The front door's cherry-red surface was battered and faded. The winner of the 'biggest shit pile on the street' award on a street where many houses were fighting for the honour.

Ryan's phone rang. Unknown number. He answered anyway.

"DI Hale." His tone made it clear that this better be important.

"Detective Inspector." Sophie's voice came through the speaker, crisp and professional and so similar to Jaime's. "I'm looking for a quote regarding your investigation's treatment of William Norris. Nearly twenty-four hours in custody while grieving his murdered wife. The emotional trauma of being treated as a suspect when he'd just lost—"

"Contact the media office for any official statements." Ryan kept his eyes on the house. *Impossible to see inside with the boarded-up windows.*

"That's a cop-out, and you know it." Sophie's tone sharpened. "You held a bereaved husband and father for almost a full day. You need to own that decision."

"Media office, Sophie."

Cal had already wandered up the driveway, phone raised to photograph some graffiti that ran along the brick wall dividing the properties. The lad moved with the casual confidence of someone who'd forgotten they were investigating a potential murder suspect.

"Wait up, you muppet," Ryan yelled at Cal, but the DC didn't pay him any attention.

"Where are you?" Sophie jumped on his words. "That doesn't sound like the station."

"I'll pop round and see Ruth the first chance I get." Ryan ended the call and pocketed his phone.

Cal had disappeared from view around the corner of the wall.

"Cal," Ryan called out, but the wind snatched his voice away.

The constable didn't reappear.

Ryan's phone buzzed again. He swore under his breath and answered without checking the screen.

"What?"

"DI Hale," Digit said, unfazed by the abrupt answer. "Have you arrived at the property on Burbury Street yet?"

"Yes." Ryan started down the driveway. The wind pushed dead leaves across the stones and gravel crunched under his boots. "What've you got?"

"Exercise extreme caution. I've accessed the property records, and the house is registered to a Tracy Zutter. She hasn't paid council tax in three years, which seemed irrelevant, but—"

"Digit."

"Robert Zutter is her son. Both have criminal records. Fiona identified Robert as the man from the search party. He's Robbie."

Ryan's blood turned to ice.

"Shit."

He broke into a run, phone still pressed to his ear. The house loomed ahead, windows dark like empty eye sockets. The back door stood cracked open.

"DI Hale?" Digit's voice crackled. "Are you—"

Ryan shoved the phone in his pocket and sprinted up the three concrete steps to the door.

It exploded outward.

The impact caught Ryan square in the chest. He went down hard and his side slammed into the edge of the bottom step. Pain shot through his damaged shoulder.

A figure in a balaclava and thick puffer jacket burst through the doorway. Ryan's eyes zeroed in on the bloody knife in his assailant's hand.

The blade slashed towards Ryan's face. He jerked his head back. The knife whistled past, close enough he felt the displaced air.

The figure didn't pause. They launched down the steps and sprinted across the overgrown garden. With one hand on the wooden fence, they vaulted over in a fluid movement that spoke of youth and practice.

Ryan's legs tensed to pursue. Then his brain caught up with what he'd seen.

Blood on the blade.

"Cal!" The shout tore from his throat. "Cal!"

Silence answered him.

Ryan hauled himself to his feet. His shoulder screamed in protest. He ignored it. "Cal!"

Nothing.

Somewhere down the street, a dog barked.

Ryan's heart hammered against his ribs. His hands shook as he pulled out his phone. His fingers felt thick and clumsy as he fumbled for the radio instead.

"Officer potentially down. 15 Burbury Street. Requesting immediate backup and ambulance."

The dispatcher's voice responded, but Ryan wasn't listening anymore.

He moved to the doorway. The door hung crooked on its hinges from the violent exit. Beyond it, darkness pooled thick as oil.

Ryan's damaged hand throbbed where he gripped the door frame. Every instinct screamed at him to rush inside, to find his constable, to fix whatever had happened.

But training held him back for one more breath.

He thought of the Met. Of the raid that went wrong in his first year as a DI. A young DC paralysed. Because he'd been too confident, too bloody stupid. The smell of copper, sweat, and the stink of his own fear.

Not again. Not on his watch. Not another one.

"DC Pine, if you're just messing about with your bloody phone I swear to God—"

The dark swallowed his words.

No cocky response. No embarrassed laugh. No sound of footsteps on the floorboards.

Just a terrible silence.

"Fuck it!" Ryan yanked the door open and stepped inside.

CHAPTER FORTY-FOUR

RYAN WAS THANKFUL HE'D TAKEN A DEEP BREATH BEFORE he went in. The smell hit him like an assault.

"Christ," he muttered. He buried his nose in his elbow. A bouquet of rotten food, musty mildew, and a distinct eau de rodent swirled around him. The kitchen was empty. No sign of Cal bleeding out on the floor, thank Christ.

Ryan flicked on his penlight. The beam was weak. *Must be nearly out of battery.* It didn't seem to do much in the gloom besides telegraphing his exact location. *Great.* He turned it off and put it away.

"Chesterfield Police," he yelled into the gloom, baton ready in his right hand for any sudden movement. He ignored the stench and pushed deeper into the house, trying not to think too hard about what was making his shoes stick to the carpet.

A cry for help sounded from the room at the end of the hallway. Too high-pitched to be Cal. The door was open, and soft light flickered beyond. A wave of dread flooded down Ryan's back. "Please!" a woman's voice rang out, then was muffled.

"Shit!" Ryan said under his breath. It had to be Emily, but who was with her?

Wasn't he repeating what he'd done wrong that fucked-up night in Silvertown? An image of his hands tied to a chair as he dripped puddles of blood on the concrete floor flashed into his head. He shook it away. Cal could be dying inside that room. He raised his baton.

"Cal, Emily, can you hear me!" Ryan shouted. Lawrence or Robbie be damned. The girl needed to know he was coming for her.

Through the gap, Ryan could see clusters of candles scattered on the windowsills of the boarded-over windows and across the fireplace mantelpiece, bathing the room in an eerie shifting glow. The scent of damp decay and burnt wax mingled with an underlying current of something metallic.

Blood.

On the floor, a familiar Italian brogue peeked out from behind a threadbare sofa.

Ryan shouldered the door open. His pulse hammered in his throat.

The scene inside ambushed his senses all at once. A cluster of candles behind the door toppled onto the carpet. Flames caught on the strips of dry wallpaper that had been piled in the corner with a hungry *whoosh*.

"Cal!"

No response from his detective constable, but Ryan could make out his crumpled form. A heavy brass candlestick lay half-rolled under the sofa beside Cal's head, its base darkened with what could only be blood.

The acrid smell of smoke and burning synthetic fibres joined the already putrid cocktail of odours. Ryan scanned the room for immediate threats, baton raised. The fire threw grotesque shadows that danced across the peeling wallpaper.

"Police! Show yourself!" His voice sounded scared even to his own ears.

No movement. Just the crackle of spreading flames.

The dining table dominated the centre of the room, its surface covered in small bronze statues arranged around a prone figure.

A man's body. Not Emily.

As Ryan edged closer, his stomach clenched. Lawrence Potts stared upward with sightless eyes, a deep gash carved across his throat. The wound gaped, deep enough to expose the white cartilage of his trachea. What Ryan had taken for varnish was a dark pool of blood spreading across the table's surface and dripping onto the carpet. The liquid had soaked into the man's plaited blonde beard, turning it the colour of rust.

"Shit," Ryan muttered.

A woman's plea came from somewhere on the far side of the corpse.

Ryan moved forward and leaned across Lawrence's body. A small black tape recorder had been tucked against the dead man's side, its buttons depressed. The recording played again. A woman's voice crying for help, then abruptly silenced.

He grabbed the device and stuffed it into his pocket. No time for proper evidence collection. No time for anything. The flames had already spread to the tattered curtains and thick smoke banked against the ceiling.

"Cal," Ryan called again. He ducked back to his unconscious detective. "Cal, wake up!"

The young man's face remained slack. A livid bruise formed at his temple. Ryan hooked his hands under Cal's armpits, his damaged fingers struggling to grip, and dragged him backward towards the door, his nostrils burning with smoke.

The fire had already caught the sofa. Orange flames licked

upward with unnatural hunger. He could only pray no one laid in wait for them in one of the other rooms.

Ryan's eyes watered as he hauled Cal's dead weight into the hallway.

Ryan coughed violently, the smoke now filling the narrow corridor. The heat pressed against his back as he struggled towards the back door, muscles screaming at the effort of moving Cal's solid frame.

"Nearly there," he wheezed, though he knew Cal couldn't hear him.

A scream sounded from his pocket. He'd forgotten to turn the damn recorder off.

Ryan kicked the back door open wider and dragged Cal down the concrete steps then collapsed onto his knees beside the young detective once they were safely outside. He pressed his fingers to Cal's neck, relieved to feel a strong pulse.

Cal's breathing seemed regular, but a sizeable lump had risen where the candlestick had connected with his skull. Ryan gently turned Cal's head to examine the wound. It had stopped bleeding but would leave Cal with the mother of all headaches.

Behind them, orange light flickered inside the house as the fire took hold. The distant wail of sirens grew closer.

Ryan stared at Cal's pale face, unnaturally still without its usual cocky grin. An intense wave of guilt crashed over him. How had he allowed this to happen? Cal was his responsibility. He should have made sure the DC waited outside, should have anticipated the danger. Instead, he'd been distracted by Sophie and all their complicated history.

He'd failed to protect a member of his team, just as he'd failed to protect Jaime.

The emergency vehicles arrived and snapped Ryan back to the present. His knees were damp from kneeling on the damp concrete. Smoke billowed from the doorway behind them, carrying the stomach-turning scent of Lawrence's burning flesh.

The woman's pleas sounded again from Ryan's pocket. Taunting him. He took the device out and hit the stop button. The recording fell mercifully silent.

CHAPTER FORTY-FIVE

Ryan stared at the empty hospital bed in Cal's room. The sheets were rumpled, bunched where his colleague had laid. A drip stand stood to one side, its plastic tubing dangling. A discarded gown lay crumpled at the foot of the mattress. The only sound in the room was the faint beep of a disconnected monitor.

He'd missed the signs, and a man had lost his life.

He dropped into the vinyl chair beside the bed and rubbed his face. The bitter scent of antiseptic couldn't quite mask the lingering smell of smoke in his nostrils.

It had been a trap. An elaborate, sadistic trap, and he'd walked straight into it. No, he'd led Cal straight into it. Driven by his constant drive to solve the puzzle before anyone else could.

Ryan squeezed his eyes shut, but it didn't block out the image of Lawrence Potts sprawled across the dining table, throat slashed open like a grotesque second mouth. The killer had known they'd find Lawrence's van. Had known they'd enter that house. Had even positioned that bloody tape recorder to lure them deeper inside with its manufactured screams.

The same killer who'd arranged eyeballs in a star pattern at the Nine Ladies stone circle. Who'd cut out Amanda Norris's eyes and replaced them with coins. Who'd murdered the Boltons and posed them like some twisted tableau.

It wasn't just killing. Someone had put on a show.

A cold realisation settled over Ryan. The killer had orchestrated every move and placed each piece on the board, Ryan included. And while Ryan fumbled around in the dark, people died.

Perhaps Lampton had been right. He should never have come back to Chesterfield. His judgment was compromised, and his presence put his team at risk. In London, it had been faceless Russian women who'd paid the price for his arrogance in Silvertown. Now it was his own people.

The door swung open. Fiona stood in the entrance, her blonde curls escaping from a hastily arranged ponytail, her eyes soft with unspoken sympathy.

"How's the patient?" she asked.

Ryan raised his head. "Moaning about the blood on his blazer and complaining that his arse was hanging out of the hospital gown when they wheeled him off for his CT scan."

He almost smiled at the memory of Cal's indignant protests.

"Doctor said he took a decent blow to the head, but he'll be okay. The scan is a precaution."

Fiona sat in the chair opposite Ryan. "Good. I'd hate to think he lost more brain cells than he can spare." She patted Ryan's arm. "I'm glad he's all right."

"Me too."

The words felt inadequate. Cal could have died in that house. Lawrence Potts had.

She leaned forward. "Fire crew found a plastic canister of petrol in the woodshed outside. Luckily, it was far enough away not to be part of the blaze. Forensics think it was placed there recently based on the crushed weeds around it."

Ryan straightened. "He planned to booby-trap the house and lure us there, but we interrupted his plans?"

"That's what it looks like. I think you got there early. It was just by chance that patrol spotted Lawrence's van when they did."

Ryan's phone vibrated in his pocket. He pulled it out and frowned at the unfamiliar number.

"DI Hale."

A panicked voice blasted down the line. "Detective? It's Todd. Todd Mathers. I've... oh Christ. I've found him."

Ryan pressed the phone harder against his ear. "Found who?"

"That Robbie guy you were looking for. He's in Emily's cottage. I'd come to do some more searching in the woods, and I noticed the door to Emily's cottage was open." Todd's breath hitched. "He's just lying there on her bed. Blue and not moving. There's a needle sticking out of his arm. I think... I think he's dead."

Ryan locked eyes with Fiona. "You're at Emily's cottage right now?"

"Yes. What should I—"

"Don't touch anything. Don't go near him." Ryan was already on his feet.

Fiona pulled her radio out of her bag and stepped away to call in the situation. "This is DS Bennett requesting immediate ambulance and uniform backup to 21 Daisy Lane, Narrowmoor, by the entrance to Flowerbank Woods."

"Todd, I need you to leave the cottage. Wait outside in your car for us. We're on our way." Ryan grabbed his coat. "Do not approach him, understand? Just get outside and wait."

"Right, yeah." Todd's voice trembled. "I can do that."

———

THE DRIVE to the cottage stretched Ryan's nerves taut. He gripped the steering wheel tighter as each minute passed, pressing his foot harder on the accelerator as they hurtled down narrow country lanes with the siren blaring.

"Hey, slow down. I'm supposed to be the rally driver here," Fiona said, bracing herself against the dashboard.

"If Robbie's dead, we might have lost our best lead to Emily."

"And if we wrap ourselves around a tree, we definitely won't find her."

Ryan eased off the accelerator. She was right, but the frustration gnawed at him.

By the time they pulled up outside Emily's cottage, two police cars and an ambulance were already parked along the narrow lane. A blue Nissan Ryan assumed belonged to Todd sat pulled onto the grass verge, its hazard lights still flashing.

An ambulance crew emerged from the cottage doorway, their unhurried movements told Ryan everything he needed to know even before the lead paramedic shook his head.

"Too late?" Ryan asked, showing his warrant card.

"I'm afraid so." The paramedic peeled off his gloves. "Been dead at least an hour, maybe two. Looks like an overdose."

Ryan nodded grimly. "Right. We'll take it from here."

Inside, the cottage felt colder than Ryan remembered from his previous visit. Their footsteps echoed on the wooden floors as they made their way to Emily's bedroom.

Robbie lay sprawled across Emily's pillows. His long black hair formed a dark halo against the floral fabric. A tourniquet hung loosely around his left bicep, the rubber tubing slack. A needle protruded from the crook of his elbow. White foam crusted the corners of his blue-tinged lips, and his eyes stared vacantly at the ceiling.

"Heroin overdose?" Fiona asked.

Ryan studied the room. "He was a known user."

He pulled on a pair of latex gloves and lifted Robbie's right arm. Old track scars latticed his forearm from years of favouring the same vein. Beneath it lay an oversized leather-bound book, its cover worn and cracked with age.

"That's Lawrence's missing grimoire," Fiona said, leaning in for a closer look.

Ryan straightened and pulled off his gloves. "Let's talk to Todd."

Outside, Todd Mathers leaned against his car, hunched forward as he stared at the ground. He looked up as they approached, his face ashen.

"Is he...?" Todd's voice cracked.

"Yes, he's dead, but he was before you arrived," Fiona confirmed. "There was nothing you could have done."

"Todd, we need to ask you a few questions about how you found him," Ryan said.

Todd nodded jerkily and pushed himself away from the car. "I came to search the woods again. For Emily." He gestured vaguely towards Flowerbank Woods across the lane. "The front door of her cottage was open when I was driving past. I thought maybe..." His breathing quickened. "Maybe she'd come home."

"So you went inside?" Fiona prompted gently.

"I called out first." Todd's words tumbled out faster. "I swear I did. I shouted, 'Emily?' but nobody answered. So I went in and that's when I... when I found..." His breaths turned into sharp gasps. "He was lying there and I... I couldn't..."

Todd's face contorted. He doubled over, hands on his knees, wheezing for air.

Fiona moved closer and placed a steadying hand on his shoulder. "Todd? Focus on my voice. You're having a panic attack."

Ryan stood back and watched as Fiona guided Todd through controlled breathing. Her voice remained calm and level, a stark contrast to Todd's ragged gasps.

"That's it. In through your nose, hold for four, out through your mouth. Good. Again."

Gradually, Todd steadied. He unfolded and wiped his forehead with a trembling hand. "Sorry. I've never found a body before. And it brought back everything with Kyle. I know he hanged himself, but..." His voice trailed off.

"It's normal to be shaken up," Fiona assured him. "Do you feel able to continue?"

Todd nodded weakly.

"Searching for Emily again?" Ryan said. "You seem to have taken quite an interest in finding her."

Todd's gaze dropped to his shoes. "I just want to help."

"That's commendable." Ryan folded his arms, Cal's comments from yesterday in his head. Maybe he should have given the DC's opinion more weight. "But Emily was Kyle's girlfriend, not yours?"

A flush crept up Todd's neck. "It's not like that."

"No? Because I've known blokes who've put in less effort into looking for their own wives than you have for your brother's missing ex."

"Ryan," Fiona warned under her breath.

Todd's shoulders slumped further. "Look, I... I care about

what happens to Emily, all right? Kyle treated her like shit. Controlling, jealous, all that stuff. She deserves better."

"Better like you, perhaps?" Ryan pushed.

"I never—" Todd kicked at a stone on the path. "Fine. I like her. Have done for ages. But I won't act on it. She was Kyle's girlfriend, and I'm..." He gestured down at himself. "And after he died..." He gave a slight shake of his head. "She needs a friend, not another guy making a move."

Ryan studied him. The man looked defeated.

"So you've been searching because...?"

"Because I want her found safe," Todd mumbled. "And yeah, maybe if I find her, she'll look at me differently. Stupid, right?" He laughed hollowly. "Knight in shining armour fantasy. God, I'm pathetic."

Ryan exchanged a glance with Fiona. The man's self-awareness was almost painful to witness.

"When you went into the cottage," Fiona asked, "did you touch anything besides the door?"

"No. I saw him on the bed, and I backed out straightaway. Called you."

"Did you notice anything unusual? Anyone hanging around the area before you found the body?"

"No, nothing. The place was dead quiet." Todd winced. "Sorry, I didn't mean—"

"It's fine," Ryan cut him off. "What about the book? Did you see that?"

Todd looked confused. "What book?"

"There was a leather book under Robbie's arm."

"I didn't notice. I was too busy trying not to throw up, to be honest."

Ryan nodded. He took in the pallor that still clung to Todd's face. His hands trembled even now.

"Right. You'll need to make a formal statement, but that can wait until later in the week."

Todd sagged with visible relief. "Thank you."

"And Todd?" Ryan added.

"Yes?"

"Next time you feel the urge to play detective, call us first."

CHAPTER FORTY-SIX

<hr>

THIS WAS HOW HIS FIRST CASE BACK IN CHESTERFIELD ended. Not with sirens or handcuffs, but with the team eating gourmet sausage rolls in the incident room.

The frantic energy of the past few days had evaporated, replaced by the low hum of computer fans and the shuffling of papers.

Cal scrolled through his phone, probably live-streaming the results of his brain scan to his followers while he tried not to get flaky pastry on his suit.

The hospital had released him the previous night after ruling out any swelling. This morning when Fiona had grinned at him and asked, 'How's the swollen head?', he'd looked only slightly miffed.

Ryan glanced over at Sheri. She nursed a cup of tea, her notebook closed on the desk beside her and half a sausage roll abandoned next to it.

Only Digit seemed animated. He'd accepted a sausage roll —for the purpose of camaraderie—his fingers dancing across his keyboard between delicate bites as he chased up the last loose ends.

"HOLMES cross-references complete and the scene logs updated." Digit declared to the room at large. "I've scheduled an integrity check for two a.m. as a belt-and-braces."

"Thanks, Digit," Ryan replied. He looked back down at the photocopy on his desk, his fingertips hovering over the edges of the paper. Spidery handwriting sprawled across the page, words slanting sharply to the right as if they were trying to escape the confines of the lined paper.

> *never meant. I NEVER. sorry sorry. Im so sorry the voices*
> *the VOICES wont STOP telling me terrible things terrible*
> *terrible. I don't listen but they SCREAM all the time cant*
> *think cant hear myself the eyes EVERYWHERE following*
> *watching even when I close mine theyre INSIDE my*
> *eyelids watching watching watching had to make them*
> *SEE had to make everyone SEE the truth THE TRUTH!*
> *they dont understand but theyll see now theyll all see now*
> *they have to*

Ryan's sausage roll sat untouched. The buttery pastry unappealing. Pins and needles fizzed along his left hand. Fatigue made the rewired nerves misfire, so he curled it into a fist he couldn't quite make. He kept reading.

> *my beautiful Emily. my BEAUTIFUL Emily we can be*
> *together now FOREVER forever and ever and ever shes*
> *with the spirits now the spirits of Flowerbank Woods thats*
> *where she is thats what she WANTED what she always*
> *wanted the spirits called to her and now shes there and*
> *nobody NOBODY can take her from me not anymore not*
> *EVER. theyre all gone now everyone who tried to keep us*

Ryan's jaw clenched. Had the search party, tramping through those same woods, walked over her grave and not known? Or had she still been alive at that point? Dogs were being sent to recover her body, but Flowerbank Woods was a large area to search.

"Staring at it won't change what it says," Fiona said, sliding into the seat next to him and placing a mug of strong milky tea by his hand.

Ryan rubbed his face, the scars faint bumps beneath his fingers. The note had been found tucked inside Lawrence's grimoire along with locks of hair from each victim. Why had Robbie put it there? In his experience, objects that didn't belong together meant staging.

"Ah, Sir?"

Ryan looked up to find Digit hovering on his other side, clutching a printout. "I've found a correlation between Lawrence and Robbie."

He handed Ryan a printout of a bank statement with five transactions highlighted.

"Mr Potts's ex-spouse allowed me access to his accounts. These transactions transferred five thousand pounds each time to Robbie Zutter's bank account. The most recent was Monday."

"Blackmail," Fiona said. "Probably threatened to expose Lawrence's drug side-hustle."

"Which explains the argument at the Inn. He didn't want to keep paying up."

"And why Lawrence lied about knowing Robbie."

Ryan's gaze drifted back to the page. A spree killer's confession, laid out in blue biro on lined paper torn from a school exercise book. The banality of it. No grand manifesto, just a weak and twisted justification for the horror he'd inflicted in the grips of a psychotic break.

The whiteboards had CASE CLOSED slashed across them in red marker. Courtesy of Cal. Emily's face stared down from her headshot behind the scrawled 'D'.

"Could he be making it up?" Ryan asked Fiona. The memory of the photo of Emily backlit in the woods, carefree and laughing into the camera, ate him up inside. He might have saved her life if he'd reacted quicker and caught Robbie when he'd surprised him at the search party. Another young woman missing with no body for her family to grieve over.

Fiona shook her head. Her face sympathetic as she guessed his thoughts. "I don't think so, Ryan. There was a lock of blonde hair in the grimoire too. DNA will tell us for certain, but..."

DCI Lee walked into the incident room. "Good work, everyone," she announced, her voice echoing in the subdued atmosphere.

Cal put down his phone while Digit took off his headphones.

"We have our killer, Robbie Zutter. We have his written confession. Forensics think the hair samples in the spell book will be a match for Emily Astley and our murder victims. The note he left gives us a motive, however scrambled. A drug-induced psychosis led to a belief he was 'punishing' bad people he met through Emily's unofficial Narcotics Anonymous group."

She paced in front of the boards and then tapped Lawrence's photo. "A simple case of greed. Blackmail gone wrong. Robbie got in over his head and saw a way out. Overall, a quick, tidy result on a nasty case. The brass are pleased. The press will have its story. We can all breathe a little easier."

Ryan scanned the boards. The red letters felt like a desecration. "It's not tidy."

Lee turned to him, her expression patient. "When is it ever?"

"Robbie Zutter was a heroin addict with a history of petty theft. Everything we uncovered about him suggested a disorganised individual. You're telling me he graduated to orchestrating six murders and four ritualistic displays, all without leaving a shred of forensic evidence until he was found overdosed with a convenient note?"

"He had a history of violence. Arrests for aggravated assault. He was blackmailing Lawrence Potts, and Lawrence was pushing back," Fiona countered. "Desperate people do desperate things."

"Desperate people are messy," Ryan said. "Whoever did this was meticulous. The strangulations, the lack of defensive wounds on the victims, the post-mortem mutilation. It was all controlled. Clinical, almost. Why the ritual? Why the coins for eyes? The tarot cards? Addicts don't suddenly develop a flair for macabre theatre."

Cal straightened up. "Maybe he read a book? Or watched a dodgy film? Got ideas."

Digit chimed in. "Statistically, killers who engage in ritualistic behaviour often have a long history of paraphilias and escalating violent fantasies. Zutter's record shows only minor acquisitive crimes and violence when cornered."

"Thank you, Digit," Ryan said.

Lee looked thoughtful. "He mentioned voices. He heard the victims' stories at the NA meetings, twisted them in his head, mixed it all in with the Wiccan rituals he'd attended. It's possible the rituals were the trigger, and he decided they all needed punishing."

"And Emily?" Ryan's voice was tight. "She was his friend. She tried to help him."

"Addicts often betray the people closest to them. It's part of the disease." Lee's tone was final. "Look, I get it. It's not wrapped up with a nice little bow. But we have his confession. We have the stolen items and the victims' hair in his possession. The CPS will have a field day. Unless Robbie comes back from the grave to enlighten us further, this is as good as it gets."

She looked over the team. "You've all put in a Herculean effort. Take the rest of the day. Get some sleep. See your families. Come back tomorrow, refreshed. We've got plenty of other cases that need our attention."

Ryan's eyes flickered to the whiteboard pushed against the far wall. It was still covered in notes and timelines detailing the string of medical break-ins. The thefts seemed petty now, almost innocent compared to the blood-soaked tableau of the last few days. Minor crimes committed by a small-minded person for addiction or profit. It would be hard to switch his brain over.

The team packed up. Cal stretched and cracked his knuckles. "Few pints and a curry sounds like a lunch plan. Anyone?"

Sheri offered a shy smile. "Sure."

"Digit?" Cal asked.

He glanced up from his screen. "Me?"

"Of course, you. Coming?"

"Ah... I'm uncertain that imbibing alcohol is advisable given that you sustained a concussion less than twenty-four hours ago. I feel compelled to note that alcohol consumption can impair the brain's already compromised healing processes. Perhaps we should postpone our libations? I also need to finish the archiving process." He went back to his work.

"Just a couple, Digit," Cal said. "The files will still be there tomorrow, and the pub has kombucha on tap."

Digit's head popped back up like a meerkat. "Kombucha? On draught? What's the pH level?" He adjusted his gold-rimmed glasses. "I mean... maybe I could complete the archiving tomorrow?"

"That's the spirit," Cal said, clapping him on the shoulder.

Digit winced.

Ryan clocked the recoil. The lad didn't care for unexpected touch. Something Cal seemed oblivious to.

"DS Bennett?" Cal asked.

Fiona waved him away. "Family calls." She stacked a pile of files into her briefcase. "You heading to the pub or home?" she asked Ryan.

The idea of celebrating turned his stomach, but the thought of his empty flat, the silence broken only by Winston's whining, was suffocating. He couldn't face it. Not yet. The image of another family left without a body, without answers, chewed at him. Robbie's confession didn't feel right. It left a sour taste, a fresher version of the one he'd lived with for twelve years.

Sophie's face surfaced in his mind, so much like Jaime's now. He still scanned crowds for Jaime's profile. Station platforms, supermarket queues, crowds. Always searching. A bad habit he couldn't quit. Her mother's image followed. Ruth Byrne still waited for his visit, but with everything going on, he hadn't had time.

"No, thanks," he said, his voice rougher than he intended. "There's something I need to do."

Fiona's brow furrowed, but she didn't ask. "All right. See you tomorrow, then."

He watched them file out one by one, leaving him alone with Lee in the quiet room. He squinted at the boards. Trace the logic. What repeats? What's performative? What shouldn't be there?

He turned to Lee. "I want to get the handwriting analysed. I think Robbie was left-handed, and there are no smudges."

"Don't pick at it, Ryan," she warned, her voice losing its managerial edge. "Let it be."

"I can't."

She sighed, a long, weary sound. "I know." She grabbed her jacket from the back of a chair. "Try not to find any trouble before nine a.m. tomorrow. That's all I ask."

The door clicked shut behind her, leaving him in silence. He stared at the case boards, at the faces of the dead, obscured by the bloody gash of red marker, then picked up his coat.

He was going to see Ruth.

CHAPTER FORTY-SEVEN

RYAN SETTLED ONTO THE FAMILIAR SOFA IN THE FAMILY room, hands wrapped around the mug to steady it. He took a sip and looked around. The room might as well have been frozen in time. Not a single ornament or piece of furniture had changed in the twelve years since he'd last been here. The night he'd told Ruth he was leaving for London.

Running away.

"It's so good to see you," Jaime's mum said, settling into the armchair across from him.

The genuine smile of delight only made Ryan feel worse about not attempting to keep in touch. He'd made brief obligatory phone calls each year on Jaime's birthday, but he hadn't once visited in person after he'd moved to London.

He'd been too scared. Scared that he might see doubt in her eyes, or worse, belief in his guilt. In his seven years with Jaime, Ruth had become a surrogate mum to him, enveloping him in her unconditional love. That she might think he was responsible for Jaime's death had been more than he could bear.

So he'd stayed away. Like a coward.

He could see now that his fears were baseless. She looked smaller somehow, the lines surrounding her delicate features deeper, but the warmth and love on her face was unmistakable. She tutted under her breath then reached out and stroked the faint scars running down his cheek. "Look what those monsters did to you."

He made himself stay still. A hand near his face still spiked his pulse. If anyone else had tried it, he would have pulled away, but he held firm until her hand dropped back to her lap.

"Sophie told me you followed the case?" A pair of sparkly ladies' sneakers tucked under a side table caught his eye. They definitely didn't belong to Ruth.

"Yes." Ruth followed his gaze. "She lives with her husband now, but she treats the place as if she still lives here." Despite her motherly persona, Ruth was sharper than Odd Bod's scalpel. Both Jaime and Sophie came by their intelligence honestly.

"They're renting a two-bedroom in Derby while they save for a house. Around the corner from the paper's office." She hesitated and then continued. "She said she ran into you on Monday when she was working. Seems miserable of them to make you work a murder your first day back."

"Murderers can be inconsiderate like that." Ryan took another sip. "It let me see my new team in action at least."

"I saw DCI Lee on the news earlier saying your case had been solved. You must be pleased to wrap it up so quickly."

I wish I were, Ryan thought but kept it to himself. "Enough about me. How are you doing?"

Ruth's smile faded. "I thought time would make it easier, and in some ways it has. In other ways, it hasn't at all. The not knowing is the worst part. I hope she's dead." Her voice dropped. "I can't bear the thought of her suffering all this time. We both know she would have never left voluntarily."

Ryan tried to hide his shaking hands, but Ruth took them in her own.

"Go easy on Sophie. I know it was unbearable for you when Jaime disappeared, but it was hard on her too. Despite the age difference, they were so close. It's still hard for her. I think she'd swap places with Jaime in a heartbeat if she could." She paused. "Even if she is dead."

So would I. Ryan went still. *And maybe someone else had the same idea.*

CHAPTER FORTY-EIGHT

A WEAK SILVER SUN FILTERED THROUGH THE GATHERING grey clouds. Ryan cursed the flat afternoon light and his half-baked theory as he bumped over hidden ruts on the unpaved country lane. The Range Rover nearly took flight as he hit a deep trench.

"Christ!"

After a few more twists, a small lake came into view below. The water's surface mirrored the slate sky.

On the edge of the lake stood a stone-built farmhouse, draped in ivy. From a distance, the weathered stones seemed carved from the earth itself, a testament to countless seasons endured in Derbyshire's temperamental weather.

Looked like the place based on Fiona's description.

Up ahead, the lane petered out into a paddock with a sagging wooden shed. He reached the end, facing a muddy sheep. It eyed him from a patch of grass before it decided he wasn't a threat and returned to its aimless chewing. Ryan studied the property below. No vehicles in the driveway. No lights in the windows. No movement.

Perfect.

He executed a clumsy six-point turn on the tight track and parked behind a cluster of trees. Better to approach unannounced. The farmhouse loomed as he made his way towards it, gravel crunching beneath his feet. A boatshed sat at the lake edge, its weathered wooden structure listing slightly. The door hung ajar, propped half-open. Something about the angle felt deliberate. He'd start there.

The scent of lavender and rosemary mingled with damp soil as he walked along the stone pathway through an overgrown English garden. Stone gnomes peeked out of the foliage, laughing at his folly. A small flock of ducks floated on the lake. Winston would love this place. Chasing ducks was one of the corgi's top ten favourite activities, though it would only be a matter of time before his fluffy arse got stuck in a rabbit hole.

The ducks drifted closer and issued a series of warning quacks.

Ryan glanced back at the house. Still no movement.

"Shut up, you little arseholes," he hissed.

His fingers twitched towards his belt, where he normally kept his baton. He'd left it at the station, seeing no need to be armed to visit Ruth. Then, once the pieces had clicked into place, returning hadn't seemed an option. Time felt too short.

Ryan paused at the entrance and listened. Nothing but the gentle lap of water and the occasional agitated quack.

The hinges creaked as he pushed the door wider. Dust particles danced in the shaft of sunlight that cut through the dimness and landed on a car-shaped object beneath a faded blue cover.

Ryan pulled back one corner, revealing unmistakable green paintwork. He yanked the entire cover off in one fluid motion and sent up a cloud of dust that caught in his throat.

Emily's missing green Peugeot.

The confirmation sent adrenaline through him in a rush. He'd been right. Ryan circled the vehicle, noting the mud splattered along the wheel arches and covering the number plates.

A muffled sound behind him.

Ryan spun.

Todd Mathers stood in the doorway. Not the nervous, awkward gamer Ryan had met before. This version held predatory confidence in every line of his body, one arm locked around the neck of a slight blonde woman. The other hand held a knife against her throat.

Emily Astley. Alive.

Relief washed through Ryan, followed by dread. He'd hoped to find her here alone.

Her eyes were wide above the dirty gag tied around her mouth. Her long skirt and embroidered yellow blouse were filthy and torn. Dark circles shadowed her eyes, and her hair hung matted.

"Hello, Kyle," Ryan said. He kept his voice calm.

The man's face split into a wide grin that transformed his features. "What gave me away?"

"To be fair, your performance was excellent, especially at the cottage yesterday. Took me a while to see through it." Ryan adopted a casual stance, hands visible. "An offhand comment someone made about a sibling who wanted to swap places helped me make the connection. Then everything fell into place."

Emily struggled against Kyle's hold. He pressed the knife closer and pricked her skin. She whimpered and stilled as blood trickled down her neck.

"Please continue," Kyle said, eyes sharp. "I can take direction. After all, once you're dead, I'll have to keep up the role of Todd Mathers, loser brother. At least until he discovers CrossFit and transforms himself."

Ryan was happy to oblige. He needed to keep Kyle in conversation, and thankfully, Kyle was a narcissist, like most people who inserted themselves into investigations. He would be eager to boast about his masterpiece to the only person who could ever know the truth.

He had to get Emily away from Kyle, but the boatshed was cramped and limited his options. One wrong move and that knife would slice through her carotid artery. He stepped out from behind the car.

"When we spoke at the apartment, I thought it was strange you gave Kyle a few backhanded compliments." Ryan shifted forward, testing Kyle's reaction. "I passed it off as misguided family pride, but it seemed odd for someone who'd been relentlessly bullied to praise their tormentor. Then there was the scratching." He gestured at Kyle's hair.

Kyle yanked off the scraggly brown wig with a flourish, revealing a short buzz cut underneath. "Thank fuck. It was driving me mental."

"And there was a touch too much cockiness behind your meek facade," Ryan said. "Consciously I bought it, but subconsciously it didn't quite ring true."

"Difficult to play a timid slug. I mean, look at him." Kyle sneered down at his own appearance, at the ill-fitting clothes and the soft physique he'd cultivated.

"I can see why your brother was an easy target. Isolated. No girlfriend, his job and social life conducted online. Almost a shut-in. No one to notice the subtle differences in his appearance." Ryan paused. "You must have planned this for a while. You dated the dental assistant at the dental clinic you both used so you could steal her database password. Then you broke in and swapped your dental records for your brother's." Ryan took another careful step. "The break-ins at the other clinic and the vets were to cover up the important one. Handy way to source ketamine too. For Todd and the others. I assume you had to keep him drugged while you slimmed him down enough to pass for you?"

"Do you know how many calories I had to consume every day for a month to look like this?" Kyle sneered. "The damage to my metabolism."

"What I don't understand is why. To fake your death and kill your brother seems extreme because you lost your job."

Kyle's eyes narrowed, the blade pressed deeper against Emily's skin. "Why do they say people kill?" he replied, his tone almost academic. "Sex, money or power."

"Todd wasn't powerful, and from all accounts he didn't get any sex, so money."

"Over nine hundred thousand in savings and, with me now dead, this farmhouse and all the land that surrounds it," Kyle said. "My nerdy brother was brilliant at stock selection. Our mother left us three hundred thousand each and joint ownership of the farm when she died. He tripled his money in three years. While my brother squirrelled away every penny, I enjoyed the high life. Until that tosser Matt fired me because I snorted coke at a conference. Like the rest of them didn't do it."

Ryan remembered the photos Digit had shown him from Kyle's Instagram page. The champagne, the luxury hotels, designer clothes.

"At that stage, I might have owed a few people some money. Nothing major. Twenty grand here, ten there." Kyle shrugged one shoulder.

Ryan realised Kyle was the one who owed Jack Stalker.

"But after I lost my job, they wanted to collect. Figured I'd reconnect with Todd, convince him to sell the farmhouse. But the sap wouldn't sell. Said it had too much sentimental value. Then one day he's in the bathroom and I see a bank statement on the kitchen bench."

Ryan inched closer, measuring the distance between them. "I was stumped about the book club regulars for a while until I realised Emily had told the book club you'd died of suicide. Then Amanda saw you at the video game store when she brought Carter's birthday present. You could tell she'd recognised you despite your changed appearance. Maybe you told her you were Kyle's brother, Todd, but you could see she didn't believe you. The entire house of cards could crash down."

A flicker of surprise crossed Kyle's face, replaced by a smug smile.

"Amanda didn't have any friends," Ryan continued. "So if she wanted to tell anyone she'd seen you, it would be the others at the next book club meeting. The day after they met, you went to Emily's cottage to find out if Amanda had spilled the beans. And she had. Once you knew Amanda had blabbed, you decided you had to kill Isabel and Lottie too."

"Did you like my little rituals? I do love to create drama. It was all of Emily's junk that gave me the idea. Bet I had you running in circles." The arsehole beamed with pride.

"How do you think this ends, Kyle?" Ryan locked eyes with him.

Kyle's grip on Emily loosened. "It ends with—"

Emily stomped down hard on his instep, her heel grinding into his foot. Kyle swore, and his hold slackened just enough for her to twist sideways. The knife scored a shallow line across her collarbone as she jerked away.

Ryan lunged forward and tackled Kyle around the middle. They crashed against the wall of the boat shed, old fishing equipment clattering down around them. The knife sliced across Ryan's forearm as Kyle's knee connected with his stomach and drove the air from his lungs. They grappled, rolled across the dirt floor and banged into the side of the Peugeot.

Ryan grabbed Kyle's wrist and slammed it against the

concrete floor. The knife skittered away into the shadows. Kyle head-butted him, and stars exploded behind Ryan's eyes.

"Run!" Ryan shouted to Emily, who stood frozen next to the wall.

She darted towards the door, hampered by her long skirt. Kyle's leg shot out and tripped her. She sprawled on the ground with a muffled cry.

Ryan scrambled after Kyle, but his left shoulder seized with white-hot pain as he tried to push himself up. The momentary hesitation was all Kyle needed.

Kyle's fist smashed into Ryan's injured shoulder, sending agony radiating down his arm. While Ryan gasped, Kyle rolled away and lunged for the knife. He snatched it from under the car's tire.

In two strides, he was at Emily's side. He yanked her up by her hair. The knife pressed to her throat once more.

"Not quite the hero today, are you, Detective?" Kyle panted, his face flushed but his eyes gleaming with triumph.

CHAPTER FORTY-NINE

"Get up." Kyle waved the knife. "To the car."

Ryan's shoulder throbbed as he pushed himself to his feet. He kept his eyes on the blade that hovered near Emily's throat. Blood trickled from her wound and stained the collar of her once-yellow top.

"What's the plan here, Kyle? Kill a detective inspector? That'll bring every copper in Derbyshire down on you."

"I looked you up. You're a lone-wolf kind of guy. No one knows you're here." Kyle gestured with the knife towards Emily's green Peugeot. "Into the car. Driver's seat."

Ryan weighed his options. The pain that radiated from his shoulder limited his movement. At least the cut on his right forearm appeared shallow. Kyle had the knife. Emily was in immediate danger. For now, compliance seemed the safest approach.

He shuffled over to the car. Kyle manoeuvred Emily behind him, using her as a shield. The door creaked as Ryan pulled it open and slid into the driver's seat.

"Emily, be a love and secure our detective friend to the steering wheel," Kyle said.

Emily's eyes darted frantically above her gag as Kyle pushed her forward, pressing the blade against her spine. She stumbled, her legs weak from days of captivity.

"There are cable ties on the passenger seat," Kyle said. "Use them on his wrists. Tight to the wheel."

Emily's hands trembled as she picked up the plastic restraints. She looked at Ryan, a silent apology in her bloodshot eyes.

"It's all right," Ryan said.

She looped the first tie around his left wrist and the steering wheel, pulling it tight. The plastic bit into his flesh.

"Sorry," she mumbled through the gag.

"Both hands, Emily." Kyle pressed the knife against her back. "Don't try anything clever."

She secured Ryan's right wrist, her fingers cold against his skin.

"Good girl." Kyle patted her head like a dog. "Now back up."

Ryan tested the restraints. No give at all. The cable ties were industrial grade and cut into his flesh when he pulled. The water in front of the boat slip looked deep. He wasn't getting out of this.

He'd made a stupid mistake. A mistake that might cost him his life.

"Glad to see you're so cooperative." Kyle leaned forward, his breath hot in Ryan's ear. "Being a detective, I'm sure you know all about death by drowning. Panic will set in as your body fights for oxygen that won't come. Your chest will feel like it's being crushed from the inside. It should take about four minutes for your brain to shut down. I researched it when I made plans for my brother."

Ryan needed to keep Kyle talking. Pray an opportunity to take him down presented itself before he and the Peugeot plunged into the lake.

"Was Robbie always supposed to be the scapegoat?" Ryan said. "Your plan was meticulous."

Kyle smirked and placed the knife tip against Emily's spine. "After I found the statues and the book at Emily's, I was going to frame Lawrence. High priest of a pagan cult with his ritual items at a murder scene? Perfect set-up." He chuckled. "But then Robbie fell right into my lap, so easy to manipulate. He was blackmailing Potty over his little secret. That's when I knew I had a better patsy."

"So you planted the grimoire with the hair."

"Among other things." Kyle's eyes gleamed. "I think the overdose was a nice touch. I found the heroin in Robbie's jacket after he got high on the ketamine I gave him. Fitting end for a junkie murderer, don't you think?"

Emily twisted away and lunged for the boat shed door. For a second, Ryan thought she might make it.

Kyle was faster.

He swung around, and the hilt of the knife connected with a sickening crack against her temple.

She collapsed with a stifled moan, blood seeping into her blonde hair.

"Emily!" Ryan yanked against his restraints.

Kyle shook his head, tutting. "She never learns." He knelt beside her and checked that she still breathed. "Shame. We could have had something special if she wasn't so bloody stubborn."

He straightened and dusted off his knees. The wig and glasses lay forgotten on the floor, his transformation from Todd back to Kyle now complete.

"Well, this has been entertaining, Detective." Kyle circled

back to the car. "But I think it's time we wrapped things up. You can go join that wife of yours." He leaned in through the window, his face inches from Ryan's. "Poetic, isn't it? The detective involved in his wife's disappearance also disappears without a trace. Did you kill her, by the way? I've wondered."

The words hit like a physical blow. Ryan struggled to maintain his composure. He refused to give Kyle the satisfaction of seeing him react.

Would he see Jaime on the other side? He stared past Kyle into the distance and smiled.

Kyle frowned, his eyes darting down to check Ryan's hands were still secure. He relaxed and grinned back. "Don't worry, I'll take good care of Emily after you're gone. She'll come around to my charms. One way or another."

Ryan felt his control slip, anger rising like bile in his throat. How to turn this around? Get under Kyle's skin instead.

"Why keep Emily alive?" Ryan said. "No one walks away from Kyle Mathers? Is that it? You're the one who always does the walking, not the girl? But she saw straight through your act. She and her sister called you 'Kyle the Penis' after you broke up. You can't kill her until she changes her mind. Any luck there?"

Kyle's smile faltered. The vein at his temple pulsed.

"Guess not," Ryan added.

Kyle's knuckles whitened around the knife handle. "You think you're clever, don't you? But you're the one who's going to die today, knowing one more woman wasn't found on your watch." He leaned closer. "I'd slit your throat, but it would be too quick. We're done. Goodbye, Detective."

He reached past Ryan and inserted the key into the ignition. Ryan braced himself as his mind raced for any way out of this nightmare. He slammed his foot on the brake, but the pedal pressed down with no resistance. Kyle had cut the brake lines.

Then, with a dull *thunk*, a stone garden gnome connected with the back of Kyle's skull. His eyes rolled back as he crumpled to the ground beside Emily.

Fiona Bennett stood in the space Kyle had occupied, gnome still held at the ready.

"Christ, you took your sweet time getting here." Ryan exhaled, relief flooding through him. "I thought you said you'd only be five minutes behind me?"

CHAPTER FIFTY

RYAN SAT ON THE EDGE OF THE HOSPITAL BED, RESISTING the urge to rip off the itchy paper gown they'd forced onto his top half. His shoulder ached despite the painkillers, but the nurse had insisted on examining it after Fiona mentioned his recent gunshot wound might have reopened during the struggle.

"Stop fidgeting," Fiona said from her seat by the window. "You'll tear the stitches."

"They don't need to keep me here." Ryan glanced at the bandage wrapped around his forearm. "It's just a scratch."

Fiona raised an eyebrow. "You got pretty banged up out there."

Ryan shook his head. "And you brought a garden gnome as backup?"

"It was the first thing I saw outside the boat shed." Fiona shrugged. "Better than bringing a baton to a knife fight."

"Remind me to thank the gnome for saving my life," Ryan muttered. He sobered. "How's Emily?"

"Stable. They're keeping her under observation for the

concussion, dehydration, and malnutrition. She was down in that cellar for over five days."

Ryan winced. Five days of fear and uncertainty. And they'd almost let Kyle get away with it.

A knock on the doorframe drew their attention. DCI Lee stood there, arms folded.

"Holding up, Hale?" she asked, stepping into the room.

"Ready to be discharged, Ma'am."

Lee gave him a sceptical once-over. "Kyle Mathers is in custody. We've found significant evidence in the cellar of the farmhouse linking him to all the murders, including Emily's phone. He'd used it to message the victims and gain access to their homes."

She summarised what Forensics had uncovered. Kyle's notes on the book club and the coven. Loose strands from the hair he'd collected as souvenirs to place in the grimoire. Originally, he'd planned to frame Lawrence for killing Emily and the others. Emily talked about the coven often enough to make it work. But then Robbie had appeared at the search party, and Lawrence had turned up at Robbie's house uninvited.

Ryan's stomach turned. He'd pointed Kyle straight at Robbie and then painted a target on the kid's back.

"What about Emily?" Fiona asked. "Was she taken because of the book club?"

Lee nodded. "Kyle told Emily he needed to 'silence the book club' after Amanda Norris recognised him. Emily was his final loose end."

Fiona's phone buzzed. She checked it, then stood. "I should get this. It's the childminder."

After she left, Lee fixed Ryan with a stern gaze. "You're not to set foot in the station for at least two days, and I've booked you an additional session with Dr Hope."

"But—"

"That's an order, Hale. We've got this covered. Mathers has confessed to everything, though he's trying to paint himself as mentally unstable to avoid a life sentence."

Ryan leaned back against the pillows, wincing at the pull in his shoulder. "He seemed methodical to me. Calculated."

"The CPS will handle that part." Lee moved towards the door. "Get some rest. And Hale?"

"Ma'am?"

"Good work." She paused. "But next time, bring more backup than one sergeant and a gnome."

After Lee left, Ryan closed his eyes, exhaustion catching up with him.

Lee's press conference to correct the public record would be a spectacular mess. The department looked like a bunch of amateurs after pinning the string of ritualistic murders on the wrong man. Again.

He knew Lee would get over it. She understood that justice was more important than saving face. The brass, though. They wouldn't be so forgiving.

Back on his superiors' shit list, and it hadn't even been a week.

But reputations could be mended. The image of Emily collapsing under Kyle's blow kept replaying in his mind. He should have seen through Kyle's disguise sooner.

A nurse popped in to check his blood pressure. "Your colleague asked me to tell you she'll be back to drive you home in an hour," the nurse said, pressing the band around his arm. "And you have another visitor if you're feeling up to it."

"Who?"

"Miss Astley. She's been asking about you since she woke up."

Emily. A surge of guilt washed over him.

"I'd like to see her."

The nurse nodded. "I'll wheel her in. She's still quite weak."

Ten minutes later, the door opened again. The nurse pushed in a wheelchair carrying Emily, who looked pale and fragile in her hospital gown. White bandages covered the gash on her temple and wrists, and someone had washed her blonde hair.

Despite her injuries, she managed a small smile when she saw him.

"I'll leave you two for a bit." The nurse positioned Emily's wheelchair beside the bed. "Press the call button when you're ready to go back."

When the nurse left, an awkward silence filled the room. Ryan wasn't sure what to say. *Sorry I didn't figure it out sooner?*

Emily broke the silence first.

"You look terrible," she said, her voice hoarse.

"You should see the other bloke," Ryan replied, then winced at his own tactlessness. "Sorry. That was—"

"It's okay," she interrupted. "I hope your colleague hit him hard."

"She's a third-dan black belt in Aikido, and she's got a good arm on her."

Emily looked down at her bandaged wrists. "They told me everything. About Kyle killing his brother and pretending to be Todd. I met the real Todd once. He was sweet." Her voice faltered. "The other murders. The book club members, Robbie. They were my responsibility. I should have protected them better."

"This isn't on you," Ryan said. "Kyle Mathers is a manipulative murderer. He fooled everyone, even his own brother."

Emily shook her head. "Robbie came to see me at the cottage earlier in the week. Brought me the grimoire and the statues. Said he'd stolen them from Lawrence's van back in

August, during the festival." Her fingers twisted the tassels on the blanket on her lap. "He was working to get clean, and he wanted to make things right. I was going to return them to Lawrence at the Twelve Apostles on Sunday. I didn't know Robbie was blackmailing him, though."

Kyle had found those items at Emily's cottage and recognised their value as props for his frame job.

"Robbie was so young and so lost," Emily continued, tears welling in her eyes. "And Kyle used that to murder him."

Ryan gave her a moment.

She lifted her gaze to meet his. "I wanted to thank you. For finding me. For not giving up." A tear slid down her cheek. "I thought I would die down there in the dark."

Ryan swallowed the lump in his throat. "I almost didn't find you."

"But you did." She reached out her hand, and after a moment's hesitation, he took it in his. "My mum said you kept looking even after they closed the case."

"I don't give up on people," Ryan said quietly.

Emily's lips quirked in a sad smile. "Even flaky wellness influencers with dodgy exes?"

"Even them." He squeezed her hand and then let it go. "How are you feeling? Really?"

She sighed, letting her brave front slip for a moment. "Like I'll never feel safe again." Her voice trembled. "Every time I close my eyes, I'm back in the cellar. I keep hearing his voice, that knife against my skin."

Ryan nodded. He knew that feeling all too well. The nightmares, the phantom sensations, the constant looking over your shoulder.

"It gets better," he said, though the words felt hollow. His own demons still haunted him most nights.

"Does it?" she asked, her eyes searching his face.

He hesitated. "The fear changes. Becomes something you can manage. You'll carry it with you, but it won't always control you."

Emily let out a slow breath. "The doctors say I can go home tomorrow." She gave a humourless laugh. "Not that I want to live in the cottage. Not after—"

"That's understandable."

"Mum's offered to have me stay with her and Felicity. She's already packed up most of my things." Emily winced as she shifted in the wheelchair. "I might even take her up on it this time."

The nurse appeared in the doorway. "Emily, time to get you back to your room. The doctor wants me to check your vitals again."

Emily nodded, then turned to Ryan. "Thank you. For everything."

As the nurse wheeled her out, Ryan settled back on the mattress, the weight of the past week pressing down on him. They'd caught the killer. Emily was safe.

So why did he feel like he was still waiting for the other shoe to drop?

CHAPTER FIFTY-ONE

Ryan stood before the whiteboards, the red words 'CASE CLOSED' now sitting right with him. He still needed to figure out where Sophie was getting her information and decide how to navigate working with Lampton, but these were problems for another day.

Fiona came over to stand beside him. "Do you have the pathology report for Robbie?" she asked, fiddling with her necklace.

She continued speaking, but her words faded into white noise as Ryan felt his blood pounding in his ears. He blinked, unsure if his sleep-deprived brain was playing tricks on him.

No.

He blinked again.

Fuck.

"Can we talk?" he asked her.

"Isn't that what we were doing, Professor?" She must have read something in his expression because her demeanour changed. "I have an amendment to file on the discovery of Robbie's body, then sure."

"Now." He grabbed her by the arm and pulled her into his office, which was still serving as a break room. He knew the rest of the team were watching, but at the moment he didn't give two shits. He shut the door behind them.

Fiona yanked her arm free, a wounded look on her face. "Ryan, what the hell?"

"Where did you get that?" Ryan pointed to the necklace around her neck.

Fiona folded her arms. "It was at the front desk for me. It's our anniversary today. More thoughtful than Nathan would normally manage."

Ryan opened the photo app on his phone and tapped on an album called 'Jaime'. He scrolled down and brought up a close-up photo of Jaime in his arms, her head thrown back in laughter. He zoomed in on the part of the photo he was interested in. At the base of her throat lay a white gold and diamond horseshoe charm threaded through a delicate silver chain.

He showed the photo to Fiona. "Jaime wore that necklace the day she disappeared. I had it custom-made for her as a birthday present the month before."

The colour drained from Fiona's face, making the freckles on her cheeks stand out in stark relief. "God, Ryan. In the case file, it's listed as a silver horse pendant. I just assumed Nathan sent the package." She whipped her head around. "Get me an evidence bag."

"That can wait. Tell me about the package first."

Ryan saw Fiona's panic fade as she settled into the role of analytical detective. "It was delivered by mail to reception. Plain brown package with my name and the address of the station typed on the front. No return sender. Goody called me on an internal line to tell me about it. Inside the package there was a note and a jewellery box with the necklace."

"What did the note say?"

"It was a few lines from a Vicious Hearts song. It seemed a little intense for Nathan, but software developers aren't the most romantic guys, you know? And they are one of my favourite punk bands. I figured he was trying to do something different. The note's in my bag. I'll get it."

Fiona went back out into the incident room, ignoring the team's curious looks. She came back with her handbag, pulled on a pair of disposable gloves, and took out three clear evidence bags from a zipped side pocket. Carefully, she extracted the note and placed it in a bag. She glanced at it, grimaced, then handed it over to Ryan. "I can't believe I thought Nathan chose these lyrics."

Ryan read the lines printed on the card.

And you mean more to me than breathing
And if this feeling isn't real love, then I know
That nothing else will match this bleeding
Until the knife comes home

Fiona put a hand on his shoulder. "I can tell what you're thinking, Ryan. This is going to screw up your ability to discreetly investigate Jaime's disappearance, but we have to take this to Lee." She removed the necklace and lowered it into the second evidence bag. The jewellery box went in the third bag.

Ryan sighed. "You know it'll fly around the station. The minute I'm back in town, new evidence mysteriously appears. People are going to say that it's not a coincidence."

"No one who matters will say it. I also think you aren't giving Lee enough credit. She knows how to be discreet. I can call Eloise directly to process these." She held up the bags. "No one outside the four of us needs to know about the necklace until Lee decides otherwise."

Ryan nodded, holding his hands over his face.

"At least you now know one thing for certain," she said, her voice soft.

He dropped his hands and looked up.

"Jaime never left you. She was taken."

ABOUT THE AUTHOR

R. K. Lynott is a crime thriller author writing mystery and crime fiction featuring compelling, quirky characters and stories packed with suspects, clues, and unexpected twists.

She lives in the South Island of New Zealand with her husband, two young children, and a grumpy Australian terrier who knows where all the fictional bodies are buried.

rklynottbooks.com

@rklynottauthor

ACKNOWLEDGMENTS

To my husband, thank you for your patience, love and good humour each time I disappear into "just one more chapter" for weeks on end. You have been a very understanding 'writing widower', keeping our life ticking along while I'm off chasing killers across Derbyshire.

Huge thanks to my mum and my sister, Briony, for bravely reading an early version of this story and pretending not to notice quite how many typos and repeated words had snuck in. Your feedback and enthusiasm helped me believe this book might actually work, even when I was convinced the plot was held together with caffeine and wishes.

And finally, to Harry, my four-legged friend of fourteen years. Without you, Winston wouldn't be half as funny, and far fewer plot holes would have been untangled if we hadn't been on our many walks.

9 780473 767525